Royal RETELLING

LOVE IN LAANDIA
SWEET ROYAL ROMANCE

HOLLY KERR

Also By Holly Kerr

Royal Rumble

Royal Retelling

Royal Rising

Royal Reluctance

Royal Rebel

Royal Replacement

The Love in Laandia spinoffs:

Coffee Break with the Billionaire

Babysitting the Grumpy Billionaire (coming soon!)

plus

Suitor Science series

Love & Alliteration series

Don't series

Royal Retelling

Prologue

Once upon a time, a girl walked home from a disappointing first date.

First dates should not feel like this.

First dates should leave you with a giddy excitement, like wanting to skip through the mountains singing *Do Re Mi* a la Julie Andrews. Not leave you with a sense of dread like when you had to tell your high school geography teacher exactly why you didn't finish your homework.

I adjust my AirPods and turn up "We Are Never Getting Back Together."

Not that there's an issue with us wanting to get back together—that would be impossible since we were never really together.

One date. And it was a *real* date, not hanging out at a party or a pick-up at The King's Hat. Liam came into the rescue shelter *three* times with his sister to pick the perfect dog for his mother. And then after they took shaggy Beaker home, he *came back* and asked me for dinner.

That was tonight. Dinner at *Nonna's Ristorante*. I had the seafood linguine and Liam had the lasagna. We split a half carafe of house red and the lemon torte for dessert. I ate most of it.

I can't put my finger on what was wrong, but something wasn't right.

Liam and I—we weren't right.

I don't know if it's worse staying single or trying with someone like Liam, who is nice and kind and who didn't ask me out because he felt obligated or because he wanted something from me.

In the two years since I graduated high school, I've been asked out for eight first dates. Not one second date.

Two of those were the aforementioned obligations—both set up by our mothers. One was like Liam: *Let's take Stella out for lunch because she owns the rescue shelter and I love my new dog.*

Two more were interested in my then seventeen-year-old step-sister Daphne and thought going through me was a solid way of getting her attention. Another one asked me out because his sister was interested in Daphne.

The remaining two claimed to be big fans of my father.

Never, ever, ever...

I think I've confirmed the fact that dating is not for me. Re-lationships? Also a no-go because how do you start a relationship when you can't even manage a second date?

I like dogs. Dogs like me. And maybe I will never be able to find that simple, sweet-singing-along-a-mountaintop happiness after a date, but at least spending time with dogs and cats and even the new parrot dropped off at the shelter never makes me feel slightly sick to my stomach like I do now. And it isn't because of the seafood linguine.

I'll stick to dogs because I'm not the type of girl who gets second dates. And I'm going to be okay with that.

I turn the corner onto Ontario Street. It's an easy but not short walk home from downtown Battle Harbour—to the house my mother refuses to part with even after the acrimonious divorce from my father and subsequent remarriage to the mayor of the capital of Laandia. I skirt through the quiet side streets, enjoying the brisk April evening chill and Taylor singing in my ears.

Until I see him.

Prince Gunnar.

Prince Gunnar, fourth son of King Magnus of Laandia, steps out of the door of a house, his customary knapsack slung over his shoulder.

A girl follows him and she doesn't look happy. I stop a few houses away.

Prince Gunnar is a frequent sight in Battle Harbour, as are his brothers. His sister Lyra isn't as common since she left for school in America. Before that, I couldn't go anywhere without seeing Lyra and her best friend Kate McKibbon, often with Prince Gunnar's arm slung around her shoulder.

Prince Gunnar and Kate have been the Barbie and Ken of Battle Harbour for almost a year now.

And like Ken, Gunnar doesn't seem to have much purpose other than being arm candy. He plays at racing—motorbikes, cars, boats, and who knows what else—bopping around the world with his jet-setter friends, and generally enjoys his life of leisure.

As someone who is working day and night at getting Catch a Pet rescue shelter up and running, all I can say is it must be nice.

I don't have many warm and fuzzy feelings about the royal family of Laandia, but Gunnar irks me the most of all.

And seeing him tonight doesn't help endear him to me. With the dimpled smile, blond hair that flops just so, and those blue eyes, he's Prince Charming personified. Just like his three brothers. Even with Kate in the picture, there is a lineup of women who want a first date, a second, and a marriage proposal from the prince. Not that he's about to drop down on one knee— everyone knows Odin is the prince for long-term prospects. Gunnar and his eldest brother, Kalle, are there for a good time, not a long one.

Because… lookee here: the girl who followed Gunnar out of the house isn't Kate. Nor isn't she anyone associated with Kate, like a friend or a family member.

It's Mabel Crow.

It's Mabel Crow's house and Gunnar is leaving with his bag. Mabel looks quite upset that he's leaving, like she really wants him to stay.

It almost appears as if they're arguing about his leaving.

I'm not one to slut-shame a woman, but Mabel has a bit of a reputation. An impressive one. She's a few years older than Gunnar and has made it clear that she's up for whatever the princes have to offer, whether it's for a short time or the endgame.

I wonder what Kate thinks about this.

My phone is in my hand before I think twice and I take a picture of Prince Gunnar and Mabel while I'm partially concealed behind the huge oak tree

If my first date with Liam had gone better, I might not have taken it. If I had been in the singing-atop-the-mountain haze of happiness, I might have skipped by the house and ignored Prince Gunnar because that's what we do.

We pretend we don't know each other, that we weren't friends years ago.

At least *I* pretend.

That is not the reason I take the picture.

I take it because if Prince Gunnar is arguing with Mabel about leaving her house at the time of the evening when it's a little late for a casual drop-by without a six-pack and a group of friends, what is Kate doing? And does she know that her boyfriend is at the home of another woman?

If not, that's not right. It's not fair, or good boyfriend behaviour, and the one thing that seriously annoys me about Prince Gunnar is that he never gets caught for his bad behaviour.

So I take the picture.

And when I finally get home, I find Kate's number and I text her the picture of Prince Gunnar.

King Magnus of

The Kingdom of Laandia

and Lord Prefect Arnaud Ousain

of Saint Pierre and Miquelon

are proud to announce the wedding of their children

Prince Odin Maximillian Patrick Henri

and Lady Camille Elisabeth

June First,

Battle Harbour, Laandia

1

Stella

"**I** CAN'T BELIEVE PEOPLE still read newspapers," I grumble as I lay out a thick layer under the puppy playpen. "It's such a waste of paper. Kills trees."

In the big crate in the corner of the room, six pairs of eyes watch me intently. The puppies have been here for three weeks, rescued with their malnourished mother from under one of the piers, and already they know the schedule: family time in the big crate at night, puppy pen during the morning with the hopes that we'll have visitors that may want to adopt one or more, and then outdoor time in the afternoon if it's nice.

It's late May in Battle Harbour, which means most days are nice, albeit a little cool. This far north, the constant breeze from the Atlantic always has a bite.

"Yes, but it's better than having to get new pee pads," Ajax says in their sing-song voice that will grate my nerves by the end of the day. "Expensive."

That's like a four-letter word in the shelter. I came up with the idea to save the stray dogs that migrate south from the First Nations reserves in Northern Laandia near the Arctic Circle when I was still in high school. Some girls mooned over boys—I fell for a pair of sad puppy eyes. My mother finally cut me off from taking food down to the docks or to the cliffs, or, god forbid, being seen around town with a bag of kibble.

I just made sure she didn't find out about it.

It took three years of plans and plotting and begging for money—which is also called fundraising—to get things running.

Five years later, Catch a Pet Rescue has never looked back. We've expanded and expanded until we're bursting at the seams, but the doggy day care offsets most of the rescue expenses, which is helpful, because I'm terrible at fundraising. I never thought operating a non-profit would be so exhausting—and yet so fulfilling.

It helps that I like dogs more than people.

I wiggle my fingers at the eyes watching me and finish the set-up. We spread paper or pads thick when the puppies come out because I've learnt my lesson on what urine does to hardwood floors the hard way. Six months after taking over the house, I had to get the floor ripped up and vinyl put down. Another expense, one I've been trying to avoid for the second floor where we house the cats.

Catch a Pet is a full-service animal centre—we take in cats as well as dogs, the odd rabbit when the owner graduates into "cute bunnies are too much work with a social life", three rats that Ajax convinced me to accept when the family moved out of town, which quickly became a family of nine and then dropped down to six before we realized we needed to separate the daddies, and a parrot that we got when Captain Bill passed.

The parrot could and did swear more colourfully than any of the fishermen down by the docks. Even I learned a few phrases in the year we had him.

But thanks to some well-needed advice and mentoring from Lady—soon-to-be Princess—Camille, we now have an updated website to promote adopting the animals, and the parrot has found his forever home in Ottawa, Canada.

It's been a learning curve but the animals need someone on their side. And the shelter has been noticeably quieter, thanks to so many dogs being adopted in the last three months.

I love that the dogs are happy and I do everything I can to make sure they're placed well, but when you rescue a stray or have a pet surrendered, or even, in the worst case, have the police bring in an abused animal—after feeding and caring and teaching them, sometimes it's really hard to let them go.

I take a moment to scan the front page of yesterday's newspaper before I lay it down. Local news has been all about the upcoming wedding, and this is no exception.

IS THE PLAYBOY PRINCE OUT OF LUCK?

Laandia is readying for its first royal wedding since King Magnus came to power as second son Prince Odin prepares to marry Lady Camille Dusain of Saint Pierre. Their surprise engagement came at the heels of Prince Odin's abrupt dismissal from the reality show, The Suitorette, where he was one of twenty-five contestants competing for true love, or what constitutes it on reality television.

The swiftness of the engagement has royal watchers questioning the viability of the match, but none as polarizing as the speculation on whom playboy prince Gunnar will bring to the wedding as his date. With only nine days until the wedding and with no announcement on who will be his guest, one can only assume the Playboy Prince has left it too long to ask someone special—or even a suitable someone—to be his date.

And from one who has followed the romantic exploits of the royal family for many years and seen many heartbreaks, going solo to any big event, is not Prince Gunnar's style.

"I can't believe this constitutes as news," I cry, but Ajax has left me alone in the puppy playpen. The only ones who listen are the puppies, the three dogs in the neighbouring crates watching me with soft eyes, and Bear, the one-hundred-and-sixty-pound Great Pyrenees who has been here from the beginning.

I'm not sure Bear can hear me over the music constantly playing. Music relieves stress, both the dogs and mine. When I came in, I switched from Chris Stapleton to a Lizzy MacAlpine playlist but she's not doing much to relieve the irritation over what's staring at me from the newspapers I'm laying out for the puppies to pee on.

Or who.

I flip over the page with the huge picture of Prince Gunnar and hope that page is peed on first.

Four more articles in the same paper basically say the same thing: the wedding is coming and who will survive? Or rather, who will be going? All week, the newspapers have been chock-full of the movements of the royal family, so I know the youngest royal, Princess Lyra returned from Chicago a few days ago, and Prince Gunnar flew home from his latest travel sojourn soon after. Bo, the royal recluse, and the one I totally relate to, is in residence at the castle. Finally, the heir apparent, Prince Kalle, has hardly been seen at his pub, The King's Hat, because of all of his royal duties.

There had been a rush of media presence when Camille and Odin announced their engagement back in February, but it was quick to die out because Battle Harbour is more of a small town than a city, and the royal family, while royal, is just a family and kind of a boring one at that.

Except for Gunnar and Lyra.

This coverage is different. Every day, pictures of Odin and Camille smile out from newspapers and magazines. Social media is full of posts and stories, and people claiming to be sisters of a cousin of a best friend of a royal person crying because they didn't get an invite. I can't even check my Google feed without a story about them popping up.

The media frenzy, like so many other things these days, irritates me. The town of Battle Harbour has watched the relationship between Prince Odin and Lady Camille unfold with interest but not obsession; with happiness but not the fever pitch of other royal weddings. The town watches because they call Prince Odin one of their own, and they're pleased that he's found love—and not on a reality show.

The rest of the world are the ones with the unhealthy obsession that I can't begin to understand.

I'm torn about what I think of Lady Camille: on one hand, since Prince Odin brought her to Catch a Pet and she adopted a puppy, we've gotten a ton of publicity. People are a bit like sheep in that way—if the royal family gets a dog from us, everyone else wants one too. And that's good for the dogs we rescue and the puppies that are born without someone to love them. Even our population of cats kept upstairs in the cattery—except the huge ginger, Cat Sheeran who roams at will—has seen a steep decline as everyone is Battle Harbour and the rest of Laandia has flocked to get a "royal pet".

There's nothing royal about my animals. I don't need the help of anyone living in the castle.

But I took the help from Lady Camille because she runs the SealSave wildlife rescue centre in Saint Pierre and she knows what she's doing. Hello, website. I wouldn't have figured that out on my own.

Okay, I would have, but an international adoption site wasn't on my radar.

Lady Camille has influence and the animals are better off for it. I can't dislike her for that. Plus, she seems nice, albeit a bit cool when you first meet her so we're not at the friendship bracelets stage yet.

But everything else about her is part of my Things-I-Don't-Approve-of List, which has the royal family right smack-dab at the top.

"Who cares who stupid Prince Gunnar is taking to the stupid wedding!" I ball up the page with the last article and toss it out of the pen. Of course it lands in the other puppy playpen, and three bundles of energy gallop across the small space, sliding headlong into the fence surrounding them.

"Are you talking to me?" Ajax asks, sticking their shaggy head back into the room.

"No," I grumble. "I'm merely bemoaning the lack of control the world has when it comes to the royal family of Laandia."

"Ooo, did you see that Prince Gunnar doesn't have a date to the wedding?"

I roll my eyes and swing a leg over the pen walls. "There are two other brothers in that family, you know? Plus Princess Lyra. Why all the fuss about Gunnar?"

I know Prince Gunnar, and I know he doesn't need the concern of the people. The man can crook his finger on a street corner and the women will flock to him.

I have never been one to flock. I'm not a flocker.

"Yes, but they have dates," Ajax reports as they fill bowls with kibble. Once the dogs realize it's feeding time, the cacophony of barking begins and I hurry to let the last caged puppies into their pen so they can be fed.

"Who?" I ask before I can stop myself. "No, don't tell me."

"You'll find out soon enough," they remind me happily as we finish feeding. "Just over a week to go. I think it was so nice of Lady Camille to invite us, don't you? Did you find a dress yet?"

The thought of a dress deepens my scowl. I'm not a dress girl; I'm not a girly girl. I wear baggy black jeans with unfashionable rips and combat boots with a three-inch platform sole from the last decade, my currently purple/blue/green hair is pulled up into uneven space buns and I bite my nails down to the quick. I work with animals and a royal wedding has long been on the list of Things-I-Don't-Want-to-Attend. "I might care about a dress if I were going."

"Stella!" Ajax makes it sound like I waltzed in wearing a Dalmatian fur coat. "You have to go. No one cares that you don't have a date. I mean," they backpedal quickly, "you could find a date. Lots of people would take you if you wanted them to."

"I really don't." To my mother's utter dismay, dating is another one of those things on the Things-I-Don't-Give-a-Flying-Fart-About list. I see the dogs first thing in the morning and last thing at night, and I'm happy with that.

"I'm kinda glad you don't want a date because then you can go with me," they admit. "You're still going with me, right?"

I glance sympathetically at Ajax. "You don't need me there," I tell my much more outgoing co-worker. "And you'll know as many people there as I will since it sounds like they've invited most of the town."

Except for my family.

Well, they had to invite the mayor but Peter's name was the only one on the invite. I've avoided any discussion of the wedding at home so I'm not sure if my mother will be going.

Once the dogs have been fed, Ajax follows me into my tiny office. I moved the shelter here four years ago after finding a house a few blocks from the centre of town. A fisherman had planned to renovate but sadly, lost his life in a storm at sea. It had been gutted down to the studs and his wife wanted nothing to do with it. We had just enough to buy the house. Ajax's brothers helped us fix it up, and we moved the animals in by the winter, dogs on the main floor and cats upstairs.

The basement is bare bones, but there's enough down there for those on the overnight shifts to be comfortable.

"Yes, but you have a connection to the family—" Ajax claps their lips together after a second, much less sympathetic, glance from me.

"I'm not going to the wedding," I say, sinking into the chair behind the desk and hauling the day's to-do pile in front of me. "End of discussion."

"We actually weren't discussing it at all," Ajax whispers.

"And we won't be."

"But you must have an opinion on who Gunnar is bringing."

"Why would I have an opinion on that?" I demand.

Ajax looks at me knowingly and I look at them with disgust. "Stella," they plead. "Just give me a little."

"Because..."

"You love me," they wheedle. "And this way I can show up at The King's Hat and sound like I know what I'm talking about." They smile winningly at me.

They are annoying, but I am fond of them, as much as I'm fond of anyone these days. "Fenella Carrington," I concede. Rifling through an old pile of *People* magazines on the floor that Ajax keeps for whatever reason, I easily find one with the Carrington twins on the cover and hold it up. "Part of the Billionaire Brats squad. I think he'll end up taking her."

Ajax studies the cover. "Didn't they date a few years ago?"

"Find me someone the prince hasn't dated," I scoff. "I'm sure you've heard she's in town. And I'm guessing she won't need to run out to find a dress suitable to wear since she's probably got a closet the size of the castle."

I could find a dress to wear if I really wanted to. But I don't.

I'm not going to the royal wedding.

And I don't care whom Gunnar, or any of the royals, are bringing as their dates. It makes no difference to me since I won't be there to see it.

As much as I sort of like/tolerate Lady Camille, I have no desire to subject myself to being in the company of the royal family if I don't have to. If Lady Camille were to command me, then maybe, but I don't think she can.

I'm not going to the wedding, and that's final.

2

Gunnar

"I can't take you to this wedding," I tell Fenella as we stop in Battle Harbour to get the second dose of much needed caffeine on the way to the airport.

I pride myself on keeping up with anyone and everyone, but then I remember Fenella Carrington. She's been staying with me for three days and I think I've drunk more in that time than the seven weeks I've just spent touring the United States.

Drying out will be necessary, but more importantly, I need sleep. Lots of sleep, without Fenella on the floor above me waking up hungry for adventure and fun and with more energy than Lady Camille's puppy, Bea Arthur.

I love Fenella—as a friend—but she does seem to have a knack for getting me in trouble when we're together.

Last night was bar-hopping. It's not the first time I've frequented the drinking establishments in Battle Harbour, but last night was the first I've visited all *five* in one night. Even Sailor's Salon—no one can remember the real name, but it's the place the die-hard fishermen and lobstermen hang out when the boats are in.

I have Fenella to thank for that one. And for maxing out my credit card when she insisted we buy everyone a round of drinks, which led to drinks on us, all night.

The girl clearly has no idea how much fishermen drink.

Minka, the one and only member of my security team, got us out of there sometime after three and paid the tab, taking the card with her.

When you're a billionaire like Fenella—billionairess?—credit card bills are never a concern.

Not that they're *that* much of a concern for me either, thanks to the well-stocked royal coffers, but I've been brought up to pay my own way.

Strange, considering I've never had a job, except my seventeenth summer spent on a fishing boat—and I don't remember seeing a paycheck for that.

I may have spent it buying rounds at the Sailor's Salon.

Fenella glances at me, her startling violet eyes full of amusement and possibly a bit of pity. "Is that because you're still mad at me for making you buy our new friends all those drinks?"

"I'm not sure you quite understand the term 'new friend.'"

"What do you mean? They loved us."

"They loved *you*. I'm the lazy prince who bops around the world and takes pictures of it."

"You do more than that. You were in that race in Miami and you did really well." The thing with Fenella is that she means it. She can't comprehend why a group of grizzly fishermen who battle the sea and the elements and really nasty things in the ocean every single day wouldn't automatically embrace me as their newest best friend.

I may be popular, but I know what the blue-collar population of Laandia thinks of me.

Lazy. Selfish. Only out for a good time. Anti-commitment.

Playboy. Player. This was apparent last night since the only conversations I had in the bar were about the women I knew. And when I say *knew*, I mean *intimately knew*.

I don't kiss and tell, so there wasn't much to discuss.

"I'm not mad about the tab," I tell her because it's true. Fenella and I are better as friends than when we were dating and it's impossible to be angry at her. The world may see her as a silly socialite with more money than brains, but she's got a huge heart and does a lot of good when she's not leading a chorus of fishermen in a rousing rendition of "Sweet Caroline."

"I'm glad you had a good time," I finish, throwing my arm around her.

Which is promptly photographed by a wandering photographer. I'm happy for Odin and Camille, but I'll be happy when this wedding is over and I can get back to my life hiding in plain sight in any place other than Laandia.

But back to the pressing concern. "I still can't take you to the wedding."

Fenella lowers her oversized sunglasses and gives me that look that makes her a mainstay of fashion magazines. "Darlin' Gunnar. No one asked you to," she says sympathetically.

"In case you were thinking about it," I add.

"I think of lots of things," she says, the hint of one of the southern states of the US evident in her voice. "You taking me on a date, whether it be for dinner or to the biggest royal wedding this side of Harry and Meghan, hasn't been something I've thought about for a long time. In case *you* were wondering."

I give her a smile of affection because that's the best way to deal with Fenella—keep her sweet. Keep her happy. "You always know how to make a guy feel good," I say, keeping the sarcasm to a minimum.

"Ditto, beautiful boy. What's the fuss about who you're taking to the wedding anyway? Just ask someone. Coral or Lavinia will go with you if you like," she suggests, mentioning a few other mutual friends. "Or call in a favour with Florence."

Florence Pugh. Coral Aldershot, heir to Triple-A Winery. Model and muse, Lavinia, who now goes by one name, like Zendaya. Fenella fits in with them, being Fenella Carrington, the daughter of one of the biggest toy companies in the world.

None of those women are whom Odin meant when he told me to get a date for the wedding.

It's a beautiful day in Laandia, which is not always the case since the country borders both the Atlantic and Arctic Oceans and the icy wind blowing will freeze the balls off a buffalo, as the saying goes.

But the breeze is June-like for once, and the sun is warm. The town of Battle Harbour, located down the hill from the castle is at its best on days like this. Especially, when it's decorated for a royal wedding.

I'm glad I'm here to see it.

Not that I would ever miss my brother's wedding, but it's nice to be back.

For the last five years, I've been steadily travelling the world, one trip at a time. After our mother died, it helped get my need for speed out of the way and I slowed down and started seeing the world. I still race cars on occasion, and the odd boat—the only thing I haven't raced are planes and that is only because no one will let me be a fighter pilot.

No one in other countries; the king would allow it, but Laandia doesn't have an Air Force and neither Canada nor America will take me.

I'm beyond grateful for the opportunities I have, and the income to go wherever I want, but being back in Battle Harbour on a day like this makes me realize I miss home more than I think I do. I'm home from a seven-week stretch touring the States, where I picked up Fenella and brought her home for a visit, and with nothing planned for after the wedding, I find myself mulling over staying put for a bit.

When I'm not mulling over my lack of that special someone to take to Odin's wedding, that is.

I wave my phone at Fenella. "Text from big brother about who I'm bringing. Apparently, it's of the *utmost importance*," I say, mimicking Odin's somber tone.

Not that I need to tell her or anyone else this fact; the press has been very diligent in reporting all and everything about this wedding. The royal wedding that should have happened months ago on Valentine's Day.

The world thinks Prince Odin of Laandia—second son, third tallest, and my big brother—reconnected with Lady Camille Dusain of Saint Pierre after he attempted to find love as a contestant on the reality dating show *The Suitorette*.

Everyone loves that story.

The truth is that Odin was trying to save face after being sent home after only one day on the show, and Camille needed a husband. The advisors of King Magnus—otherwise known as my dad—and the prefect of Saint Pierre thought it made sense to arrange for Odin and Camille to be married.

On Valentine's Day, to make the story look really good.

Only, Odin and Camille didn't want to make it *look good*. They wanted it to feel good and real. The original wedding would have worked out, but big brother and his lady had only begun to develop true feelings for each other and wanted the time to get to know each other and truly mean their vows.

As someone who has watched the blossoming love story play out on my trips home and numerous FaceTime calls, the real thing between them is better than any reality-show romance.

This wedding is going to be epic.

For them, anyway. Not so much for me unless I find a nice girl who will put up with the three-ring circus that is a royal wedding.

I can only assume it's going to be a special kind of chaos because we've never actually had a royal wedding in the kingdom of Laandia.

All I know is that I'm expected to bring a date.

Normally, that wouldn't be a problem for a prince, and it's not a problem for my brothers, Kalle and Bo because Kalle can get anyone he wants, and Bo is practically a hermit and no one will care who he brings.

I'm not sure why it's different for me. There are betting odds on who I'll bring, with Florence coming in at 5-1, and Sabrina Carpenter and Olivia Rodrigo both at 8-2, which apparently, has created a social media war between their fans. Also on the list are

Camilla Cabello, the girl from the "Never Have I Ever" TV show, and even Zahara Jolie-Pitt, only because I happened to be standing next to Angelina at the Cannes Film Festival and someone took a picture.

"I need a date," I say unnecessarily.

"So you say. Find someone to ask."

"It's not that easy."

Fenella gives me a look. "I dated you. It's not that difficult."

"And that's why I can't take you. The world can't handle even a mention of the possibility that the two of us might be getting back together."

"Oh, sweet boy." Fen laughs loud enough for Ernie from the candy shop to look up from his sweeping. I nod a hello but don't stop to talk since Ernie is one of the biggest gossips in town. "It's not the world that can't handle *this*." She swipes a hand down her very lovely figure. "It's you."

"You are so right," I say in a monotone. "You are too much woman for me."

Actually, it's true. Fenella Carrington is a lot. *A lot* a lot. I'm not sure if that's because she was born into the Carrington family—known for the Carrington toy cars, those little cars that I and everyone else in the world played with as kids—or because that's just how she is.

Fenella is a New Year's party, during Mardi Gras, in the middle of a hurricane.

I didn't come up with the description but it fits.

I'm just glad I made it through six months of dating with all my appendages intact. The fact that we're still good friends is nothing short of a miracle.

"She's got to be local." I switch back to my usual voice.

"And, from what I recall, you've burned some bridges with the local girls, hmm?" Fenella raises an eyebrow, and I wince.

Kate. Years later, I'm still not forgiven. "Yes, well, I can't pick up just anyone on the street."

At that moment, a trio of girls who can't be more than sixteen steps out from the juice shop in front of us with shrieks of delight. "Prince Gunnar!"

"It's him!"

"Take us to the wedding!" one of them cries. "Please?"

"Take all of us," a second one chimes.

I manage a lackluster wave. "You should be in school," I tell them under my breath as we sidestep the group, and Fenella laughs.

"Looks like you shouldn't have a problem," she says without an ounce of sympathy.

I jerk my thumb toward the girls. "That is the problem. I need someone... suitable."

"What's suitable for you? A nice girl who won't make a scene after you let her down ever so gently after rocking her world at the wedding of the year?"

I grimace but I can't deny it. Fenella knows me too well. "Yeah. That."

Unlike my brother Odin, I'm not on the hunt for commitment or long-term or even a relationship that lasts over the weekend. I'm not looking for anything these days, but the problem is that anyone I ask to be my date will see that as a declaration of lifelong adoration.

"Poor Gunny. Got *any* options?"

I really wish I could say Kate because that would be so easy. Kate, as my sister Lyra's best friend, has known the family forever. She's working PR for Odin now, which means she's part of the inner circle.

But three things stop me from inviting her as my date: the media circus me showing up with her would entail, my brothers would have my head, and Kate's already got herself a new guy.

"There are none," I say morosely as I open the door of Coffee for the Sole for Fenella. "And therein lies the problem."

3

Stella

I SPEND MY AFTERNOON break from the shelter at Coffee for the Sole. My sister, Sophie, joins me. She's the manager of Ye Olde Fish Shoppe, and two p.m. isn't a very busy time for her, so that's when we meet for coffee. Sometimes, if I'm peopled out, we take it to go; other days, we stay for a snack and a chat with Silas, which is a treat on its own.

Coffee for the Sole has the best coffee in Battle Harbour and the best barista. Silas took over the coffee shop about ten years ago when his parents retired, and I would bet money that there isn't a woman in town who hasn't had her fair share of fantasies about the tall drink of water manning the frother.

He may be super nice but he's also really hot.

And hasn't been out with anyone since he got his heart broken when Mia Khan left Battle Harbour, shattering Silas's heart in the process. It's a good thing she's gone since the townsfolk would have come after her with pitchforks if she'd stuck around.

The people of Battle Harbour are very protective of their own, and Silas, as well as Coffee for the Sole, belong to us all.

My stepsister Daphne works at the coffee shop. I wasn't really into having a step-sister when Mom married Peter Luute, now the mayor of Battle Harbour, but Daphne was quick to grow on me.

We're not as close as Sophie and I, but she's my sister in every sense of the word.

My mother feels Daphne still needs supervision, and I have to agree. Even though she's twenty-two, there is an innocence about Daphne that worries both me and Sophie. She's too sweet for her own good, just asking to be taken advantage of by some wealthy sophisticate who undoubtedly works at the castle and thinks it would be fun to sweep a local girl off her feet.

I'm cynical like that. Plus, anyone who has anything to do with the royal family is persona non grata for me. As Ms. Swift says in the song, the castle is on my list and underlined in red. Or something like that. Daphne is a bigger Taylor Swift fan, so she would know the correct lyric to describe it.

Because everything can be described with a Taylor Swift lyric.

The only problem with my—let's not call it hatred; apathy, perhaps—of the royal family is that Lady Camille is kind of growing on me too. And Odin isn't that bad.

He did get her a puppy as a present, after all.

But it's too nice of a day to dwell on the people up the hill. It's a good day. The June sun is warm enough to fill the few tables on the sidewalk patio, although it's too crowded for me to want to sit outside; none of the puppies peed on me yet, although one of the latest took a dislike to the puppy kibble which led to a mess that forced us to prop the door open for most of the morning, and Sophie is bringing fish and chips home for supper even though it's only Tuesday, and I prefer takeout on Friday.

Still, a good day, for the most part.

Sophie sips her latte with a smile on her face. "The coffee is always so good here," she says. "Hot and strong, like the princes."

I do my best not to gag. "I can't believe that just came out of your mouth."

"A lot of things come out of my mouth that you find unbelievable, including my opinions on Those Who Live Up the Cliff."

Sophie knows I don't like to discuss the castle dwellers.

And yet— "Who do you think Prince Gunnar will bring to the wedding?" she asks.

"Why does everyone feel the need to ask that of *me*?" I demand, a little too loudly.

"C'mon, Stella. You're the perfect person to ask, because, you know—you and Gunnar..."

I roll my eyes so violently that I worry they may roll back into my head. "Seriously?" I hold my hand up and begin counting. "That was fourteen, almost fifteen years ago!"

Sophie's smile is wide and teasing. "Still."

"Still nothing, because there was *nothing*. Plus, kids."

Both Sophie and I had been part of the pack that ran riot through the castle in the summers when we were kids. Our mother was officially a lady in waiting for the queen— and unofficially, her best friend, so it was natural their children would be friends. The castle had been like a summer camp back then, with Mrs. Theissen the head counsellor we tried to avoid.

Especially when we did things that would get us into trouble, like playing Truth or Dare in the dungeons.

But friendships don't last forever.

I don't like being reminded of the fact that Prince Gunnar kissed me—on a dare from his brother Bo—when I was twelve.

A girl always remembers her first kiss and mine was with Gunnar.

There are a lot of emotions to unpack about that.

My sister leans back in her chair, one of the comfy armchairs by the window. "So you admit you had a girlhood crush on the youngest prince?" she asks with a teasing grin. "Maybe you should ask him to the wedding."

"No. You will never hear such a confession come out of my mouth. And *no*. Not on your life. Not even if your life was in danger and your survival depended on me going anywhere with him." To emphasize, I take an aggressive bite out of the soft pretzel we're sharing.

"We were sharing," she pouts.

"Sharing is caring, and you just destroyed it with that suggestion."

"It may be time to get over your heartbreak," Sophie suggests. "Or at least stop taking it out on my afternoon snack."

"There was no heartbreak," I tell her with a grim note in my voice. "And I don't understand why you won't share my—"

"Continual and irrational anger toward the royal family?" Sophie interrupts. She shrugs. "Maybe because I don't see the point? Not anymore."

It's too nice of a day to get into this. There is a reason for my aversion toward King Magnus and his family, and it's not because of a girlish crush on the younger prince.

Also, I would never call it a crush. More like a lack of judgment, but I've learned many lessons since I was twelve and to never trust a royal is only one of them.

Because I don't want to ruin the day, I decide to ignore Sophie instead of heading into one of my almost weekly rants and sip my coffee in silence. Sophie waves down Daphne and asks her to bring us another pretzel.

As well as making belly-warming coffee that can change a good day into a great one, Silas also has the best treats in town. I'm partial to the jumbo cinnamon buns but need to skip a meal to even share one of them, and I plan on enjoying my fish and chips tonight.

But then, the pleasant afternoon suddenly changes. Like an icy wind sweeping in through an open door, Prince Gunnar, fourth son, shortest, smiliest, and one of the banes of my existence, saunters into Coffee for the Sole like he owns the place.

The fact that he doesn't acknowledge our mutual animosity is like a popcorn kernel stuck in my teeth.

To give Prince Gunnar credit, it might be possible that he doesn't realize just how much I loathe him, even though I do my best to show him whenever we meet.

"Oh, joy," I say, reaching for the last piece of salted dough to stuff in my mouth to stifle the litany of complaints that brews like bad coffee.

"Share!" Sophie pulls the plate away from my grasping fingers before glancing up. "Ah. Only your favourite person. His ears must be burning."

"I'd be fine if the rest of him was in flames." I glare at my cup instead of the prince. I may hate him with all the depths of my soul, but he is a prince, and shooting daggers across a coffee shop may be illegal in Viking circles, for all I know.

"Stella. That's not nice."

"I take it back. I wouldn't want him to be on fire in here because it would wreck the place and Silas doesn't deserve that."

Sophie shakes her head as she studies Gunnar intently enough for the both of us. "She's new."

I glance up to see her attention is focused on the woman at Gunnar's side—tall, raven hair, wearing a sundress with all the colours of my mermaid hair, and platform sandals. Like my clumpy combat boots, they give her an extra couple of inches she doesn't need. Unlike me.

Beautiful, like most of Gunnar's bevy of female companions.

The man is as shallow as a saucer of milk.

And yet, every woman in the place tries to catch his eye because he's Prince flippin' Gunnar.

"Not new, just hasn't been around for a while," I say with a grimace. "That's Fenella Carrington."

Sophie's eyes widen at the name. "I didn't recognize her with long hair. Is her brother here?" For someone who has been raised in the shadow of the castle, Sophie is sweetly oblivious to the comings and goings of the royal family and friends.

Or maybe I'm just a little too focused, thanks to Ajax's never-ending fascination and non-stop attempts to engage in conversation about them.

That must be the reason. I'll tell them I saw Gunnar with Fenella and hopefully, that will stop the questions for a few days.

Everyone in the world knows the Carrington twins: Fenella and Ashton, heirs to the Carrington model car dynasty, and part of the group of socialites and heirs to family fortunes, with the odd model and Instagram influencer thrown in, that cavorts across the world in their search for fun. The press dubs them the Billionaire Brats.

Gunnar, close friends with Ashton and one-time paramour of Fenella, is a card-carrying member of the group.

I shake my head. "I haven't smelt the stench of sulphur, so I don't think so."

"Ashton may be unpleasant, but still, oh, so pretty."

I make a face at Sophie. "You really have horrible taste."

"You have *no* taste unless it's for something made of dough." She attempts to rip apart the remainder of the pretzel and I grab for it before it makes it to her mouth.

"Stop fighting, I'm bringing you another to share," Daphne calls, setting the plate down beside me and bringing with her a whiff of sugar-sprinkled vanilla cookies.

I don't know if it's Daphne's perfume or shampoo that makes her smell so sweet. I have a feeling it may just be her general sunny personality. She's one of those people who look at the world through rose-coloured glasses that are half-full of sparkling glitter that trails in her wake.

If she smells good because she's nice, it means there's a great chance that I smell as foul as that puppy pooing accident from this morning.

Daphne is blonde and can be somewhat bumbling and possibly a little...dim... but she's as sweet as my mother's rhubarb pie so no one ever takes offence or makes fun of her. She's loved by everyone she knows, admired by those she doesn't, and a people-pleaser in all the best ways; plus she's caring, considerate and makes a really amazing caramel latte.

She stars in every theatre production in the area, volunteers at the Home of Aging Residents, and was, of course, crowned Sea Queen for the annual Battle Harbour holiday celebration.

It's a thing. And Daphne has won it three years in a row.

Despite all those awesome things about her, Daphne *does not* annoy me like most of the world's population. I suspect she's magical in some way.

"Do you have time to sit with us?" Sophie asks her.

Daphne shakes her head, high ponytail swishing back and forth. "I'd love to, but I need to help Silas. He hasn't had a break since lunch, poor guy. But there will be lots of time to hear about your days at supper tonight." Soft blue eyes sparkle. "Fish and chips!"

With a blinding white smile that doesn't come from Crest Whitening Strips, Daphne floats back behind the counter.

Her magic doesn't rub off on me. While I break apart the pretzel as unfairly as I can get away with, I switch on my glowering gaze while Gunnar and Fenella Carrington order their drinks.

Why such a basic interaction grabs my attention is unknown but probably because people like Gunnar and Fenella Carrington don't make it a basic interaction.

Gunnar, who oozes charm like a slug oozes slug-goo, speaks to Silas behind the coffeemaker like they are old friends, asks Daphne about her latest performance, teases barista Jacko about his boyfriend, and makes every single person in the line feel like they are an important part of his life.

I know Gunnar does this because he's done it with me. It's a gift—or a curse, depending on how much you like talking to people.

I'm the same age as Gunnar, born three days earlier, and as the story goes, I was his first play date at four days old. We lay swaddled beside each other, alternating sleeping and crying—I'm sure he slept while I cried—while our mothers had tea and discussed epidurals and episiotomies, and hey, did you poop on the table giving birth?

Later in life, Gunnar was in my class at Leif Erickson Public School because the queen insisted that the royal kids got a regular education. It worked for the regular kids of Laandia because twice a year King Magnus opened the castle for a party—at Christmas, which became the annual Battle Harbour holiday party, and again in June to celebrate the end of the school year.

Even I have to admit they were great parties—scavenger hunts, obstacle courses, and jumpy castles dotted across the castle backyard, plus cupcakes and the best sundae bar.

Gunnar and Fenella move off to the side while Silas makes their drinks, probably super complicated with multiple pumps of multiple syrups and a double load of the unicorn froth Coffee for the Sole is famous for. Fenella doesn't give off the "I'm friendly when I'm trying to be a regular person" vibes that Gunnar does, but she more than makes up for it with sheer nosiness. She saunters off to look at the fish net dangling in the corner, the paintings on the wall—one of which I'm proud to say belongs to my sister— and laughing at the flipping fish, with more than a little condescension in her voice.

I don't like her, which isn't surprising because I don't like many people.

"That one is by a local artist," Gunnar calls to Fenella, who is back to studying the painting. "And she's sitting right here. Hello, Sophie." Gunnar smiles at my sister and even under my glowering glare I see her melt like the ice in her iced matcha.

I want to pinch her back into the reality where we hate him. At least where I still hate him. Unfortunately, she's been out of that world for a while now.

"Your Royal Highness." If Sophie had been standing, she would have curtsied. And if she had, I might have kicked her.

"That's so funny." Fenella glides back to Gunnar's side with a smile. "He's just Gunnar to me." Her smile has teeth, warmth and smiley eyes; a very different expression than the rest of the world gets.

I hate to admit it makes her look even more stunning.

If Fenella were blonde, the two of them would be dead ringers for Barbie and Ken. Gunnar isn't clone handsome like Odin, or has the bad boy sexy looks like Prince Kalle, but he's got a cheerful boy-next-door good looks meets mischievous devil-may-care vibe that is irresistible to most women.

Except for me. Even with the Jeff Probst deep dimples and the dark blue eyes that laugh more than they are serious because Gunnar can't be serious about anything.

"We were taught to respect the crown," I say, oozing my own brand of slug-goo. "Whether they deserve it or not."

"And there she is." Gunnar's smile is still present, but tight. His entire expression tightens. I do that to him. "Stella."

I nod, not willing to degrade myself with the niceties. Luckily, Daphne drops off their coffees at the side counter so he doesn't have to be close to us for long.

"Thanks, Daphne." Gunnar's smile is back, or maybe he's just under Daphne's influence. More than Princess Lyra, Daphne rules the town with her sweet nature and endless good humour.

Plus, she's Cinderella-like beautiful. Better than Fenella with her expensive creams and exfoliating machines and army of make-up artists to make her Insta-perfect.

"She's a pretty one," Fenella gazes after Daphne, and for a moment, I give her credit for admiring another woman rather than disparaging her with put-downs.

Only for a moment.

"She belongs to them." Gunnar nods at me and Sophie, his gaze lingering on me. I raise my chin, preparing for battle.

"Oh, really?" Fenella's violet eyes—such an amazing colour that it *can't* be natural—sweep over us, and I can tell what she's thinking: that there is no way the Blonde Beauty can possibly be related to us.

"Stepsister," Sophie explains unnecessarily.

"Daphne is the Helen of Troy of Battle Harbour," Gunnar explains. "Men would go to war for her. Luckily, it's never come to that, although Uhtred of Lichtenstein offered a private island for her when she was only sixteen."

Fenella sniffs. "No one has offered an island for me."

"I don't remember anything about a private island," I snap.

"He offered it to my father since Daphne is a citizen of Laandia." I open my mouth to let out a cry of injustice, and Gunnar holds up his hand. "Dad refused, of course, and suggested Uhtred speak directly to Daphne and her father if he was serious about her."

"And you didn't think the kingdom needed a private island?" I ask with a heavy dose of sarcasm.

"We already have a private island." Gunnar smiles but his eyes are cool.

"In the Arctic Circle," I scoff.

"We have two. You might want to check out that map you always carried around. Or have you forgotten your dream of travelling out of Laandia?"

I open my mouth but can't come up with a retort because *what*? How does he remember that?

Sophie interrupts/saves me. "I don't mean to be rude, Your Highness," she begins.

"Rude?" A pointed glance at me, and then he turns to Sophie with a grin. "You? Never."

"Rumour has it that you're looking for someone local to take to the wedding."

I marvel at Sophie's boldness. But— "You're not serious?" I demand. We're fourteen months apart and share twin-like extrasensory perception.

Sophie lowers her voice, even though Gunnar and Fenella are standing beside us and can hear every word. "You have to admit, it's a good idea."

Just to make sure Gunnar hears *everything,* I raise my voice. "I don't have to admit anything."

"Aw, look." Gunnar nudges Fenella. "They're fighting over me."

My glare would wither a lesser man, but Gunnar only grins. "I am doing nothing of the sort."

And now the dimples come out.

"Sure sounds like you're expressing your displeasure about something, and I'd bet money that it's me."

"That's because your ego is bigger than the entirety of Laandia."

"I'm not about to deny that I have a considerable ego because I know it only irritates you when I don't engage in your little insult war." Gunnar sounds way too delighted about our exchange and I grit my teeth.

"You annoy me," I mutter into my latte.

"That all you got?"

I inwardly growl but don't give Gunnar the satisfaction. "Sophie?" I force my tone into politeness. "Where is this idea coming from?"

"She really wants to go," Sophie pleads.

My gaze slides to Daphne who is with a customer, so sweet and happy and *good*. "She has no idea what she wants."

"She?" Gunnar asks.

"Not us," Sophie assures him. "No offence, of course."

I don't mind offending him. "There is no *us* in this," I add, crossing my arms across my chest. "I am not part of this. Anything relating to this."

"*This* sounds like it's right up my alley then." He motions to Sophie to continue.

Sophie gives me a long, hopeful look and I can see the battle in her eyes. I think for a moment that I'm about to be on the winning side, but then—

"Daphne doesn't have a date for the wedding," Sophie explains with a glance over to Daphne behind the counter. Gunnar follows suit.

He looks. Looks a little longer before turning back to Sophie. Sophie. Not me. Because he knows I do not agree with this.

What is she *doing*? This is our sister she's trying to set up with my worst enemy. That's like the worst kind of sister betrayal. Where is her loyalty? Her allegiance? Her—

"Let me get this straight." Gunnar's navy-blue eyes narrow like he's seriously considering the idea, and *he can't be.* "You're suggesting I take *Daphne* to the wedding? Your stepsister. As my date?" He glances at Fenella, who shrugs.

"She looks the part," Fenella concedes. "The pictures of the two of you would be amazing. Royal Barbie and Ken."

I *hate* that she's read my mind about Gunnar as Ken. "And that's all that matters," I drawl.

Gunnar glances at me, then back to Sophie, over to Daphne, and then back to Sophie.

Fenella, clearly bored of the conversation, examines her nailbeds.

"She's not interested in me, is she?" Gunnar leans close, and for a moment I smell something amazing. Clean and citrus and woodsy, and manlike—

Nope. Not possible. Prince Gunnar does not smell good. There must be something wrong with my olfactory senses today. That puppy poo must have broken something up there.

"I don't think so," Sophie says in a quiet voice. She glances at me, and I finally get what her endgame is.

I still don't like it.

"Has she said anything about it?" Gunnar asks. "About *me*? Because maybe it's a good idea, but honestly if she's interested, it would complicate things. I do need a date but I'm not looking..." Gunnar shifts, as uncomfortable as I've ever seen him, which is the only thing fun for me about this.

Nothing else is fun about this. Just the thought of Daphne and Gunnar—

Still...

Sophie shakes her head. "She's only said that she'd love to go to the wedding. Many, many times. At least ten times a day. But nothing about you. I really don't think she's interested in *you*." She gives me a sideways glance, warning me to keep my mouth shut.

I bite my tongue only because Daphne going to the wedding with Gunnar means she won't be going with someone else. A specific someone else.

Because someone else might be becoming a problem.

Gunnar seems to be seriously contemplating the idea, which is insane because who he's taking to the wedding has become a national obsession and deserves to have more consideration than being asked if he wants sugar in his coffee. There should be a connection and interest, not because of convenience or the prettiness of the pictures.

"It might work," he muses. "You really think it's a good idea?"

"Yes," Sophie says as excited as if Gunnar were asking *her*. "I do."

Not that Sophie and Gunnar should excite *anyone*, especially not me. "No," I insist. "Not a good idea."

"So you—" —he points to Sophie—"think I should ask her. But you—" —points to me—"don't think I should."

"That's right. And if I give you a moment, I'm sure you'll say something to convince Sophie how much of a bad idea it really is." I glare at my sister.

"Well, I'm not about to give you that moment. Daphne?" Gunnar calls and heads to the counter. "Got a minute?"

4

Gunnar

A Prince of Laandia and the Sea Queen? It's not the worst idea.

Much better than the idea of me taking Stella, which is where I thought Sophie was going.

Stella is... I've known her forever and I've always found her slightly terrifying.

She's so sharp-tongued and quick-witted and smart and well-read and can talk rings around me. And she knows it. We were friends when we were kids, and then we weren't and I've always felt awkward about the things I confided in her.

To be honest, it was more than friends. I spent my pre-teen years, and a few of my teen ones completely infatuated with Stella Laz and got mercilessly teased about it by my brothers. Lyra too.

And then there's that kiss... We were twelve, but still. Bo didn't need to dare me, and he knew it because I headed into pre-puberty wanting to kiss Stella.

So there's that.

It's never easy knowing someone doesn't like you, and you have no idea why. To be honest, I usually don't have that problem. I'm a likable guy.

But Stella—no idea what goes on in her head. And I hate the thought that I *want to know* so I've found the best way to deal with that is to give her the business as much as she does to me.

Stella would never be an option to take to the wedding.

Now Daphne, on the other hand...

Daphne Luute, is the Regina George of Battle Harbour without the petty selfishness. She's the Cher from Clueless, but not as dim—

That may be debatable.

She's got the pretty/popular/perfection of Taylor Swift but without the pipes.

Who knows? Maybe she can sing.

Taking Daphne to the wedding is a solid idea, and I should have thought of her earlier. She's pretty and popular and all of Battle Harbour loves her. She'd be great with the media because of her experience with the local pageants, and she's *nice*, so much nicer than her sister. Stella would be my first choice for the role of the wicked stepsister, so it's fitting that she wants to deny her sister the fun of going to the wedding with me.

And it would be fun.

Even if Sophie isn't telling the whole truth and Daphne does have a thing for me, I'm confident we'd be able to sort it out without too many hurt feelings. She's sweet and personable, and familiar enough with the family not to be too freaked out about the idea about being on display.

And honestly, she'd look great standing next to me. She'd look terrific standing next to anyone, but my average-sized ego tells me we'd look amazing.

Now that I've said I'd do it, I've got to do it.

I don't look back at Stella and Sophie, but I know they're watching me. They used to look like twins—same curly reddish hair cut in a chin-length bob, same big, curious eyes, the only difference being the colour. Sophie with her chocolate-button brown and Stella a silvery grey that may have been the source of my earliest fascination.

They were so pretty; Sophie still is, but it's hard to tell with Stella with the black eye makeup and slick of dark lipstick. The nose ring is new, as is the multi-coloured hair pulled back into little buns perched on the top of her head, but the mulish expression has been there for quite some time now.

It's hard to find Stella's prettiness when she's mean to me, but every time I look at her, I still try and find it.

So I don't look back.

Fenella, on the other hand—tall, gorgeous with her own set of uniquely coloured eyes—is most likely scrolling through her various media accounts, looking to post the pictures she took on the way here.

My focus is on Daphne. Because this is a good idea.

"Daphne. How're you doing?" I grin at her over the counter, appreciating how very pretty she is, even wearing the apron covered with grinning cartoon fish.

She could land a toothpaste commercial with that smile. "What can I help you with, Your Royal Highness?"

I can't hide the grimace. "Just plain Gunnar."

"But you're a prince," she protests. "Prince Gunnar. Not just plain anything."

"I can pretend, can't I?" Which is my favourite thing to do these days. "How has your day been?"

Daphne doesn't even try to hide her expression of confusion. "Fine, thank you. Do you need anything, Your... Prince Highness Gunnar?"

"I need a date." I might as well lay my cards on the table since Daphne seems busy... and a little confused.

"We have some nice date squares."

Okay, a lot confused. "Not a snack. A real date." I take a deep breath. "I am in desperate need of someone to accompany me to my brother's wedding. Prince Odin," I add, in case she's missing the point.

Maybe I shouldn't have mentioned the desperate part.

"You don't have a date for the wedding?" Daphne looks pointedly at Fenella standing by Stella, scrolling on her phone.

"Oh, I'm not taking her. I can't," I say quickly. "We're just friends. I'm not looking for anything more than a friend to take to the wedding, but not Fenella. I need someone from here. The people—Laandia—kind of expect it, you know?"

"That makes sense." Daphne nods like it does make sense. "I'm sure that it won't be too hard for you to find someone. Maybe I can help you with that."

"I would love that."

She's even prettier with a big smile across her face. "I might have some friends who would—"

I hold up my hand. Whoever thinks it would be easy for me to find a date needs a one-way trip to the castle dungeons. "It's okay. I think I have found someone."

"That's great. You should ask her." Her excitement seems so real, and for a moment, my heart gives an *awww* tug, like it did the first time I saw Camille's puppy.

"I agree. Daphne, would you like to go to the wedding with me?" I ask in my best princely voice. "As my date?"

"Me?"

Her voice rings out through the shop and a glance over my shoulder shows Stella's shoulders hunched as she laughs into her coffee.

Is this as big a mistake as it seems? "Yes, you," I say, fighting for patience. "Is that something you'd be interested in?"

"Being interested in you?"

"That's not a requirement," I rush to say. "You don't have to be interested in me. In fact, it's better if you aren't. Other than friends. We can go as friends. I think that's best, anyway."

Daphne frowns. "But we're not friends. You don't like my sisters."

"That's not true, I think Sophie is terrific. And we might not be friends *yet*." I stress the word. "But we could become friends and go to the wedding together. What do you think?" I give her my most winning smile.

I have asked out supermodels, an Oscar winner, and the highest-paid social influencer in the world. Every one of those times was so much easier than this.

Daphne pauses and *holy crap, she's going to say no*. But then she pulls her phone out of the pocket of her apron and checks it.

This just keeps getting better and better.

And I can hear Stella's laugh getting louder. I hope she's enjoying herself.

I'm about to tell Daphne to forget it in an attempt to save whatever dignity I may have left, but Daphne looks up from her phone. "The wedding is at the castle?"

"It's a royal wedding, so yeah, we thought we'd have it at the castle," I say casually. "Thought it'd be a good idea."

"I'll go with you."

The about-face throws me off-guard. "You—really?"

"Really. You must need someone if you're asking me. Neither of my sisters wanted to go?"

"I didn't ask them. I asked you."

"And I say yes." Daphne gives me the smile that won her the Sea Queen title, which thankfully masks the last few *WTH* moments I've just experienced.

But I have a date.

And my smile is one of satisfaction as I head back to where Fenella is still standing by Stella and Sophie. They look awkward; Fen just looks bored.

"Done," I tell them.

"Don't look so smug," Stella snaps. She's always so snappy, much like Betty White. But I've won over Camille's elderly dog. I'm not about to try to win over Stella.

I suspect she bites.

"I seem to recall how it was the wicked stepsisters who tried to stop Cinderella from going to the ball," I muse. "I have to say, you really fit the role."

"Ha ha," Stella makes a face, but I notice she doesn't protest.

On the other hand— "I'm not wicked," Sophie protests. "Much."

"No, I apologize for including you." I stare pointedly at Stella. "Daphne isn't Cinderella."

Is Stella *grinding* her teeth? "And yet, you're not denying you're a wicked stepsister?"

"You are definitely not Prince Charming."

I raise an eyebrow and glance at Fenella. "I think I might have hit a nerve."

"I have no idea what's going on," Fenella sweeps her hair off her neck. "Nor do I really care."

"What's going on, fair Fenella, is these two loyal Laandian citizens have just suggested their sister attend the wedding as my date. I asked the fair maiden—"

"You can't call both Fenella and Daphne *fair* in the same sentence," Stella bursts out. "It's like bad grammar or something."

"Okay," I say slowly, as Sophie looks incredulously at her sister. "I asked the beautiful maiden to be my date, and she said yes."

"Why can't I be called the beautiful one?" Fenella asks.

I don't understand women *at all*. "I think we're missing the point here. The point being *I got a date.*" I'm about to fist-pump but then I realize Daphne is probably watching and she already thinks I'm desperate. "And I owe it all to you." I tip an imaginary hat to the sisters.

"I want no part of this," Stella hisses, giving me her Black Glare of Death. If she didn't look at me like that all of the time, I might be slightly nervous.

"Fine," I say.

"Fine," Stella echoes, but louder for more emphasis.

Thank *you*, Sophie." I turn to Fenella. "Ready to get you back home?"

"If I must. So nice to meet you both," Fenella says with one of her tabloid-ready smiles. But then her eyes narrow at Stella. "Even though *you* seem to dislike Gunnar more than anyone I've ever met."

5

Stella

I REALLY DISLIKE FENELLA Carrington.

And it's not because her surprisingly protective side came out toward Gunnar but... I just don't like her.

I don't technically *dislike* Gunnar. I just...

I don't like him. Much.

He unnerves me with his ease with people and places and things. And I don't like what he stands for—the principles of the royal family.

I definitely don't like the royal family.

And now, my stepsister, the one, according to my mother, I'm supposed to look after, is going to the royal wedding as Gunnar's date.

"He actually asked her," I hiss as Gunnar gallantly escorts Fenella out of the coffee shop without a backward glance at me. Not that I expect him to give me any glances. Nor want him to.

But I still watch them leave with a touch of unease in my stomach that feels a little like disappointment but more likely is caused by too much pretzel.

"You told him to." Sophie blinks at me. "You practically dared him to. Even I know Gunnar Erickson takes every dare he's given."

I am well aware of that. It's the only reason he ruined my first kiss by being the first boy to kiss me. On a dare. "That doesn't make sense—that I told him. I told him *not* to ask her. And it's *Prince* Gunnar."

"Stel, you held hands with the guy when you were seven and kissed him when you were twelve. I don't think he'd mind you calling him Gunnar. It's not like King Magnus goes around beheading people who are a little too informal with the princes."

"I wouldn't know who he beheads."

"No one, that's who." Sophie shakes her head. "You've got to get over this thing you have against the royal family."

"It's not a thing."

"It is so a thing. And especially with Gunnar. I don't get it. You're so..." I know she wants to say *mean* but won't. Sophie isn't as nice as Daphne, but she's so much nicer than me.

"He's the same way to me."

"I think he likes you. That's how boys treat girls when they like them."

"Yes, when they're twelve," I chide. "And that is the most un-feminist thing you can say. Women shouldn't allow men to be mean just because they might like them. It's so immature and *wrong*."

Sophie blinks. "You're right about all of that, but I still think he likes you. He *looks* at you."

Why would Prince Gunnar look at me? "Why?" I ask aloud just to reiterate how silly that is. "Especially when he has someone like Fenella? And now Daphne." There is a look in Sophie's eyes that I don't appreciate, the little, almost pitying glance that suggests I'm being too hard on myself or not seeing my potential or something that a therapist would say.

I don't want to hear it.

"Nothing positive can come out of Gunnar *looking* at me unless he's in awe of my quick wit and wants to learn from me because his comebacks are pretty darn lame."

"Stella!"

"Stella!" Daphne echoes as she appears by my side. "Did you tell Prince Gunnar to invite me to the wedding?" She's beaming and it's like the sun coming out from behind a cloud, making her seem like she belongs on the cover of one of the magazines Fenella graces.

I shake my head. "Wasn't me."

"Sophie!" Daphne throws her arms around her. "Thank you!"

"It made sense. You're you, and he's a prince." She shrugs. "Maybe he'll end up being your Prince Charming."

I can't help the scornful scoff. "Gunnar? Gunnar is a cheat, or have you forgotten him messing around with Mabel Crow when he was supposedly in love with Kate McKibbon? You need to remember that *at all times*. You can't trust him."

"That was a long time ago," Daphne argues in her mild, I-don't-do-confrontations way. "I'm sure he's made things right with Kate. She's working at the castle now, so I'm sure they're fine."

Sophie shoots me a look. "That was a long time ago," she echoes. "They were kids."

"It wasn't that long ago," I remind them with a mulish tone in my voice that I wish would go away. It's as if I'm personally offended at Gunnar's actions like it was *me* he betrayed.

It wasn't.

"Prince Gunnar is a sweetheart, but we're going as friends," Daphne says. "And that's fine with me. Because I just need to get to that wedding and my own Prince Charming is going to be there waiting for me." She clasps her hands under her chin. "It's going to be perfect."

My expression mirrors Sophie's worried frown as we watch Daphne dance back behind the counter. "That doesn't sound good," I mutter.

"I thought this would be a good way to get her mind off him," Sophie frets. "Gunnar is a *prince*."

"In name only." I can't help myself. "In reality, he's a spoiled, selfish little boy who can't handle a real relationship, which is why he's scrambling for a date less than two weeks before the wedding."

"Stella," Sophie hisses. "You're going to get thrown in the royal dungeon someday if you don't stop saying things like that."

I stand up. "The king would never do that." I take a deep breath, flaring my nostrils. "Our father wouldn't allow it."

Our father, right-hand and best friend of the king.

Our father is Duncan Laz, the man who abandoned our mother to raise two- children alone. He picked duty to the king over his own family.

I haven't spoken to him in over ten years.

6

Gunnar

MINKA DRIVES US TO the airport. Fenella is used to being chauffeured, but I'd rather be doing the driving. Or the flying. Or anything that gets me from one position in the world to another as fast as possible.

But Minka is a good driver and more than capable when it comes to my security detail, which has become mandatory since the castle announced Odin's wedding. King's orders. I haven't gotten to the bottom of *why* and probably won't bother unless Minka starts to annoy me.

She's pretty cool, so I'm not worried. I'm also not worried about anything happening to me on her watch, since who would try to get a piece of me with a six-foot-two Amazon who fought in the UFC in their way? I've no idea how Dad found her.

"Thanks for the coffee," Minka says, driving with one hand and guzzling the extra-large coffee with three shots of espresso. We leave colourful Battle Harbour and head inland to the airport on a road full of dips and curves winding around the bigger hills. Laandia is covered in trees, mountains, and rocks and is a prime example of the power of glaciers that moved over the country during the Ice Age.

It's a very pretty place to live.

"It's the least Fenella can do since you're the reason she's going to be on time for her flight," I tell Minka from the backseat behind her.

"I'm not that bad," Fenella protests, sipping her own coffee. "What does the guy put in this? I'm not even finished and already I want another one."

"Silas makes good coffee," Minka states. "He's also very attractive."

"Minka!" I chide. "Do you have a crush?"

"Just because I find someone attractive doesn't mean I'm interested. I merely stated that for Ms. Carrington's benefit."

"Thanks, but I've done pretty well with finding attractive men," Fenella replies in a wry tone.

"You haven't been doing a great job of that recently," I point out. "I'm sure they're attractive, but not exactly *good*. Imma right?"

Fenella wrinkles her nose at me, the only outward indication that I've annoyed her. "Instead of discussing me, which I have no interest in doing—"

"For once," I say under my breath. And then I grin at her.

"—let's talk about what just happened in that cute little coffeehouse. Impulsive, wouldn't you say?" The reprimand in her tone is rich, coming from Fenella.

"I'm an impulsive guy."

"Darlin', you know you've opened that girl up to a world of hurt."

"How do you figure?"

I see Minka's suspicious gaze via the rear-view mirror. "Is there something I need to be aware of?"

"Gunny's got a *date*," Fenella coos. "He just up and asked this blonde Cinderella-type who made my coffee."

"Cinderella," I chuckle. "She's definitely got the wicked stepsisters. Stepsister," I correct. My thoughts swing back to Stella, which is the worst place for my thoughts to be.

"Daphne Luute?" Minka guesses.

I let out a belly laugh. "Love it!" I cheer. "You've only been with me a few months and already you've got Stella pegged. She is *not* a nice person."

"I also am aware that Daphne works at Coffee for the Sole," Minka points out. "I think you're too hard on Stella."

"Too hard? Do you know what she said to me last time I was home?"

"We're not talking about the wicked stepsisters, although the one needs a spot of colour in her wardrobe," Fenella interjects before I can get into my past back-and-forths with Stella, some of them quite amusing. "It's the blonde that I'm concerned with."

"Daphne? And why?"

"She's about to fall for you," Fenella continues, her attention caught by the sight of the castle, high on the hill in the distance, the bright sun turning the old stone white. "You're a very fall-able guy. And—need I remind you?—a prince."

"You haven't fallen for me," I point out. "In a while."

"Because I'm your friend. Now. Your best friend, some could say," she points out.

I met Fenella right after Kate and I imploded and then my mother died and Fenella spent the following year trying to distract me from my grief. Our relationship spanned six countries, one Met Gala, and sold enough tabloids to feed a small country. We were photographed drunk, arguing, jumping off yachts sans clothes, out of an airplane (fully clothed), and right after the car crash that gave Fenella the row of stitches at her hairline.

I'm still amazed that I got to keep her as a friend.

"And yet, you still haven't fallen for me in a long time," I remind her with a teasing grin.

"Yes, and thank goodness for that. I am proof that you're a guy women fall for, Gunny. Because I don't fall for just anyone."

True. Fenella is even more anti-commitment than I am. She flits from man to man as quickly as she travels the world, and has flings with actors, musicians, and princes—not just me. Not to mention an Italian race car driver, a Swedish hockey player, and too many football players to count.

"Daphne knows the score. She's doing me a favour—that's it." I sound like I know what I'm talking about, and I really hope I do. I don't want the complication of having a local girl hung up on me. Ever since Kate—

There's that sadness that I can't seem to shake when it comes to Kate.

The folks of Battle Harbour are quite protective of their own, and after I broke Kate's heart, I was *persona non grata* in town for a good long time. This was at the start of my travels, so it was easy to forget when I wasn't around.

It was easier for Kate when I wasn't around as well. But she left anyway, only to come back when Dad called.

I don't blame him because Kate is very good at what she does. But I don't want to cause her any more pain.

And that pang that stabbed my heart when I first saw her and Jackson? Well, folks would say I deserved that, and more.

"She seems like a nice girl, but I don't think it's a good idea," Fenella insists.

"Why does it seem like a bad thing?" I wonder, honestly confused. "I think I'm lost."

"We're still on the road to the airport. ETA seven minutes," Minka announces helpfully.

"Dating Daphne," Fenella says. "That's a bad idea. Even without her wicked sisters."

"Stella and Sophie." Our little conversation this afternoon wasn't the worst one we've had. My mother taught me not to talk ill about anyone behind their back, but I'm not sure about the sisters, since Stella has no problem saying what she feels to my face. And everyone else. "Sophie is nice enough but Stella hates the world."

"Why? The world has issues but this part of it is beautiful."

"It won't let her save it. Plus, she seems to get personally offended by everything I do."

"So you decide to make it worse by taking her sister to the biggest social event in the Western Hemisphere?"

"I wouldn't go that far. Maybe biggest in North America."

"Do you think it'll be bigger than Mase Stirling's non-wedding?" Fenella asks.

"Yes, because I wasn't invited to that."

"What did you do to get her panties in such a twist? Wicked stepsister Stella, not Mase."

"What makes you think it was something *I* did to Stella?" Fenella stares expectantly at me. "I didn't do anything. We were in school together and we used to be... friendly. And then." I glance at Minka, who is once again watching in the rearview mirror. I wonder if I should be worried that she doesn't have her eyes on the road so often.

"I read the extensive dossier on Lord Duncan and the rest of the castle staff and residents when I started," Minka informs me.

"Lord Duncan? You mean Mr. Yummy himself, Duncan Laz? What does he have to do with this?" Fenella demands.

I heave a sigh. This isn't my story to tell but it's public knowledge. Just not outside-Laandia public. "Duncan is Stella's father. And Sophie's."

"Okay…"

"Dunc met and married Stella's mother when he was working for Dad. Being the advisor to the king takes some time, and Signe—Stella's mother—was always upset about the time Dunc spent with Dad. And she was angry that she was raising Spencer because *his* mother had no interest in him."

"How many wives did Duncan have?"

"Two. Spencer's mother and Signe, who is now married to Peter Luute, the mayor of Battle Harbour who spends more time at work than Duncan ever did." It's hard not to sound judgmental because I'm Team Duncan all the way. Not only is he an important part of the family, but so is Spencer. He lost a stepmother, which might not be a bad thing, considering what she's like, but Signe was the only mother he knew. And I may not think much of Stella, but Spencer lost her and Sophie as sisters too.

"I know there's more to the story, but the gist of it is that Signe demanded Duncan leave his advisor role, and well, Dunc picked Dad. He brought Spence to live at the castle and Signe stopped being friends with my mother because she was very angry at anyone associated with the royal family for a very long time. It rubbed off on Stella."

"But you didn't do anything wrong," Fenella points out.

"I got Duncan and Spencer," I say ruefully. "They were pretty close and when they moved to the castle, Stella never saw them. But I got to see them all the time and she never forgave me for that."

"So that's why she looks at you like she wants to poke out your eyes?"

"Pretty much, at least I think so. I don't really understand all of it, but Stella Laz really seems to hate me."

Fenella throws back her head and laughs. "Oh, my prince, trust me, that woman definitely does not hate you."

I spend the rest of the drive to the airport arguing with Fenella, just to find out the reasons why she thinks Stella doesn't hate me.

There aren't many but... maybe?

And why do I think that's a good thing?

7

Stella

I FIND UNNECESSARY JOBS to do at the shelter but I still make it home before Sophie. Which isn't good because she needs to be the one to tell our mother about Daphne and Gunnar.

I can't imagine our mother is going to be pleased.

If she had an ounce of witchcraft running through her veins, she would have cursed every single person living or working in the castle after my father left us.

That included the queen, her former best friend.

"They took him away from us," she announced the day after he moved his things out.

"They have everything. They didn't need to take your father from us. It's selfish, so very selfish. We need your father and they don't." This was the second night, amid a howling burst of sobbing, that left Sophie and me wondering what to do to help her.

"I'm not allowing him only a few hours with you. What's the point of that? It'll only do more harm than good, seeing how upset you'll be at seeing him. If he wants more time with his daughters, he'll soon realize he made the wrong choice," she told us after cancelling a planned visit.

"He loves them more than he loves us. If he ever loved us at all."

I heard that one throughout my childhood, and even to this day whenever someone is thoughtless enough to bring up Duncan Laz in her hearing.

I'm not looking forward to telling my mother Daphne will be Gunnar's date to the wedding, the wedding she's refusing to attend, even though Peter, as mayor of Battle Harbour, needs to be there.

I unlock the door, trying to be as quiet as I can, and once again kicking myself for still living with my mother at age twenty-six. Not that I can really afford my own place, since I don't take much of a salary from the shelter, but Sophie and I together might be able to scrape together enough for a small place to share in town.

But no. Every year I tell myself to make the move, and every year I let months go by until it's the next year and I'm still living at home.

It's a comfortable home, large by Battle Harbour standards, and located on the outskirts of town as far away from the docks as possible. My mother grew up in a nearby town, the daughter of a fisherman, and she wanted no part of that life. And then she met my father at the final farewell concert of Kräftig's—the heavy metal band he played with along with King Magnus.

As unbelievable as it may be that Laandia's king was once a member of a heavy metal band that featured long-haired, leather-clad men screaming into the microphone between shrieking guitar solos, I still can't get my head around the thought of my *mother* at one of their concerts.

But she was there, because that's where she met Duncan and he made sure my mother had a very different life than the one she had been heading toward.

"Stella?" my mother calls.

"It's me," I mutter as her footsteps approach, wishing I were anywhere else.

Signe Luute reminds me of a 1950s housewife—the kind that does her hair and makeup before her husband is awake so he never sees her when she's not at her best. Appearances matter to her—which is part of the reason I dress like I do. And she hates my hair.

It's my little rebellion.

As well as appearances, Mom cares way too much about what other people think of her. It amazed me that she cut ties with the castle, since for someone who craves admiration and social status, a relationship with the royal family is a big deal. It took years and some growing up on my part to realize that Mom refused to become a pariah after Dad left; instead, she sought others in Laandia who had issues with the monarchy. They might be petty or political, but there are a lot of fires that have been stoked by my mother over the years, including the Odinites. This is the group that has been calling for Prince Kalle's removal from the line of succession in favour of Odin.

I really hope no one knows that my mother was ever involved with the group.

"Stella," she repeats, a glass of wine in her hand. As well as hair and makeup first thing, Mom also greets Peter at the door with his favourite cocktail.

Never Sophie and me—just Peter.

Tonight, she's wearing a silky pair of pants and a matching tunic, which kind of looks like pyjamas and is probably just as comfortable, only a lot more expensive. The outfit is a pretty purple-blue colour, which goes well with her blonde hair but does nothing for the scowl twisting her still-beautiful face.

"Tell me everything," she demands.

If the word *demanding* could have a picture beside it in the dictionary, it would be Signe Luute.

She is my mother and I love her, but she wants what she wants when she wants it: whether it be six-year-old me to make my bed in the morning, for her husband, newly elected mayor of Battle Harbour to organize a holiday party better than the one the castle used to hold, or for Daphne to be crowned Sea Queen. And what she wants, she usually gets.

I assume her question is regarding the Daphne-Gunnar date and I don't even bother asking how she knows. It's six o'clock; four hours is plenty of time for her network of spies to get the news to her.

At least I don't have to tell her. *Kill the messenger* is a very real thing in our house; not *kill* kill, but flay with sharp words and a flurry of passive-aggressive insults.

If anyone wonders how I came to be the wicked stepsister of the princess of Battle Harbour, look no further than the woman with the cold eyes and piercing tongue standing before me.

"The prince invited Daphne to the wedding as his date," I tell her, unable to keep the note of scorn out of my voice.

"*No.*"

"Yes." Obviously, I'm not about to out my sister as the instigator.

"Daphne is going to the ball with Prince Gunnar?"

"Last time I heard, it was a wedding," I correct.

"How did this happen?"

Her spies aren't as good as she thinks if no one has told her that Sophie and I were there when the plan was hatched.

I shrug and slide past her to take off my boots, noting Mom's sniff. If it were up to her, I'd wear ballet slippers all the time to avoid the "horrible clods and clumping."

"Maybe this could be a good thing," she muses and takes a sip of her wine.

She approves of Daphne and Gunnar?

Not that this is a "Daphne and Gunnar". And why would I care if it were? I can only blink with surprise and wonder how much wine she's already had.

My mother is the reason I loathe the royal family.

My father may have committed the unforgivable sin of abandoning his family, but she blamed the king for this decision, and for everything else wrong in her life.

According to my mother, it was the king's fault that she had a falling out with Queen Selene. The king was the cause of Sophie being passed over for a scholarship that would have allowed her to study art in Paris for the summer when she was sixteen. It was his fault that Peter lost the mayoral election the first time, that I turned down acceptance to veterinary school in Halifax, and that Daphne lost the Sea Queen crown that first year. Every storm, every bad internet connection, and the slightest bit of traffic fall under the control of the king, and she never hesitates to find him responsible for every bad thing that happens.

It's a lot for a daughter to listen to. And yes, even though I can think for myself, my mother's irrational hatred has had an effect on my thoughts on the matter.

"Excuse me?" I manage. "You think this is a good idea?"

"It's a good move," Mom says.

"For... Daphne?"

"Of course Daphne. Her profile is at an all-time high with her latest crowning and being seen with Gunnar will only help her."

I narrow my eyes. "You know she's not a real queen, right?"

"Stella," she chides. "Your sister's popularity will soon make her a force to be reckoned with in Battle Harbour, and being seen as a special friend of the castle will only help. And Daphne's popularity will definitely impact you and your sister, in a very positive way." Mom practically rubs her hands together with anticipation. I feel like checking to see if this woman is wearing a Mom-mask, like on Mission: Impossible, but I don't expect she'd appreciate me pinching her cheek.

"I don't need anything rubbed off on me. Just so you know, I am quite okay not being popular."

Mom rolls her eyes over the rim of the wineglass. "Stella, your social life is atrocious."

I lift my chin. I may be argumentative by nature, but if there was one thing my father insisted on when he was my father, it was that I temper my temper when speaking to my mother. "I'd say non-existent," I say in a mild voice. "Atrocious is going a little overboard."

"Have you ever considered your combative nature is keeping away the men?"

I laugh. I have to, because my mother is... laughable. She's like a Mean Girl, solely concerned with being better than everyone else. Hating the castle has always defined her. I have no idea how she got on board with a Gunnar-Daphne non-pairing date so fast. "I need a little clarification, please. Are you trying to tell me that you think it's a good idea that Daphne is planning on going to the wedding as Gunnar's date?"

"I do."

"But you don't want *me* to go to the wedding, even though Lady Camille invited me." Not that I want to go, but it might be nice for once for Mom to encourage me to attend the social event of the year rather than pointing out how my wardrobe wouldn't be suitable.

"What benefit would that give you?" she asks in all seriousness. "Now, if the prince invited *you*—"

"Gunnar?"

"But you had your chance with him years ago."

My laugh is more of an amazed snort. *My chance* was a clumsy first kiss between two pre-pubescents in one of the castle dungeons that we used as a clubhouse.

And how did she know about that? I certainly never told her.

Maybe her spies are better than I thought.

"I think this pairing has its merits," she continues. "Things have changed. Peter needs more of a connection with the castle, and this could be a good move for him. Gunnar will fall in love—"

"They're going as friends," I interrupt in a flat voice. How can a lame invite change years and years of thinking Gunnar and the others were no better than the spawn of Satan?

I've long believed that Daphne was the favoured girl, but this goes too far.

"It's Daphne. Everyone loves her. Daphne and Prince Gunnar?" Mom spreads her hands. "It's perfect. *They're* perfect."

None of my objections form into words since I can't really find the right words for them. I don't think it's a good idea for Daphne to have anything to do with any of the princes. My stomach twists with something akin to jealousy. I may not be as pretty and sweet and nice as Daphne, but this is *my* mother. "Yes, but she's fixated on Daulton right now," I tell her spitefully. "I think it's a bad idea."

"You don't," Mom corrects. "Because it's going to help Daphne get over Daulton." She looks worried at the mention of his name.

My sweet, naïve little sister fell head over three-inch heels last December for one Daulton Drake, the latest addition to the King's staff. Daulton is suave and sophisticated, happy to tell anyone who would listen about his life in Toronto, with his burgeoning law career that he gave up to come work for the king of Laandia.

The hard and fast facts of the case are that Daulton is twelve years older than Daphne, and he's married—and not to Daphne. His wife—and daughter—are still back in Toronto and will be joining him this summer. Daphne swears there's been nothing between them save hours of conversation and enough stolen glances to make even a semi-romantic like me sick to my stomach, but it's enough to make Daphne believe Daulton is the man for her.

"It *is* a good idea," Mom decides. "I'm afraid Daphne is too close to Daulton."

"Tell her not to see him."

"Obviously, you're not a mother. I can't do that. Do you think I can just lock her up like some wicked stepmother in a fairy tale?"

What's with the wicked stuff today? First Gunnar, now my mother. Is there a fairy tale fad that I'm unaware of? "You're the one who told us no one from the castle could be trusted and now you're willing to let Daphne do this with Gunnar?"

"It's a wedding, so they'll never be alone together. Gunnar is…" She hesitates, carefully picking her words. Whenever that happens, I wonder if it really might be an act of treason to badmouth the royal family. "He takes after Magnus," she says finally. "He's personable. Charming. He'll be able to woo Daphne without even realizing he's doing it."

"You want her to fall for him?"

"Just enough to make her stop obsessing over Daulton Drake."

I have to agree with that.

Daphne needs a distraction. Someone to take her mind of the horrible, terrible, awful bad idea that is Daulton Drake, and I hate to admit, Prince Gunnar may just be it.

"What if he falls for her?" I ask.

My mother's expression of scorn isn't attractive. "So what if he does? Those boys deserve to know what heartbreak feels like."

Despite what I think of Gunnar, that doesn't sit easily with me.

8

Gunnar

"JUST SO YOU ALL hear it from me first because I know how concerned you all are," I announce to the group collected in the dining room, spreading my arms wide. "I have found a date for the wedding."

There are a smattering of golf claps and a few boos.

I grin at my oldest brother, Kalle, he of the boos as well as the owner of the King's Hat pub in Battle Harbour, a favourite hangout of mine when I'm home. He's also the heir apparent to the throne, a little fact he's never been happy about.

Tonight's family dinner takes place in the small dining room, which is bigger than some bachelor apartments, and has a table big enough for twenty. Right now, it's set for nine, with enough bottles of wine on the table to start a proper wine cellar. Everyone is already here, holding glasses of Barolo, save Dad and Duncan, who are always late.

I travel a lot, and so I miss a lot of the family dinners organized.

And I do miss them. There's a tug of something inside me to see my family together. I'm pretty sure it's happiness.

For a few years after our mother passed, family dinners were tough to get through. The queen didn't have the presence Dad did, but she was a calm, constant figure in our lives, and at the table when we gathered. Her place at the table stays empty even after almost seven years.

Things have gotten livelier lately, especially now that Camille has joined us, and Odin has loosened up a bit.

I love my big brother, but Odin has to be the stiffest stoic among us. Bo may live as a hermit, but at least he shows emotion.

I look forward to spending time with my brothers, but I still glance at the empty place where Mom always sat.

And Odin must see me do it because he's the first to step forward. "Finally, a date. We were getting worried."

"It was a difficult decision," I protest.

"I'm glad you found someone." Camille elbows Odin. "There's enough time to get her dress ready."

"Who's the unlucky lady?" Kalle wants to know.

I resist the urge to flip him the finger. "We're going to have royalty in our midst. I'll be escorting Ms. Daphne Luute, the Sea Queen herself to the wedding."

The lack of reaction tells me they already knew.

"You're taking my sister to the wedding," Spencer says with a hint of brotherly suspicion as he hands me a glass of wine, poured right to the rim in the Viking way.

Maybe the Vikings didn't drink much wine, but I'm sure they agreed that space in your drinking horn is only a waste of time because you have to refill it more often.

"No, I'm taking Daphne, not Stella. Or Sophie. Definitely not Stella." I give a mock shiver. "Last time I heard, Daphne was *not* your sister," I correct him. "Or even technically your stepsister?" Either way, I'm not getting involved with any woman related to

Spencer. Some guys like the challenge of dating the sister of a friend, but it sounds too complicated to me.

I'm not dating Daphne. She's doing me a favour.

And I'm absolutely not dating Stella.

I didn't even want to bring a date to the wedding. My love life has been hit or miss lately, and I planned on going solo. But that was before I talked to Odin when I got home last week and he set me straight, i.e. I need to bring someone.

"Who are you taking?" I ask Spencer after I've cleared some wine out of my glass. "I've been out of the loop."

"Touring around America will do that to you," Spencer says.

"That's because you don't read the weekly wedding emails sent to you," Odin points out as we begin to find our seats at the table.

"You email about who we're *dating*?" I demand.

"Not you, because we're able to read all about it," Spencer says. "I think you made the covers for four magazines last week? Miley Cyrus, huh?"

"I was impressed with the Olivia Wilde picture," Bo cuts in.

It's almost painful to have to deny the stories because Miley and Olivia? I look pretty good standing beside those ladies. But I pride myself on being nothing if not a gentleman. "I'd love to tell you it's all true, but no. I stand beside someone, and they decide we're madly in love. You know the drill."

"Yes, but you stand beside more people than we do," Kalle says.

"Maybe if you actually left Battle Harbour you'd get your own covers," I tell him.

Kalle lifts his glass to me. "And that's why I like it here."

"What's going on with Fenella?" Lyra asks, looking up from her phone and joining the conversation. My little sister has gone back to her natural strawberry blonde hair colour, but the way she's cut her hair makes her look like a pixie or a fairy. With her big blue eyes and suitcase full of sass, Lyra is the best-looking of all of us, including Bo, who was the first of us to hit People's Sexiest Man list.

They got a picture of him in full lumberjack garb, and you can't really compete with rugged masculinity, flannel and an axe.

But Lyra's always been a handful, which is another reason I'm glad that Spencer has the same issue as I do about dating one's friend's sisters.

Spencer and Lyra? What a nightmare. They snip back and forth more than Stella and I.

I wish I didn't bring her up in my internal monologues so much.

"Same thing that was going on last time you bugged me about her—nada," I tell Lyra. "We're friends. I have that ability to stay friends with my ex-girlfriends, you know."

"Does Kate know about this ability?" Lyra shows a little of that sass and my mouth does the twist it does whenever anyone brings up Kate.

Dating one's sister's best friend? Not suggested or recommended, and it's why the closest I'll get to Spencer's sisters is for a waltz at the wedding. Or even non-sisters. Too many potential problems to do that again.

Not that the problem was with Kate. I may be the only one to say it, but we were good together. We were a couple for almost a year, longer than any of my brothers' relationships, and at nineteen, that was pretty impressive. I like to think Kate was happy with me, at least until the end...

Which was mostly my fault. I mean, I know what I did wrong, but the *ending*... To this day, I still don't know how that happened. Someone saw me leaving Mabel Crow's house at midnight and the rumours spread from there. No one thought to ask *why* I was there, they just jumped to the easiest conclusion—Mabel with an empty house plus Prince Gunnar with the playboy reputation equals the two of us having a good time.

Only thing? I didn't have the playboy rep before that night.

I'll probably never know who took the picture of me leaving Mabel's that night, which is fine because I'll never be able to tell the truth as to why I was there.

Instead of answering Lyra, I drain my wine glass and she goes back to her phone.

"What did Daphne say when you told her about being a bridesmaid?" Camille asks. I'm so grateful for her getting the conversation off of Kate that it takes me a second to fully comprehend what she says.

And then I think it's maybe because of the wine because—pardon? What did she say about *what*?

"I asked her to be my *date*..." I stammer. "Not even a date *date*. Just—like an escort date. Like you wanted. So I have a dance partner and—"

"But whoever you bring needs to be part of the wedding party." Camille looks confused and more than a little stressed, which the closer the wedding gets, has become her usual expression. "As one of my bridesmaids."

I blink, and then blink again. "I'm sorry, what? You said *brides-maid*?"

"I need another bridesmaid. You knew that."

Wide-eyed, I look at the faces of my brothers. No one seems surprised. "I did not know that," I say slowly. "I had no idea that I had to provide Camille with a bridesmaid. Because—what?"

Daphne as one of the wedding party? That's more than even a *date* date. That's magazine cover worthy? That's—

Spencer coughs into his fist. "Emails."

"I don't have many friends," Camille says in her no-nonsense way. "Not enough to make up the wedding party." She spreads her hands to indicate Kalle, Bo, me and Spencer. "I have Kate and Lyra. I need two more."

There is nothing in Camille's tone to suggest she wants pity for this fact, but even if we hadn't developed a good friendship, I'd feel a sympathetic tug for her.

And—I consider us to be friends so *why* wouldn't she say any of this to me? "Let me just get this straight," I say, struggling to absorb it all. "You needed me to ask someone to the wedding so you could get another bridesmaid."

"To make up the numbers."

"I could be paired up with Kate," I suggest.

"No," Kalle and Odin say in unison. "Spencer is paired with Kate," Odin adds.

"She's my maid of honour," Camille adds.

"Wait a minute. Does that mean *Spence* is your best man?" I demand, giving Spencer, my brother-of-another-mother a dirty look.

Odin looks pained. "Jackson put all of this in the email. It was easier to have Spencer than pick one of you oafs."

That makes sense, but still. Maybe I didn't expect to be Odin's best man, but I had a hope. At least I thought it would be Kalle, as the oldest. I turn to Camille and try again. "You have Kate and Lyra—"

"Bo is paired with Lyra," Odin supplies. Bo shrugs and drinks his wine.

"Who are you with?" I ask Kalle.

"I'm bringing Edie." Edie, who manages his pub. Kalle has been friends with her forever, so it also makes sense.

I sink into the closest chair, shoulders slumping. "So I wasn't looking for a date, per se, but someone to fill up the numbers for the wedding party."

"I don't have a lot of friends," Camille says again, this time with a note of defiance in her tone. "You have a big family and they need to be included."

I raise my hands. "Don't mean to tick you off, Cammie—just a little surprised. I might have picked differently if I'd realized what was going on."

"I think Daphne will be perfect. She's very nice. And she's fourth in line."

Which means I'll be at the end of the line as well.

A commotion at the door catches my eye. Dad bursts in, followed by Duncan. "I know, I know," he says, hands up in surrender. "Late again. But I'm happy to see my girl, and all my boyos back." He slaps me on the back as he heads for an open bottle of wine on the table. "Glad to see you home, Gunny."

Duncan takes the seat beside me as Dad sits at the head of the table. "Interesting choice," he comments, lifting a silver eyebrow.

"I didn't know she was going to be a bridesmaid," I whisper.

I had no idea my date was slotted to be a bridesmaid, but even if I did, who else would I have asked?

9

Stella

THE NEXT DAY IS a day for angry and angst music, and I play the entire Jagged Little Pill album—the original, not the musical—before Ajax and Lennie arrive at the shelter. Eli is still asleep in the basement; he often does the overnight shift because he lives with his aging parents.

I expect whoever stays the night to sleep, which is why I invested in the many baby monitors set up on both floors, so the whimper of a scared dog or the crash from a mischievous cat upstairs in the cattery could be easily heard and dealt with.

No one got much sleep when we had the parrot since he often spent the night muttering to himself.

I keep the music down so as not to wake Eli even though I'm in the mood for loud and angry, with some boot stomping and arm shaking.

All because of my mother.

Or rather her reaction to Daphne and Gunnar; so technically, I can say the fault lies with Gunnar.

Like I told Sophie last night, I'm completely dumbfounded by Mom's switch from castle hater to castle promoter in less time than it takes a litter of puppies to soak one of the precious pee mats. And I'm not happy about it.

Not even the excited yips and yaps of the dogs can clear my foul mood, so I know it's pretty bad.

It gets worse when Ajax reads the newspapers before they lay them down for the puppies to pee on.

"Your sister is going to be a *bridesmaid*?" they ask incredulously with more than a little awe and envy.

"You know you shouldn't believe everything you read in the news," I chide them as I cuddle one of the newest puppies brought in. Four of them were found down by the pier three days ago.

That's how we get most of the dogs; there are quite a few strays in the area and when someone finds a litter, they call me so the puppies have a chance at a home. Once in a while, we'll catch an older dog who has been injured, or one that their owner can no longer care for, but most of the time it's puppies.

"This isn't the gossip, it's a wedding update from the castle." Ajax holds up the page. "It lists who is going to be in the wedding party, and here—Daphne Luute."

I frown as I scan the article. "She didn't say anything to me about that." This is a surprise because when she got home last night, it was all she'd been able to talk about, including texting me sixteen times, trying to convince me to go to the wedding.

Unfortunately, there's not a lot I can deny Daphne. For now, she has to be content with a half-hearted *maybe*.

The only good thing about it is if she's so excited about Gunnar, then she's not thinking about Daulton.

But it's also a bad thing because I really wasn't planning on putting myself through the circus of the royal wedding because—

Well, just because.

"She would know if she's going to be a bridesmaid, right?" Ajax asks with a nervous laugh. "Daphne is really sweet but..."

Not the sharpest knife in the drawer. "I was there when Gunnar asked her and I didn't hear anything about being a bridesmaid," I admit.

"Maybe they talked about it later."

"Maybe." But Daphne is open about almost everything, and she didn't say a word. And this is worth several words. "I don't think she's even said anything to my mother."

I check the clock—only ten thirty. Hours to go before my break. "I could use a matcha latte," Ajax suggests, catching me checking the time. "If you wanted to duck out and grab one for me. Eli is waking up downstairs, so I can get him to stay until you get back."

I give them a tight-lipped smile and head for the door.

The shelter is situated on one of the furthest streets from the town square, but Battle Harbour is small enough that it only takes a few minutes of walking at warp speed for me to get to Coffee for the Sole. I'll find out from Daphne what's going on and if she doesn't know, suggest she get hold of Gunnar tout de suite.

I'm sure he's the reason there's a mix-up in the papers. Daphne doesn't even know Lady Camille—why would she want her as part of the wedding party? Who does that?

And who asks a perfect stranger to be his date for his brother's wedding, royal or not?

It's strange—my warp-speed walking only fuels my annoyance to anger-like levels. Not even yesterday's sun and warmth are helping. And when I get to Coffee for the Sole, I see that Daphne is talking to the devil himself.

Gunnar.

He's with Lady Camille and hopefully fixing this mess up.

"You want me to be your bridesmaid?" I hear Daphne ask just as I step up to the counter behind Gunnar. It's hard to tell if she seems excited or scared or upset or happy—

She actually has no expression, just her usual pretty face.

I was right. She didn't know.

"If you don't mind. We'll provide the dress," Camille says quickly. "It's ready except for any alterations you might need. It's a little embarrassing, but my friend group is a little small, so we decided Kalle's and Gunnar's dates will be included to make up the numbers. I hope you're okay with that."

"Of course. Thanks for thinking of me," Daphne says with an impressive smoothness. "But..."

Why didn't you mention it yesterday? Her expression says differently.

"There was a miscommunication," Gunnar cuts in. "I thought Camille was going to talk to you, and Camille thought I had covered it, so we both came to see you."

"Good timing, considering the news is all over the newspapers," I say.

Both Camille and Gunnar turn around. Camille with a happy expression and Gunnar without.

"Stella!" Lady Camille exclaims with a warm smile. "I was coming over to visit the shelter next."

I start with surprise at her obvious happiness. "Uh, sure. We're always glad to have visitors. How is Bea Arthur?"

"Perfect! She's bonded with Betty White and getting so big."

"There are more puppies if you want to add to the family," I offer.

"Believe me, I've been working on Odin. The last bunch you had were so sweet."

My eyes flick to Gunnar, but I don't say a word to him.

Camille steps to the side of the counter with Daphne, leaving me with Gunnar. Now that I know it was a "miscommunication," I can go back to work. But my feet aren't moving to the door and Gunnar isn't moving from my side.

I should get Ajax their matcha latte at least.

"Hello, Stella," Gunnar says, somehow taking my glance as an invitation.

"Did you forget the bridesmaid part when you asked Daphne to be your date?" I ask, hoping if I irritate him, he'll go away.

Gunnar's jaw tightens almost imperceptibly. I wouldn't have noticed if I hadn't been looking for it. He's always hated being called out.

"Seems an important thing to mention when you invite someone to be your *guest*," I add, keeping my voice low so Camille, who is discussing dresses with Daphne, doesn't hear.

"Like I said, it was a miscommunication," he says, his voice cool.

"I'm sure." I smirk.

"And what business of this is yours?"

"My sister's happiness is very important to me."

"I'm sure it is. As it is to me."

This time I laugh outright. "Since when? Twelve hours ago, when you found out she was playing a big role in your brother's wedding?"

The mask slips into place. "The happiness of our citizens is always of the utmost importance to my family."

"*So* happy to hear that."

"Do you think you'll be able to stop by the castle tomorrow to try on the dress?" Camille asks Daphne. "I could bring it to you, but the seamstress is working on Lyra's dress and there's a bit to do, so she's a little pressed for time."

"I can come up after work," Daphne offers and Camille beams.

How strange would it be not to have friends and family with you on the biggest day of your life? Who would I have with me? Sophie, obviously, and Daphne, but as for friends, I may be as desperate as Camille.

"Stella, why don't you come with Daphne?" Camille turns to me before I can answer my rhetorical question. "You can see how Bea Arthur is doing."

"That's a great idea." Gunnar is wearing his own smirk because he knows very well that the castle is the last place I want to be.

"Sure," I say, surprising everyone with the ease of my agreement. "That's a great idea."

"Exactly what I said." Gunnar grins evilly at me.

"Stella can drive me," Daphne cuts in. "Please, big sis?" she adds in a low voice, not wanting everyone to know she's had her driver's license for a year and is still not comfortable behind the wheel.

"Sure," I repeat because it's Daphne and I'll do just about anything for her.

"Wonderful." Camille smiles at both of us, so sincere in her happiness. "We'll see you around five. Are you sure we can't send a car for you?"

"That's not necessary," I say quickly. "I'm happy to drive."

I manage to keep the smile on my face as she leaves with Gunnar, both with drinks in hand, chattering about wedding details, until the moment they get to the door.

I'm going to the castle, number one on my list of things I don't want to do. But I don't say anything to Daphne. "You're going to be a bridesmaid," I mutter instead.

"Isn't it great?"

I look at her with surprise because Daphne shows more emotion now than when Gunnar asked her. "You're okay with this? He didn't say one word about it when he asked you? Did he forget, or not think you were important enough?"

"I don't care," she says gaily. "If I'm part of the wedding, I have a good reason to be at the castle. Maybe I can even stay overnight there."

"Why on earth would you want to be at the castle more than you need to?"

Her smile is like a streak of sunlight straight through the clouds. "Because Daulton is there."

10

Gunnar

I HOLD THE DOOR of Coffee for the Sole open for Camille and we step out into the late May sunshine.

Two beautiful days in a row is almost unheard of. Stella would say we're due for a storm where I'm just going to enjoy the nice weather. I hoist the canvas bag filled with dog food and treats onto my shoulder. It would have been ungentlemanlike to give the bag to Stella to take to the shelter, especially since I know Camille was looking forward to visiting the dogs.

If I'm being honest, I am too. Who doesn't like puppies?

It's who looks after them that I'm not looking forward to seeing again. "We should wait for Stella," Camille says, "if she's going back to the shelter."

"She's on a break. Who knows what she's doing?"

What does Stella do for fun? Whenever I see her, she's either with her sister or hanging out in Coffee for the Sole, and she never looks very happy.

Probably doesn't know how to have fun.

"She seems nice." Camille waves at Brian Boot, one of the regulars at Kalle's pub, as he passes us to slip into the drugstore.

"Stella?" I demand, a little harsher than I need to be.

"Her, too. But no—Daphne. She's nice."

"She is."

I wonder if it's an insult to call someone *nice* when you don't have another suitable adjective. Like a back-handed compliment. It's fine when a person *is* nice, as well as smart and funny, or maybe amazing at beer pong or ballroom dancing. Daphne may be all of those things, but right now, all I can come up with is *nice*.

Daphne is nice and sweet and kind... but I can't say much else. Or if there's something there, it's buried under the niceness, like a dog bone under a flower bed.

"Do you think you'll have fun with her at the wedding?"

Will I have fun at the wedding? Absolutely—I have fun wherever I go. I make sure of that. I'm a fun guy.

Will I have fun with Daphne?

Not sure about that.

"I'm sure I will," I tell Camille because she's planning this wedding—actually Mrs. Thiessen is, but Camille is at least involved, unlike Odin—and she doesn't need the stress of having a dud in her wedding party.

That's mean—Daphne's not a dud. She's very nice.

"When we came up with the idea to have your date as the bridesmaid, I honestly thought you'd be dating someone," Camille says, sounding almost apologetic. "Or at least bringing someone you're close to. Like Fenella."

"I can't bring Fenella. We're friends."

"You said Daphne is only a friend."

"Yes, but anytime I show up with Fenella, people start planning *our* wedding." I know the press has been hounding both Camille and Odin for comments and pictures in the run-up to the wedding, but that's only the photographers and journalists who come to Laandia, and that's not too many.

We're a quiet country, and Battle Harbour is basically an out-sized fishing village. It will be teeming with the press here for the wedding by the end of the week, but as a rule, a royal could streak through the town square and the world would be none the wiser.

I should know—it was a dare from Kalle on my eighteenth birthday. To this day, there is no record of my late-night run and I'm perfectly happy about that.

Odin got a burst of notoriety for appearing on—and subsequently being sent home from—The Suitorette reality show, but it died down after he announced his engagement to Camille. Since neither of them has travelled like I have, they have no clue what the media can be like in other places, like Los Angeles or London and the rest of Europe. I wouldn't say I'm hounded, but I'm a famous face that doesn't always make the best decisions and it gets attention. Sometimes too much.

It's not as bad as some, but there are enough lies and half-truths out there about me to make me leery.

There's only one lie about me here in Battle Harbour, but it did more damage than every other half-truth combined.

"Is there a reason for people to start planning your wedding to Fenella?" Camille asks as two cars stop to let us cross the street. "I like her, by the way. She's fun."

Fun, not nice.

"Absolutely not," I announce vehemently. "I'm not getting married anytime soon, and if I am, it won't be to Fenella. Great girl—we'd drive each other crazy."

"What kind of woman are you looking for?"

When I first met Camille, I never would have imagined her being the sort of person who would ask me about my love life. She was cool, slightly repressed because of having Lord Dusain as a father, and more than a little angry at Odin. But she's mellowed. Softened. Become fun—not as much as Fenella, but enough that I really like her company. I end up spending time with her when I'm home, plus I keep in touch with her when I'm away, more than I do with my brothers.

I sidestep two mothers and strollers taking over the sidewalk. "The kind I clearly haven't found yet," I say ruefully.

"You sure about that?"

I know she's referring to Kate. They're good enough friends for her to have heard all the dirty details, but it's too nice of a day to bring up the past. Plus, lately, when I think about Kate, there's not the hollow, sinking feeling I used to have. I feel bad about how things went down, but there's no longer the same pull toward her.

I think I'm actually over her, and that's a good thing, especially since she seems happy with Jackson. According to Camille anyway, who seems to enjoy dropping tidbits in my ear about them.

"Positive. Besides, I'm only twenty-six. I've got loads of time before I need to settle down. And after we get your wedding over with, this town isn't going to want one for a long time."

"Don't be so sure of that."

I laugh as we turn onto Fourth Street where the animal shelter is. Catch a Pet is at the end of the street, housed in a two-story monster house, the biggest on the street with a yard on each side. It's as colourful as the rest, but most of the homes of Battle Harbour are attached, crowded together like plastic soldiers on display.

"I've never figured out how Stella could ever afford this place," I muse as we walk toward it.

"Donations." Camille shifts Betty White in her arms. "There's a spot on their website asking for money, and the adoptions help. Fundraisers, same as SealSave. They also get a big donation a few times a year. It's anonymous but Stella says she tracked it down to the castle." She looks expectantly at me.

I shake my head. "I don't know what the castle does with the money unless I'm spending it."

"Do you spend a lot of it?"

I grin. "Not anymore."

"She also got a good deal on the house," Camille continues. "A fisherman had gutted it and had planned to renovate it for his wife, but he was lost at sea. She didn't want anything to do to with it, and was happy to see it become a good home for the dogs."

"It's all about the dogs for Stella," I mutter. "I think she likes them more than people."

"Do you blame her?" Camille steps up to the door, painted fuchsia that clashes slightly with the bright blue walls.

The people of Battle Harbour paint bright and paint often.

Inside is more subdued, with pale gray-green walls—and quiet. So quiet I can hear the faint *yeows* of a cat upstairs. "No dogs in a dog shelter? Isn't that bad for business?"

"They must be outside. Hello?" When no one answers, Camille leads the way through the obstacle course of dog pens and feeding bowls to a back door.

"You've been here before."

"You obviously haven't."

We step out to a backyard that's as chaotic as the rest of the house. The first thing I notice is the colour—along the eight-foot-high fence that rings the property are hanging flower boxes, full of every bloom and shade imaginable.

The dogs are here; puppies make a dash toward us, two older dogs bark, sounding more surprised than fierce protectors, and a large heap of fur that resembles a bear lifts its head from where it lies in the sun watching us.

"Lady Camille," Ajax cries from the far end of the yard, walking a mid-sized dog on a leash. "And Prince Gunnar. You're here."

"Sorry to just walk in," Camille says, sounding anything but as she crouches to greet the wriggling mass of puppies at her feet. In her arms, Betty White gives a yip of warning and a few of the puppies back away. "We saw Stella at the coffee shop. She'll be back soon. We brought food and toys."

"Maybe leave that inside?" they suggest. "The puppies get excited enough out here. Just put it in the office."

I step back inside with the bag. It's a big room, with support beams marking where walls once were, and a galley kitchen at the side. Near the front of the house are three doors and I hit the office on the second try, dropping the bag on the chair not occupied by a giant orange cat.

It's a neat and tidy space; big enough for a desk, chairs and a sofa, with paintings on the walls. I recognize them as Sophie's work.

It smells faintly of vanilla and I notice the candle on the desk.

The shelter smells like dog, even with the windows open and fans blowing. But even with all the time she must spend here, Stella doesn't smell like dog. She smells—not like dog.

She smells good.

I'm glad we saw Stella at Coffee for the Sole, so I won't have to deal with her at the shelter. Maybe that's why I spend extra minutes looking around the office. The bookshelf behind the desk is full of books—thick tomes of non-fiction and dog-eared paperbacks. I recognize most of Bill Bryson's travel books because I have the same ones. The paperbacks seem to be of the romantic genre, and—oh, wow.

When I pull one out to check, I rear back because it's Duncan smouldering at me from the cover.

Stella has an entire shelf of books with Duncan on the cover, most of them with dark hair blowing in the wind and, unfortunately, shirtless.

I've seen them before; one of the libraries in the castle has a copy of every book that Duncan appeared on the cover of. Dad has told us that, for years, after the band broke up, Duncan was *the* model for romance novels.

That was before he came to be Dad's second-in-command, and before Stella was born.

For someone who claims to hate her father, it's odd that she has all the books he was a cover model for.

Something tells me Stella wouldn't appreciate me knowing that, so I put the book back exactly where I found it, and step out of the room.

Just in time to be yelled at. "What in hell are you doing in there?"

Oh my god, she's back. I can't get away from her. "Miss me?"

Stella—furious Stella—gives me that Black Glare of Death. I might be frightened if her hands weren't full of to-go cups.

I lift my hands in a gesture of peace. "Just dropping off a bag of dog stuff. Ajax's orders. They're out back with Camille."

"I know where Ajax is because they were there when I left," Stella snaps. "You shouldn't be in my office. It's my personal space."

She *definitely* doesn't want anyone to know about the books. "Trust me, I don't want to be in any space you deem personal."

"What's that supposed to mean?"

"I don't want to be in your office. Or anywhere around you."

She sniffs. "That's rude."

"Well, *you're* rude."

Another sniff— "So childish. *I know you are, but what am I?*" she mocks.

"I'm going outside," I huff. "The dogs don't bark as much as you do."

Her eyes—more silver than green today—widen. "Are you calling me a dog?"

"Well, you like them more than people, so I thought that would be a compliment. But, no, I did not, nor would ever, call you a dog. You know, you never seem happy to see me," I muse, steps halting in my attempt to leave.

"Because I'm not."

I could just walk away. There are no obstacles between me and the backdoor and yet—"Your sister smiles when she sees me."

"Am I supposed to do the same just because she's my sister? Because even if we were related, I don't think genetics work like that."

"You also don't seem happy Daphne is going to be part of the wedding," I point out.

"Why would I be happy that you completely blindsided her?" she cries. "Being a date and being a bridesmaid are two very different things."

"You suggested I ask her."

"*No*, I did not. And even if I did, I never expected her to say *yes*."

I know it would be wrong of me to smile at Stella's consternation but seeing her all flustered is amusing. "It surprises you that most women find me charming and desirable."

"The ones the palace pays to feel that way?"

The urge to smile fades. "Are you suggesting the palace compensates your sister for dating me? Because that seems an awful lot like—"

"I am not saying that," she snaps.

Score one for me.

"I explained everything to Daphne," I soothe like Stella is a snarling beast. "She's good with it. We're going as friends, nothing more."

"Because you want to be available for when you run off and start your travelling again," Stella sneers. "And get your picture taken with your myriad of girlfriends."

I cock my head and study her like she's an engine I'm about to fiddle with. "For someone who professes to hate me, you seem to know quite a lot about my life."

"Unfortunately, the trials and tribulations of your love life are all over the newspapers."

"I didn't know you were still reading paper products. Doesn't that go against you trying to save the world?"

"Newspapers are made from recycled materials, much better than the glossy tabloids you're featured in."

"And yet, you are well aware of the stories they write about me," I muse, thoroughly enjoying myself. When Stella gets mad, her eyes flash and her cheeks turn a pretty shade of pink. Not that I'm having fun solely because Stella gets more attractive by the moment, but it does help. "Interesting."

"Nothing is interesting about the royal family."

"You should work on your comebacks. Have you ever heard of flyting?" I ask with a half-grin.

"That's not even a word."

"Oh, it is. You should look it up."

Stella shakes her head and stalks away, which might have been more dramatic had she not tripped over a dog bed on her way to the back dog.

And then I might not have laughed, which causes her to give me a very dirty look, with a finger gesture to boot.

11

Stella

FLYTING, I'M QUICK TO discover from a Google search, is a poetic exchange of insults, as found in Scottish history and Norse myths. It sounds an awful lot like *flirting* and if Gunnar thinks that is what I'm doing...

I'm not. There is no *flirting* in my *fighting* with him. His ego must be huge for him to make that jump.

Plus, how dare Gunnar snoop through my things?

Granted, I don't know if he was snooping, but what if he was? What if he saw the books—

Prince Gunnar has never been a reader. I'm sure he wouldn't touch a book with a ten-foot pole.

It still doesn't make me feel better.

I made the mistake of collecting the books when I was eighteen and to this day, I still don't understand the need that drove me to buy romance books with my father on the cover.

I like to think about the why even less than I look at the books. And I hate the fact I physically can't bring myself to get rid of them. I keep them here because my mother would blow a gasket if she saw them and she's never once stepped foot in the shelter.

I stopped asking her years ago.

The dogs rush Gunnar as he steps outside. "Elrond, Galadriel—down," I order, with more authority in my voice because of my irritation. I slip my phone into my pocket so Gunnar doesn't know I checked out the word. *Flyting*...

"Elrond?" Gunnar asks.

"And Galadriel. Lord of Rings," I snap. "Merry, Pippin, Gimli, Frodo." I point to the mass of puppies with Camille. "Got a problem with how I name my dogs?"

He shakes his head with a bemused expression. "Good movie. Didn't think you have that... taste... in movies."

"Well, I do." I take a deep breath. "Lady Camille, welcome. Ajax, everything okay here? Matcha latte," I add, handing Ajax a to-go cup.

"I wanted to wait, but Gunnar said we should leave you alone because you were on your break," Camille calls from under the puppies.

"Usually a good idea," I murmur, narrowing my eyes to return to glaring at Gunnar. "Ajax? Any problems other than the uninvited guest? Not you," I add hastily to Camille. "You're always invited."

"The two of you really don't get along, do you?" She shakes her head.

"No," we say in unison. For once, I'm completely in sync with Prince Gunnar.

"You were only gone for about fifteen minutes," Ajax says wryly. "Everything okay with you? You seem a little more intense than usual."

"That happens when I find someone in my office. I'd appreciate it—"

"Do not give them trouble for that." Gunnar steps forward. "I put a bag. On the chair. With things for the dogs. You'd think you'd be grateful for that rather than getting your knickers in a twist."

"Excuse me?"

"Knickers. In a twist." His blue eyes are Atlantic Ocean cold and the shiver that runs through me might not be because of the ice in his voice.

Prince Gunnar is *very* attractive when he's mad.

I should *not* have thoughts like that.

"Are the two of you finished yet?" Camille asks, still crouched on the ground.

"Oh, Stella will never be finished with me." Gunnar reaches down to let Gimli sniff his fingers. "Hello, puppy." The puppy, long and lanky at four months, takes that as an invitation and jumps onto his jean-clad legs.

Princes should not be allowed to wear jeans because—huh. I can't admit he shouldn't wear jeans because he looks good while wearing them.

I should not think that.

I should not be thinking that *at all.*

Gunnar looks up at me with a smirk. "Puppy likes me."

"Good for puppy."

"Maybe the castle needs more dogs, Prince... er..." Ajax stumbles.

"Just Gunnar is fine. When I'm out and about anyway." He winks at them, and I lose all respect for Ajax because they practically melt into a puddle of flannel shirt.

"Have you ever thought about getting a puppy?" Ajax asks with a dreamy expression on their face.

As soon as the question is out there, I laugh. "You need to have some measure of responsibility before you can even think about getting a pet."

Gunnar stands up and once again, I'm reminded how tall he is, even as the shortest of the princes. "I'm responsible." His voice is still cold and if anyone else reacted like that, I would back off.

I can't seem to do that with Gunnar. Push push push. Needle, jab, stab. Anything to get a rise out of him.

I'm like a dog barking to go outside. If I keep barking, maybe Gunnar will leave.

"If you say so," I say, matching his cool tone. "At least you'd have to learn to stay in a place for longer than a week."

"Unlike you, who has never left this place."

"What's wrong with that?" That stings, but I do my best not to let it show.

"That's all you would talk about when you were a kid. All the places you'd go. Things you'd see. Parts of the world you'd save."

Gunnar started with a sneer but it quickly faded into what seemed like nostalgic reminiscing, so that when he's finished, there's a smile curling at the corner of his mouth.

Why is he smiling? He makes me nervous when he smiles like he knows something I don't. And how does he remember that? I barely remember my country-hoping plans, only that I wanted to see the world. All of it.

My father said he'd take me; take me anywhere I wanted to go. We had a globe, and every night before I went to bed, I'd give it a spin until it slowed, leaving my finger pointing at some country. And then I would ask him about it because, back then, his stories were like that of a superhero, jetting off to faraway countries to play for the masses.

He'd tell me about his favourite places, where he thought we should go. Because he was going to show me the world.

Another lie.

Because my father was the complete opposite of a superhero. "I was a child." I try to keep my voice even after the unpleasant memory. "Things change."

"What's that saying? Out of the mouths of babes?"

"You're calling me a child?"

"I think I just called you a babe, but I'm not about to repeat it because I'm sure it offended you."

"You offend me. Everything about you offends me."

"And for that, I apologize, even though I have no idea why my presence annoys you so much. But it is enjoyable to know that I get under your skin so much. Doesn't happen with anyone else."

"You're never getting one of my dogs."

"Are they personally your dogs? Have you named them? Do you pay for their upkeep?"

"And yes—Merry, Pippin, Frodo, Gimli." I point to the same puppies I named for him moments ago. "I'm responsible for all the animals here. Unlike you, who is responsible for...?" I raise my hands for emphasis.

"And now we're back to that."

We glare at each other for a little too long. So long, that Ajax clears their throat. "So Samwise seems to be doing better on the leash," they offer.

That gets Gunnar's attention. "I sense a theme," he says to Ajax, finally tearing his gaze away from me.

"We do the big franchises," they tell him with a shy smile. "Also, Stella, we got a call right after you left, about the dog on the side of the cliff. I called animal services and they haven't been up to check."

"I called them three days ago." All of my Gunnar annoyance quickly transfers to the nameless animal services employee. "We have an agreement. They *need* to check it out."

"What's the problem?" Camille pulls herself up from the mountain of puppies crawling on her, still with Betty White in her arms.

"We got several calls about a stray dog halfway up the cliff, on the beach side. A lot of times they go off to have puppies, so we need to check on them. Also—"

"It's not a safe place for a dog to hang out," Gunnar finishes.

I spare him a quick, glare-free glance for that. "No, it's not."

"Is this someone's lost dog?' he asks. "Should their owner be looking after them?"

"Most of the older dogs we find are runaways from the First Nations communities," I explain. "Like Elrond and Galadriel. They have a stray problem worse than we do."

"That's because they don't have you," Camille says. She brushes the grit off the back of her pants. "What do we need to do?"

"You don't have to do anything," I tell her firmly. While I appreciate Camille's advice with fundraising and the website, I am perfectly capable of doing my job when it involves rescuing a stray. "I'll make some calls. Animal services will have to do their job, and if they don't..."

"You can't pick up a stray dog and possible puppies by your-self," Gunnar accuses. It's a bit unnerving that he read my mind.

I raise my chin. "Says who? I've done it before and I'm sure I'll do it again."

"She's like the dog whisperer," Ajax adds.

Gunnar watches the puppies cavort with a sullen expression. I don't know what his problem is. Maybe, as a prince, he's too used to everyone taking his suggestions and bowing to his wishes.

I'm not about to do either.

"Find out exactly where the dog is," Gunnar instructs. "I'll pick you up first thing in the morning and we'll check it out."

I take a step away from him. "I have to be here first thing, and *no*. You're not helping me with anything."

"Now you sound like a child."

"I do not, and I'm perfectly capable of looking for a dog myself. And even if I weren't, I wouldn't ask you for help."

"You're not asking. I'm telling you I'll pick you up."

"Does this really work for you? Ordering people around?"

"Okay, that's it." Camille raises her voice and Betty White gives an echoing yip. "As unamusing and unpleasant as listening to the two of you is, I think I'll put a stop to it. Stella, you do a great job with this place, and the castle appreciates it. So please accept Gunnar's offer to help you locate the dog. You have to admit, it would be very difficult to do it by yourself."

What am I supposed to say to that?

Gunnar smirks at me. "You heard her. I'll pick you up at seven."

12

Gunnar

THANKFULLY, AFTER CAMILLE ISSUES Stella the red flag warning, we take our leave.

"The two of you really don't get along," Camille repeats as soon as we're out of the shelter.

"No." I gesture to the SUV idling across the street, where Minka is waiting for us. "We don't. I seem to bring out the worst in her."

Camille studies me. "You really do."

"I'm sure we could get along in certain circumstances," I offer.

"What would those circumstances be?"

"I have no idea," I admit with a chuckle as I open the car door for her.

"No dogs?" Minka asks, setting her book on the passenger seat. "Because Prince Odin said no more dogs until at least after the wedding."

"Oh, he did, did he?" Camille's tone is just as icy as Stella's, but in her case, it makes me smile.

"See, you don't always get along with my brother," I point out.

"That's only when he tries to tell me what to do," she huffs. "What did you do to Stella?"

That is the million-dollar question because once upon a time, I considered Stella a friend. We're the same age—Stella is three days older than I am—and she was around all the time when we were kids. But then Spencer and Duncan moved into the castle and Stella changed. It was like she developed a rock-hard candy shell over her gooey centre.

These days, I doubt there's much of her gooey centre left. "I honestly have no idea."

"Really? Is this like you had no idea of how your actions would hurt Kate?"

Kate. What does it say about me that my one claim to fame as a prince of Laandia, is that I broke local Kate McKibbon's heart? Once again, the surge of frustration wells up; not about Kate, but the fact I can't tell my side of the story.

Because my story is part of a bigger story that isn't mine to tell, and Kate just happened to be a casualty of it. "This is nothing like Kate," I mutter. "Stella and I were kids."

"Were you friends?"

I stare at the window as Minka pulls away from the shelter. "Yeah. Duncan worked with Dad and Stella's Mom was a lady-in-waiting for the Queen—my mom."

"Yes, I know your mom was the queen." But the hand that touches my arm is gentle and understanding. Camille lost her mother too, so she understands that sometimes you just want to say her name.

"Stella would play with us," I say. "Sophie was shy and she'd stick with her mom or hang out with Duncan in his office, but Stella stuck with us and Spencer. She adored him."

"What happened?"

"Duncan and Signe—Stella's mom—split up, and then I have no idea. Stella was different when we went back to school in September. I never thought much of it because a few of my friends went through their parents' divorces and I know it does something to a kid at that age. I guess any age. Stella stopped talking to me. We were paired up to do this geography project together, but she refused to lift a finger to help. Said she'd rather take a failing grade than do anything to help me get what I didn't deserve, whatever that meant."

"Did you fail?" Minka asks, as engrossed as Camille.

"Of course not. I did it all myself, and never told the teacher a thing. Stella might have hated me, but I wasn't about to see her fail."

"And that's why you offered to help her look for the dog? You didn't want her to fail?"

Even if there's an iota of truth, I'm not about to admit it. "No," I say firmly. "I don't want a dog to suffer longer than it needs to. Plus, you've seen the shoes she wears. If she wears those up on the cliff by herself, she'll end up tripping and rolling down the hill and wouldn't that put a damper on your wedding? So, in reality, I'm doing it for you," I finish with a grin at Camille.

"How generous of you. You could do something else for me."

I groan at the earnest expression on Camille's face. "I don't like where this is going."

"You don't even know what I'm going to say!"

"Haven't I done enough? I take you out drinking, help Odin get you a dog. I bring you a really good wedding present back from New Mexico—"

"What kind of present? And where exactly is New Mexico? Is that near Old Mexico?"

I knew that would distract her. As sheltered as Camille's upbringing was, her education in North American geography was even more of a crime. She was constantly asking me where countries were, or if certain American states were close to California. It didn't help that her father is passionately un-American.

"I'll show you on the map when we get home," I promise.

Home.

For the last few years, the castle hasn't felt much like home. Lyra is there even less than I am. Kalle is consumed with the pub and being as different as the heir apparent can be. Bo always kept to himself and Odin—well, O was obviously going through something if he ended up on a reality show.

I had been busy doing my own thing. But now... the castle is back to feeling like home. I would never begrudge our father for letting me flounder, because he did the best he could after Mom died. For all of us, as well as the country.

"It does feel like home," Camille says in a wistful voice, perfectly illustrating my thoughts.

It's quiet between us until we're almost up the hill to the castle. "I still haven't told you what else you could do for me," Camille says.

I hide my grimace. "As always, I am at your service."

"You could be nice to Stella."

"Why did I know you were going to say that?" I groan. "And—what? I'm *always* nice to her. She doesn't return the favour."

"No, you're not."

"No, I'm not. But I try, really, really hard." I widen my eyes and smile innocently at Camille.

"I'm sure you do. Maybe a little more? I like her, Gunnar. For a while, I thought about asking you to invite her as your date," she admits sheepishly. "I like Daphne, but I've gotten to know Stella a little better."

That might have been the end of me if Camille had followed through. There's no way Stella and I could have both survived a whole night together.

"I'm happy with Daphne," she adds. "And I don't think the two of you—you and Stella—"

"There will never be a me and Stella," I tell her flatly.

"I'm not sure about that," Camille muses. "But I hope she's coming to the wedding, so I would appreciate it if you could rein in your angry banter."

"Angry banter." I chuckle. "She does seem to be angry with me all the time."

"Consider it a wedding present."

"So I should send the other one back?"

"No, two presents are fine," she's quick to say.

I laugh. "Anything for my future sister-in-law."

13

Stella

AFTER ALL THAT WITH Gunnar, I am not looking forward to taking Daphne to the castle for her dress fitting.

Because of Gunnar and his insistence on goading me—witty banter, Ajax called it with a knowing glance, and I quickly shot down that idea—I missed talking to Camille about SealSave.

Because of Gunnar, I now have to drive Daphne to the castle; Daphne, who is practically trembling with excitement at the chance she might see Daulton.

Not Gunnar, thank goodness for so many reasons, but Daulton?

I'm not sure how long this thing between Daulton and Daphne has been going on; Sophie told me several weeks ago that Daphne had been texting someone regularly, but it was another week before Daphne let it slip who it was.

Daulton Drake—King Magnus's new PR person. First problem; he works for the royal family. Second—the twelve-year age difference. The third?

I've lost track of how many times *He's married* has come out of my mouth when I'm talking to Daphne about him.

I don't know how serious it is between them since nothing much has happened beyond a string of flirty texts. I honestly can't see the attraction she feels for him—he's smart and charming and good looking to be sure, but Daulton strikes me as the slimy type of man who goes around telling single women his wife doesn't understand him.

Of course his wife doesn't understand him. What woman truly understands men?

And I truly don't understand my sister. *He's married!*

I blame Daulton: Daphne is too naïve to be held accountable if he pulled a full-court press on her. At twenty-two, she's never had a serious relationship. She says they're just friends, but I don't trust him. There are three strikes against him, and even though the twelve-year difference in ages might work for some couples, Daphne is a young twenty-two.

Sophie and I have concluded that while it appears to have stalled at friendship, Daphne is hopelessly infatuated with Daulton, and nothing we can say seems to be able to shake that.

At least I hope it's nothing more than that, but crushes hurt enough.

This is why I reluctantly went along with using Gunnar as a distraction tactic; I am not proud of it because if this works too well and Daphne ends up falling for Gunnar, she'll be in a worse mess than she is with Daulton.

My only hope is that, somehow, Daulton remains a *married* gentleman who remembers his vows, and Gunnar tucks his charm away in the pocket of his suit on the day of the wedding. Because whatever I may think of Gunnar, he's got more than his fair share of royal rizz.

"Are you sure you want to go through with this?" I ask Daphne as we round the last curve leading up the hill to the castle.

I remember once Spencer and I tried to ride our bikes up the hill, a daunting task even for the professional cyclists who often visit Laandia to train for races. We failed—miserably—and after twenty minutes of pushing the bikes, a van appeared.

One of the princes—most likely Odin—had sent a driver to find us.

But I don't like memories like that.

"Go through with what?" Daphne doesn't look up from her phone. Texting Daulton?

"The wedding. Being Gunnar's date and a bridesmaid. It'll be awkward, won't it? You don't even know them and—"

"It's the royal wedding. Of course I want to go!" Still with her phone in her hand, Daphne bounces on her seat, eyes now trained out the window to catch the first glance of the castle.

"But with Gunnar?"

This gets a smile from Daphne and a quick glance my way. "Despite what you may think of him, Gunnar is sweet. And he needs a date. I'm happy to help."

"But you're going to be a *bridesmaid*. Of someone you don't know."

"It's like being in the Sea Queen court. No different," she says with a shrug. "And I'll get to know Lady Camille. She seems very friendly. Nice."

The Camille I know is a lot of things—strong and opinionated, sharp-tongued—but *nice* wouldn't be my first choice to describe her. Just like me.

I think that's why she's starting to grow on me.

"It'll be fun," Daphne adds.

Fun. Nice. Sweet.

Daphne's life is so easy.

We round the last curve, and like every time I see it—the simple sight of the castle takes my breath away. It's so castle-y. Imposing, but not intimidating; four stories of off-white stone that looks golden when the setting sun hits it just so—which happens as I drive through the gates.

There are turrets and towers and arrow slits for the long-dead archers to defend the throne. The outer wall was dismantled years ago but the battlement is still intact, and the portcullis is raised outside the heavy wooden door.

I have a faint memory of being on the battlement once, watching a storm roll in over the Atlantic. I'm not sure how I got up there, but the house manager, Mrs. Theissen, had been furious when she found out, so much so that she lectured my mother for at least ten minutes for allowing it.

Of course my mother had no idea where I'd been, or whom I'd been with. I've never been sure if I remembered it correctly, but I have a strange feeling that my father might have been the one who took me out to watch the clouds.

I hope he's not at the castle today.

Parents splitting up is a common occurrence; I wasn't the only one in my class to have parents getting divorced. Some claimed to grow apart, fathers left mothers for other women, mothers left fathers for other women. One kid's father was lost at sea, only to show up eight months after the mother remarried; she left the new husband for the old husband, only to split up with him six weeks later, but her new husband had already found someone new and didn't want her back.

That kid—I think it was Ivan Erickson, no relation to the king—was pretty messed up.

For my parents to divorce shouldn't have been the end of the world, but when your father leaves you for the king of Laandia, it does something to your loyalty to the crown.

It was purely platonic; my father was a bandmate and best friend to King Magnus and after his successful modelling career, followed the kong home to Laandia after their successful run as part of the heavy metal band Kräftig to become advisor to the king. He worked late hours, and while there were missed Sunday dinners and soccer games, he always apologized and said he did his best to get there.

Behind the scenes must have been a different story, and one I was never privy to.

I was twelve. I lost my father to the king, to the castle. To the royal family.

To make it worse, I lost my half-brother Spencer as well, because he went to live at the castle with Dad, and my sister and I stayed in town with Mom.

When I round the curve in front of the castle and park off to the side, I huff a sigh of relief that there is no sign of my father.

But as I slam the car door a little too hard, I notice my half-brother waiting for us halfway between us and the door. The sight of him does weird things to my insides.

Battle Harbour is a small place, but I worked hard at avoiding Spencer. His leaving for university, and then law school in Canada certainly helped.

He wrote me letters for a time. I opened a few, but I was too hurt to write back.

"I didn't expect you to meet us," I say trying hard to hide how the flutter of happiness at the sight of Spencer affects me. I slam it down because there's no sense getting excited over him. Too much time has gone by.

It's all been too much.

And he looks like he's here to block our entrance to the castle, which raises my hackles even more.

"I didn't think you were coming," Spencer admits, taking a big step forward and then a quick half-step back when he sees my expression.

I can't see myself, but I doubt it's a nice expression.

He looks nothing like the older brother I once worshipped: his floppy, dark hair is styled into one of those hundred-dollar haircuts, the T-shirts and jeans with rips as familiar as the ones I had in my own clothes are long gone, replaced by tailored suits.

This one is navy with a faint light blue pinstripe and a tie to match. He's even sporting a waistcoat.

My lip raises in a sneer because Spencer looks like he was born to wear it, born to live in the castle.

I had no idea Spencer wanted to be a lawyer, and that seems like something a sister should know. I'm sure our father, on orders from the king, talked him into it, and that Spencer had other dreams like becoming an astronaut or a farmer, or something else that would take him away from the castle.

"I'm glad you're here," Spencer adds.

"Why?"

He blinks with surprise at my cool tone. "Well... ah. It's been a long time."

"Too long, I think," Daphne says, looking over Spencer's shoulder with a big smile.

A moment later, I see the reason. Daulton Drake steps outside with a big Crest-whitening-strips smile and eyes only for Daphne. "Why, hello," he says as if this is a completely random meeting.

The way Daphne was vibrating on the drive up suggests there is nothing random about this.

This is the man who has bewitched my step-sister. I know of Daulton because a man can't move to Battle Harbour without my mother hearing about it, especially a good-looking one. And he *is* good-looking, with a bland handsomeness suitable for an animated Prince Charming in a Disney movie.

"Daulton," Daphne chirps, excitement evident in her tone, her face, and even the way she flutters her hands. "How are you?"

"Better now that I've found two lovelies at the door of the castle." His smile is wide and perfect. Too perfect.

Just looking at him—perfectly tailored suit, tie hanging ruler straight, with more product in his hair than any woman I've seen—I don't see how he has much in common with Daphne. He's a businessman, stress on the *man*, and at twenty-two, Daphne is still very much a girl.

I don't like him.

I don't know men's fashion but I would make a good guess that this suit is worth more than Spencer's. It's slim cut with a sheen to the fabric that rubs me wrong.

Daphne reaches for Daulton's hand. "You're so sweet."

"Not nearly as sweet as you."

Maybe it's not the suit fabric—maybe it's just him. I don't bother to try to hide my expression of disgust.

For the first time in over a decade, I meet Spencer's gaze. He looks like he's throwing up a bit in his mouth.

Same.

"Yes, well." My tone is curt, and regardless of how or why I'm here, I'm not about to stand around making inane small talk outside the castle door because who knows who is about to show up next? "Where does she need to go?"

"I have to make sure—" Spencer hesitates and glances at us with obvious unease. "Daphne, you know anything you see or hear at the castle—"

She reluctantly pulls her attention away from Daulton. "Do you need me to sign an NDA?" Daphne asks as if signing a non-disclosure agreement is second nature for her.

It isn't for me. "Why does she need to do that? Why would you even ask something like that?"

"It's not necessary," Spencer assures Daphne. "But there are certain protocols—"

"Are you in charge of castle protocols now?" I snap. "I thought that was Duncan's department."

The words sting as they tumble out of my mouth. As does the look of pity Spencer gives me. "I thought it might be less awkward if I met you," he says. "But Dad would love to see you if—"

"I can deal with this, Spencer," Daulton cuts in as smooth as a warm knife in butter. "There's no need to create tension here."

I can't help but notice the muscle clench in Spencer's jaw. "There's no tension."

Daulton's eyebrow rises, thick and so perfectly groomed that I wonder how often he waxes. "Oh, no?"

"No, tension," I automatically side with Spencer. "And there's no need for a NDA. We won't be here long enough." I motion to Daphne and head for the door, brushing between Spencer and Daulton like they don't exist.

"Stella, we're at the castle. Let's have some fun," Daphne murmurs as she catches up.

"How can dress fitting ever be fun?" I demand as the door swings open and my heart sinks even more.

Gunnar stands there with his usual smirk. "And you've been fitted for how many dresses?"

Instantly, my mouth twists into a sucking-a-lemon expression. "I have dresses."

"I'm sure you do." The smirk is wider, and the dimple appears. Just one, which is somehow more attractive than two set equidistantly from his mouth.

Three years ago, People magazine once selected Gunnar's mouth as the sexiest in the world. I have no idea why.

"You need something to wear to the wedding, too, Stella." Daphne sounds almost giddy, and Gunnar's smirk changes to a genuine smile.

So different than the smile I got, and the pang that courses through me at the sight—like two pot lids clapped together—sends a quick inhale of breath through my nose.

Dresses, parties, fun—I've never been that way. Like a person who enjoys that sort of thing.

Or smiles instead of smirking.

Spencer catches up to us. "You're coming to the wedding?" he asks with a tone in his voice that might be eagerness but is probably the opposite. Whatever the opposite of eagerness is.

Indifference? Dread?

"Ajax and I were invited," I reluctantly admit.

"How nice." Daulton stands beside Daphne, his height blocking the late afternoon sun.

"That's great," Gunnar offers.

"I'm sure you're thrilled," I say, heavy on the sarcasm.

"What?" Gunnar glances at Spencer, wide-eyed and innocent. "That was—maybe not thrilled, but not *not* thrilled. I do think it's great you're coming to the wedding. Everyone should come to the wedding. It's going to be a great party."

"Weddings are more than parties."

"They're kind of *not*," Daphne whispers. "Weddings are really big parties."

Whose side is she on? Last time I drive her anywhere. "I'll wait in the car," I tell her with an about-face.

Daphne snags my arm. "No, don't," she begs with a winsome smile. "Come with me. I need the moral support."

The girl could sell ice to the Inuits with that smile. "Fine," I grumble and let her lead me up the sweeping main staircase while I look around like I'm about to step into a booby trap.

This is the castle. The whole place is a trap.

14

Gunnar

I'D SAY STELLA ISN'T happy to be here.

She showed up with Daphne in a display of sisterly loyalty—or possibly some misguided idea that she needs to protect Daphne from us, the big bad Vikings in the castle. Maybe long ago, pretty maidens needed to be protected from marauding Vikings, but my brothers and I weren't raised to be the pillaging and plundering types.

She grew up here, so she should know that about us.

It doesn't seem like she remembers anything good about me.

I wish I knew why that bothered me. Because it does bother me, I'd like to needle her even more, rather than doing the smart thing which would be to ignore her and keep smiling.

I've never been the smart brother. That's Odin. Spencer. Even Bo, with his life in the woods, has more brains than I do.

The four of us—Spencer, Stella and I, with Daulton taking a solid stance at Daphne's other side— escort Daphne to the seamstress's room. I'm not sure what's worse—the stilted conversation between Daphne and me or the awkwardness between Spencer and Stella.

Or Daulton. I'm not sure why he's here. This is *my* castle and *my* date—

And *my* inner voice sounding like a child.

I blame Stella because she does bring out the worst in me. I think she has the same effect on Spencer since all of his Spencer-ish qualities making anyone comfortable enough to start talking about all their deep secrets have vanished at the sight of Stella.

Listening to them, it would be impossible to guess they're brother and sister. Half, but still. They sound like strangers making polite conversation on a plane.

Even though I don't have much to say to Daphne, she still trips lightly up the stairs like she's going on a picnic, looking like summer personified in her blue dress. She asks questions about the weapons hanging on the walls and laughs at my jokes and jests.

Stella, on the other hand, is all stomps and scowls. She's behind me but I feel the daggers of her stare on my back.

Daphne looks the part of the perfect date. She's sweet, she's nice, and there are no expectations. There's no interest.

I can tell when a woman is interested in me, and Daphne is clearly not. I'm sure she wouldn't be immune to my considerable Erickson charms, but there's nothing that gives me an indication that she agreed to this to get into my pants.

Which is great because I'm not looking for anyone to get into my pants right now. Especially not when I'm home, because that never ends well.

Cue the montage of my breakup with Kate. It was six years ago but I never like to be reminded of my mistakes. And being home and seeing Kate is a huge reminder.

Which is why I shouldn't plan to be around much after the wedding. There are too many places to visit, people to meet. If I had a role here, I could be persuaded to stay longer, but there's nothing. Everyone has a life to lead—Odin will be married and starting his happily ever after with Camille, and Kalle will continue running the pub and staying out of the spotlight. Bo will stay out of the spotlight even more. And Lyra has plans to head straight back to Chicago right after the wedding, probably even sooner than I'll be hopping on a plane.

Dad is fine with this. He lets us live our lives. He runs the country better than anyone and has his team to help.

I'm not a part of that team. I don't have a job. I've had enough education. I'm more about learning from life experiences and I do my best to get as many as I can.

Ever since Stella goaded me yesterday about my travels, I've been thinking about my next trip. The plan was to go to Indonesia, and then meet my friends Milo and Ashton, Fenella's brother, in Singapore for a Formula One race, but now there's a little voice in my head saying things like the "trip is *privileged, selfish, immature.*"

And I hate that it sounds an awful lot like Stella.

I do my best to ignore it, which is difficult when the owner of the irritating voice in my head has just shown up.

Wherever I go, I will be *going,* which means I don't want to leave something like a Daphne-Gunnar thing behind.

Not that there ever will be a Daphne-Gunnar thing. She's not interested. I'm not interested. She might *start* to get interested, but I'll do my best to make sure that won't happen. She's a nice girl who is doing me a favour, and it's a bad coincidence that she's the stepsister of my would-be arch-nemesis—if I gave Stella enough credit for that role.

It feels like forever to reach the second floor where the wedding sewing/dress fitting is in full swing but I still gesture gallantly to the door. "Your gown awaits."

"I can't wait to see it." Daphne clasps her hands under her chin.

"You'll look even more beautiful than the bride," Daulton says. Again—why is he here?

"That's sweet, but no. Camille must be in the spotlight, the centre of attention."

I agree, since that's the reason Daphne is doing me this solid, but I don't think it's gentlemanly to say that. "You'll look amazing," I assure her. "A compliment to Camille."

"I hope so. It's *her* day. I'll have my day... someday." Daphne lowers her eyes and looks up through her lashes in the classic, innocent flirtation move. "Soon maybe?"

Just as my stomach sinks, thinking that I got it all wrong about Daphne's lack of interest, she looks up at—

Daulton.

"I'd better go try on my dress," she adds with a sweet smile. "It was nice to see you, Daulton."

Still looking at Daulton. I glance at Stella, who has now directed her Black Glare of Death straight at the man in question.

"Always a pleasure." Daulton, in his fifteen-hundred-dollar suit, looks like he has every right to be included in the escort duty. He does look the part.

So does Spencer, in his suit. I look out of place in my cargo shorts and T-shirt with a swipe of grease down my arm that I missed after I cleaned up from tinkering with my bike.

Both Spencer and Daulton look like valued members of the castle staff, and I look like what I am—an entitled prince with nothing to do but play with my toys.

"Coming, Stella?" Daphne, her hand on the doorknob, is still smiling at Daulton.

Stella looks between the closed door—and the fabric and finery that waits behind it—and me and Spencer. The dress obviously wins. "Uh, sure."

"I'll wait for you out here," I tell her. "Camille won't let me see anything."

Stella looks surprised at my comment. "Why?"

Why would I wait for her? For *them*? There are no reasons, but still— "To make sure you get out safely," I manage.

"Bet you can't wait for that," she mutters as she closes the door behind her with a firm click, leaving me standing with Spence and Daulton.

"Boys." Same as Stella, it's obvious Daulton doesn't see the point of sticking around with us because he gives a curt nod of dismissal and disappears down the staircase.

Either he takes his public relations job too seriously or I'm missing something.

Spencer heaves a sigh. "It's a nice dress, isn't it?"

I think the sigh is because of Stella. "I guess so?"

"No ugly bridesmaid dress? With the big butt-bow?"

I lean against the wall, wondering how long I'm going to have to wait. "I know nothing about big butt-bows and I have no idea why you would."

Spencer shrugs. "I dated a girl who was in a wedding and that's all she talked about."

"I didn't hear anything about this girl," I say teasingly.

"There wasn't much to hear about. Plus, you're not around much these days."

There's no animosity in *his* voice. Not that my brothers ever say much beyond teasing and wanting details. "Things to do, people to see."

"People to do, things to see?" Spencer asks with a wry grin. "I hear more about you than actually see you."

"Heresay. The paps will print anything they think will sell papers."

"So those rumours about Florence Pugh…"

I heave a bigger sigh than Spencer's. "Just rumours. Unfortunately. She's great, though."

"Not great enough to be your date to the wedding?" He looks at me suspiciously.

"Spence. You got a problem with me taking your sister? Not that Daphne *is* your sister."

Spencer frowns and stares at the heavy door where Stella and Daphne disappeared. It's heavy enough for us not to be able to hear anything about what's going on inside. "She's not my sister, but she's a nice kid. I don't want anything to change that."

"To make her not nice, or not a kid?" I wonder. I'm not offended by Spencer's wariness—if half of what was written about me were true, I'd worry about me. And that's what people see, the photos and stories about me playing my way around the world.

It's sad they don't believe that there is more about me.

My life, contrary to popular belief, is not all parties and private yachts, although there are plenty of both. I make contacts, a network of important people who I can call on if needed. And they're not all the privileged, entitled brats that the papers call us. I'm friends with Alexandria Oscasio-Cortez and Leonor de Borbón, two women who I think will change the world someday. I've been interviewed by Oprah Winfrey and invited to dinner by Melinda Gates, two women who *have* changed the world.

I know a lot of important men as well, but the women are more impressive.

"There's nothing between me and Daphne," I assure Spencer. "And that's why this is a good idea. It's one day—that's it. I don't want to break any hearts when I leave."

"What about yours?"

I rein in the scoff. "Daphne is not going to break my heart. But maybe you should be having this conversation with Daulton." I look pointedly at where he disappeared down the stairs. "He didn't have to be here to bring the girls upstairs. What was that all about?"

Before Spencer can answer, the door to the seamstress's room opens and Stella flies out, eyes wide and breathing in little pants. "Are you okay?" Spencer reaches for her and then recoils when Stella scowls like he's offered her something foul.

"I'm not—it's not. It's not my scene," she finishes. "There's a lot in there."

"A lot of what?"

"Everything."

"Everything" could be anything, but I'm the ultimate gentleman and don't say a word as the horror is slow to fade from her eyes. Spencer, on the other hand, looks at this as an opportunity to bond with a sister he hasn't spoken to in years.

Both make our little group in the hall a tad uncomfortable.

I get it. They haven't seen each other in a while. It's always awkward for about a day when I see Lyra before we go back to being like a pack of puppies.

I remember Spencer and Stella once being as close as me and Lyra. Now? Not so much.

My gaze keeps stealing back to Stella and I tell myself it's because I feel for Spence.

She's the same height as Daphne but seems smaller because of her black, sloppy sweater, with sleeves full of visible holes, possibly from puppy teeth, covering most of her hands. It hangs off one shoulder, and her bra strap—also black—is noticeable.

So are the tattoos on her shoulder.

I keep stealing glances until I make out a tree and with what may be paw prints trotting along her back.

I have no idea when she got the tattoos; she obviously didn't have them when I knew her, back when she was twelve. There hasn't been much opportunity to see her skin lately.

Not that I'm looking for opportunities to see Stella's skin.

But the tattoos are there, and quickly becoming a distraction. So I look at her hair instead.

It's still purple. And blue. And green. And strangely, it provides a much-needed burst of colour from Stella's all-black attire. Even the eye makeup around her grey eyes—

Pretty grey eyes.

—is thick and black.

Sloppy black sweater. Loose black skirt hanging unevenly along her knees, and stompy boots with thick soles.

I've never seen someone dressed so casually during a visit to the castle, and my father was in a heavy metal band.

I thought goths were teenagers. Stella is the same age as me and seems like she hasn't gotten out of the phase.

"What?" she demands when my gaze skims along her hair again, sticking for half a breath too long. "You keep looking at me."

"I'm not looking at you."

"You are. I can feel the heat of your blue eyes."

"My eyes are not hot and they're not looking at you." I glance at Spencer with an expression like *she's nuts,* only to find Spencer looking at me like I have two heads. "You have tattoos," I concede.

"You wouldn't know that unless you were looking at me!"

"Well, your shoulder is hanging out of your shirt and they're *there.*"

Stella adjusts her sweater to cover her shoulder, which causes the material to slide off her other shoulder.

There are no tattoos there.

Not that I'm looking.

"How long have you had tattoos?" I'm glad Spencer asks because while I'm not interested in the ink on Stella's skin, I kind of want to know.

"Since I was eighteen and didn't need my parents' permission."

"Yeah, I can see your mom not being big on them," he says with a chuckle.

If possible, Stella's eyes grow even colder. "She's fine with them," she snaps, and I, having met her mother, know that's one big fat lie.

But I don't call her out on it. "Did they hurt?"

She lifts her chin. "Not for me."

"What, you've got some higher-than-average pain tolerance?"

"As a rule, most women do."

"As a rule?" I scoff.

"Childbirth."

"Ah," Spencer and I say together. "I like the dog prints," I offer.

"Why?"

"I like dogs."

"You like dogs?" she demands like it's the worst thing in the world.

"Of course I like dogs."

"It's not, *of course I like dogs*, like *of course I have blond hair because I'm a prince of Laandia*," Stella says mockingly. "Having Camille's dogs in the castle doesn't mean you instinctively like them."

I really don't understand the hostility here. "But I do."

"You've never even gotten a chance to get to know Bea Arthur because you're never around," she says, heaping on the scorn.

"I have. And she sleeps with the blue duck I bought her. I'm not gone all the time."

"Yeah, right. And what does that matter?"

"Stella."

We're so busy glaring at each other that neither of us hears Duncan's approach.

And I do know Camille's dog enough to recognize that Stella jerks her head toward Duncan's voice the same way Bea Arthus reacts when she's startled and scared.

Stella's mouth opens and, for once, closes without anything coming out of it.

"Hey, Dunc," I say.

And then it clicks. How could I not have realized how much Stella looks like her father?

Same square jaw, but with a feminine softness for Stella. Long narrow nose. But it's the eyes that catch you. Silvery eyes that look grey one moment and green the next.

I wonder if Stella's flash green when she laughs, like Duncan's do.

I don't remember seeing her smile in a long time, let alone laugh.

"D-Duncan," Stella finally manages. "Lord Laz."

Duncan flinches. I don't know the exact history of that family, but it's clear Duncan expected more than a cool surprise without a hint of welcome.

That must have hurt.

And she's not done yet. "I should check on Daphne," Stella adds, forgetting how she ran out of the room with her tail between her legs not ten minutes ago.

Spencer also looks like he feels the sting of that dismissal.

"Wait. Please." Duncan reaches out as if to touch her arm, but Stella steps back. "How are you?"

What do you care? her expression says. "Fine," she clips. "And you?"

Duncan lifts his shoulder. "And your sister?"

"Sophie is amazing, just like she was when you left."

He winces, so much that I want to step between them to shield Duncan from Stella's sharp tongue. "Stella. Your mother..." Her incredulous expression snaps his mouth closed. "No. Never mind."

"I would say no, never mind because you have *no* right to even mention mother's name in front of me, let alone say anything about her to me. So—" Her voice could freeze parts of a polar bear, plus just to be clear, she gives what might be the most annoyed version of a nod. "I'm out of here. So *not* nice to see you."

Stella turns to the door, and I see her expression when she realizes that, once inside, she has no way of escape if Duncan decides to wait for her.

She goes in anyway.

15

Stella

I HATE HATE *HATE* that at the first sight of him, all I wanted to do was run straight into his arms.

My father.

Dad.

Daddy.

And at the first sight of him, all I can hear is my mother's voice, telling me Daddy wasn't coming home.

He was going to live at the castle, with the king and the queen and the princes, and princess.

Why?

Because he wanted to be with *that* family more than his own. And he was taking Spencer with him—leaving me and Sophie with our mother. He left us behind because he didn't want to be part of our family anymore.

He would rather be with the royal family than us.

That's what my mother told me, and as much as the words ripped a hole in my twelve-year-old heart, I have no reason not to believe her, because Duncan Laz never made a move to try and explain things to us. Or apologize.

Nothing.

Not a word.

He stopped coming to my soccer games, stopped taking Sophie to her art lessons. No more family dinners, watching movies with big bowls of popcorn, no more Daddy-special pancakes on Sunday mornings.

No more visits to the castle.

No more Spencer.

There were only the three of us until Mom married Peter and him and Daphne moved in with us.

Speaking of Daphne—heads whip in my direction as I come through the door, probably as wild-eyed as when I burst out of the room. "Are you okay?" Daphne asks with real concern so I know I look bad.

"I—fine. I'm fine. You look—" My fluster fades as I stare at my step-sister with genuine affection in my gaze.

Beautiful. Daphne looks absolutely stunning. Her dress is a pale yellow that, with her blonde beauty, makes her look like a sunbeam.

I hadn't really noticed the dresses the first time because being back here, seeing Spencer again, had been—yeah. And now my father...

It's a lot.

"You came back." Princess Lyra and Odin's assistant and maid of honour, Kate, stand at the far side of the room, both wearing their dresses. Lyra, tall and glamourous in a pink shade that somehow does not clash with her strawberry blonde hair, and Kate's is a pretty lilac.

Lyra looks at me like I crawled in from the garden, smelling of compost. At least Kate is marginally more friendly.

How could I forget *they* were the reason I bumbled my way outside?

I do remember hearing the seamstress, Mademoiselle Zoya, explain how the dresses are all a different colour because Lady Camille couldn't decide which was her favourite shade.

The dresses themselves are amazing—tiny spaghetti straps, a ruched bodice sprinkled with diamantes, and a full skirt with layers of sheer material. Plus, there's a shrug to wear for the ceremony because the wedding was initially supposed to be in February, not that the sheer material would provide any warmth.

I could never see myself wearing anything like it.

"Stella?" Daphne makes a move to step off the tiny platform the seamstress is crawling around, hemming the layers of her skirt, but stops herself. "What did Gunnar do?"

Lyra snorts. "What makes you think it's my brother who did anything?"

"I—nothing. He didn't—" Why can't I catch my breath? It was no big deal. My father—Duncan—tried to talk to me. I didn't want it. I came back in here.

Nothing to it. I try to stop the racing of my heart because I shouldn't have this reaction. There's no point.

"You ran into your dad, didn't you?" Lyra nods with a smug smile. "Tough being estranged, isn't it?"

I stare at her. How does she know? Did she know—was this planned? Did Duncan know I was here, and did he want to—

I have no idea what he wanted.

"Your dad?" Kate looks confused. "Oh—Duncan."

"Lord Laz is my biological father, yes." The ice in my tone should warn off anyone, but not Princess Lyra.

"I'm surprised you admit that," Lyra says, meeting my coolness with some of her own. "Since you've cut him and Spencer off so completely. It's like you've denied his existence."

There's the reason for Lyra's holding a grudge—she's always been fiercely protective toward her brothers, and in her mind, Spencer is the fifth prince of Laandia.

She's not the only one. Half the country thinks the same.

Lyra considers Spencer and Duncan both to be part of her family and therefore I am the villain in this saga.

"I've had my reasons for cutting him off," I snap. "Which are none of your business. And he did it first!"

Immature, but come on. I never signed up to take on a princess. Gunnar is bad enough.

"Did he? Did he really?" Lyra practically oozes the question.

"This is your business—how?"

"They're my family, too."

"And that's because Lord Laz made his decision." To abandon his family is what I want to add but I don't because I don't want pity. I also don't want to be having this conversation but Princess Lyra can't read a room to save her life.

"Was it? Was it really *his* decision?" she pushes.

"Lyra," Kate chides. "Leave it."

"Someone should tell her she's been an idiot for years! Duncan—"

"Lyra!" When they were younger, Kate followed Lyra everywhere, including into a lot of questionable situations. It's nice to see her speak up for once.

I never would have imagined it would ever be on my behalf.

Lyra tosses her red hair and pulls out her phone. "Whatever."

Daphne stares, her expression a mix of confusion and concern. I try a reassuring smile and fail miserably. "Are you about finished?" I ask in a shaky voice.

"A few more minutes," the seamstress murmurs from her spot on the floor, pinning up the hem of the dress.

I lean against the wall behind Daphne. I'm stuck. Daphne is perched on the platform, looking like Cinderella at the ball, and I'm the sour stepsister.

I'd leave, but I *know* Duncan will be waiting for me outside. If I leave with Daphne, there will be safety in numbers and he won't try any father business with her beside me.

I don't think he will.

But I can't be in here. It's too much *girl*.

I'm a girl, but I'm not that much of a girl. Lyra has pulled me back to seventh grade when the popular girls shunned me once they heard Duncan left us.

I never told anyone how Megan Stuber said it was *my* fault he left. And Daniel Moore agreed. Even my teacher, whose husband worked at the castle, believed it was *me* who made my father leave.

Lyra thinks the same thing.

The worst thing is that *I don't know*. I don't know what the relationship was between my parents at that time, only what my mother chose to tell me. *I don't know* if there was an underlying problem or if my father just up and decided he didn't want to be a father to me and Sophie anymore.

I was twelve years old, picking sports and animals and activism over friends and pretty clothes. I had been a difficult child. I had an attitude—admittingly still do—a holier-than-thou way of looking at things that I can see now must have been annoying, and a sharp tongue that never held back. I was too smart for my own good.

I wouldn't want to parent me either.

I'm old enough now to understand it wasn't me who caused the split, but twelve-year-old-me, still hidden inside my bravado and bluster, sometimes likes to remind me that I played a part at the most inopportune times.

Like now.

I tuck in my earbuds and stare at my phone, scrolling through my playlist that I turn on when I need to calm the dogs, but I have no idea what's going to work for me.

Stella. Your mother...

It's been a long time...

Someone should tell her she's been an idiot for years...

There's more that I don't know. There has to be.

And it sounds like I'm the only one who doesn't know what really took my father from us.

It's not a good feeling.

16

Gunnar

I'VE ALWAYS THOUGHT DUNCAN had the widest shoulders of anyone in the castle, wider than even Dad and lumberjack Bo. So to see them slump, like he's carrying the weight of the world is disconcerting.

Almost as much as the expression on Stella's face when she disappeared into the sewing room.

"I don't know why I thought it would be any different," Duncan mutters.

Spencer has a matching face full of disappointment.

"Why should what be any different?" I ask. Duncan looks at me with tired eyes and I tell myself that it's because of those shoulders that I press on. "I mean, why is it like that between the two of you? She's your daughter and she makes it seem like... Not that it's any of my business," I finish, realizing this conversation might be out of the comfort zone of the playboy prince.

"It's Stella's mother," Spencer says, his voice bitter and full of frustration "All of this comes from her."

"You got a divorce," I point out. "It's not the end of the world. Sad, but still."

"It shouldn't have been, no," Duncan agrees.

"And it wouldn't have been if she hadn't poisoned the girls against Dad. And you didn't do anything to stop it," Spencer accuses.

I remember Stella's mother, and I've heard the rumours of her machinations around Battle Harbour, but for Spencer to blame or complain means she is, indeed, a nasty woman.

"There wasn't anything I could do," Duncan protests.

"You played lead guitar for one of the biggest metal bands in the world, and that's before you became the Harlequin romance book cover model of the century. There's not a lot you can't do, Dunc," I tell him.

"She would have taken the girls." Duncan heaves a sigh like he's just released a bunch of toxic gas and looks apologetically at Spencer. "I never told you. Signe threatened to leave Laandia if I ever tried to contact the girls. I would never have seen them again. At least if they're here, I can see them and know that they're close. She said she'd go if I talked to them, or tried to explain, but even with that, I couldn't let them leave."

Duncan and Spencer are tight, so knowing he gave up any chance of a relationship with his daughters to have them stay close breaks my heart. I squeeze his shoulder in sympathy.

"I thought it would get better once she married Peter," he continues, "but by then, Signe was so full of bitterness and passed it onto the girls. There was nothing to be done. They wanted nothing to do with me. Especially Stella. She was happy once," he adds wistfully. "Always laughing and running around. Hating me changed her."

There's nothing much to say after that, and Duncan takes his leave, talking in a low voice with Spencer as they head down the hall.

I stand alone outside the sewing room.

I'm not sure what I'm waiting for. I might be ahead of Duncan on Stella's least-wanted list, but she's not going to be happy to see me standing here when she finally comes out.

Will she even venture out? What would be worse for her—running into Duncan again, or staying in the castle for hours?

It's sad really, that once upon a time, Stella did spend hours here. Days, even. She would join the six of us, at times dragging Sophie into our games and little adventures that only those who grow up in castles can imagine.

That might be why seeing her so sad still sticks with me.

We would divide into teams and play Capture the Flag. We raced across the lawns in games of Manhunt. There was Hide and Seek inside when it rained, and countless hours spent playing board games.

Stella taught me how to play chess, and I was with her the first time she rode a horse. She spent so much time here and it's weird that she's back and so unhappy about it.

I hate that she's so unhappy.

Even with Stella's sharp tongue and strange need to insult me, the memory of our friendship does strange things to me. It makes me want to look out for her, to protect her.

To stop her from looking so scared.

"Gunnar! What are you doing here?" Camille calls from down the hall. I turn to see her hurrying toward me. "Are they still in the dresses?"

"No idea. You told me not to peek. Plus, Lyra's not going to let me inside."

"Stella—"

"Is inside with Daphne."

She looks at me strangely. "Why does that seem like it's a problem?"

"You know Stella. I'm sure being around dresses isn't her favourite thing to do. She said it was a lot of everything."

If Camille was a wringing-of-hands type of person, she would be doing it right now. "I saw Duncan and Spencer," she murmurs. "And they looked like someone kicked their puppy."

"Yeah, he came to talk to Stella. It wasn't pretty."

She stares at the closed door. "I have my own father issues, so maybe that's why I don't understand what's going on."

"It's not just you. I don't think anyone does." Except me, now that I've heard Duncan's side. I was always on Team Duncan, but I wanted nothing more than to sit Stella down and make her listen to how her mother kept her away from her father.

Only I can't do that. Stella may not hate me now, but that will change if I say anything about her mother. I'd be the same way.

"You know, she doesn't have to wait with Daphne in there," Camille offers. "You could—"

I roll my eyes. "I'm the last person Stella wants to see. Well, maybe Duncan. And then me. I'm right up there."

"I don't understand that either. Did you and her... like you and Kate?"

Why does Camille look excited about the thought of me and Stella *anything*? "No," I say firmly, conveniently forgetting about the kissing thing because I'm not about to get into that now, when Stella might step out the door any moment. "Nothing like Kate."

"But something. Because I can tell…"

"No. No, you can't tell anything because there's nothing to tell."

"Still…" She smiles hopefully. "You could rescue her, you know. It would be a princely thing to do."

I raise an eyebrow.

"You could *amuse* her for twenty minutes while Daphne is finishing, so she doesn't have to stand there bored out of her mind," Camille suggests. "Because you know she is. That wouldn't be so difficult, would it? A little rescue attempt?"

"That would be difficult. I'm not sure I would survive it."

"You would," she promises as she opens the door. "I'll make sure Daphne is in and out, so you'll barely have time to have your first fight."

"I wouldn't count on it," I mutter but Camille slips inside and doesn't hear me.

Why do I have to like my soon-to-be-sister-in-law so much? If it were anyone else, I'd ignore her suggestion. I'd leave all this family drama and stop worrying about girls who don't like me, and go for a ride on my bike. It's a nice day; I haven't been out since I've been home and—

Stella's face. It's like it haunts me. I can picture her stuck in that room, standing in a corner like a Betty White with her hackles raised.

I could open the door and tell her the coast is clear, that Duncan is gone. I could help her escape. It wouldn't be that bad.

But...

I also could do a lot better than just opening the door.

This is a castle after all.

17

Stella

I FLIP THROUGH MY playlist, trying to find songs that would make this bearable.

If I look up, Lyra will still be glaring at me while Kate chats happily with Daphne as she admires herself in the mirror.

I could leave. Again. Open the door and walk out, and if Duncan is still here, just brush past him like he doesn't exist. He perfected that move years ago.

Spencer as well. What could they do? Physically stop me from walking by?

I doubt it.

That's what I should do. Walk out of here and get away from Lyra's glares.

But I don't.

I stand by the wall and stare at my phone screen like I'm actually reading what's on it when in reality, I'm remembering being in this very room years ago.

There used to be a huge armoire right about where I'm standing. I would come in here with Spencer and Gunnar and Bo, sometimes with Sophie, sometimes Lyra, and we would play Narnia. As many as could fit would cram into the armoire, pushing past the old clothes left there, each of us playing a character that would soon disappear into the secret land of Narnia.

I loved those books. My father would read them to us, and Spencer introduced them to the boys.

When the air ran out in the armoire, we would tumble out and then Bo or Spencer would check the hall outside the room. If no one was there, we would carefully open the door to the secret passage, the imperceptible crack in the wall hidden in the shadow of the wardrobe.

The castle has a labyrinth of passages in the walls and we explored them all, even though Mrs. Theissen and our mothers forbade us to step foot beyond the wall.

They caught us a few times, but not many.

The memory of those days loosens the knots in my shoulders and my expression relaxes from that of a persecuted criminal to my usual face.

It's good timing because the door opens and Camille appears. "You're still here," she cries at the sight of Daphne. "Oh, the dresses are so beautiful! This is the first time I can see them all together."

Who would have worn the dress if Gunnar hadn't asked anyone to the wedding? But I don't ask because I don't trust my voice.

This is really a lot.

"Is Edie coming?" Lyra asks as Camille practically dances around her bridesmaids, a huge smile on her face.

"No." The smile drops. "Kalle needs her at the pub, but she'll have her final fitting on Monday. Edie, who works at the King's Hat," Camille says to Daphne's expression of confusion. "Do you know her? She'll be the fourth bridesmaid."

"I know *of* her." With at least ten years of age difference be-tween them, Edie and Daphne run in very different circles.

"She's nice," I offer from my spot against the wall. "She came into the shelter to get a cat for her neighbour."

"Stella!" Camille leaves her appraisal of Daphne and turns to me so expectantly that I pull out one of my earbuds. "I'm so glad you're here. Mrs. Theissen only gave me a minute to run over and say hello, but I wanted to ask you something."

I blink with surprise. "Ask *me* something?"

"You always seem so interested in what I'm doing for Seal-Save and well, I'm going for a quick visit later early next week and wondered if you'd like to come with me." Her expression is interesting—hopeful but guarded, like she wants something but is afraid to ask.

"Me?" I can almost hear the creaks in my cheeks as I smile. "I mean, sure, that would be—"

"If you'd rather not—"

"No, it would be great. Really," I tell her honestly. "I'd love to visit and see what you're doing with it. Thank you for asking."

It's amazing how that changes my mood. One minute, I was miserable and didn't hide it, and now a simple invitation—Camille invited *me*—pulled me from the doldrums.

Almost.

"Good." A satisfied smile creases Camille's face. "I thought you might. We'll leave first thing Monday morning, and be back that same night. If that works."

"It does." I can ask one of the volunteers to help Ajax in the shelter. "Thank you."

"You're going to Saint Pierre?" Daphne asks from up on the platform with the seamstress still crawling around the floor.

"You're welcome to come with us," Camille says quickly. "It's just a quick trip to check on the animals."

"I'd love to," Daphne says with her smile. "Thanks for including me."

"Of course. I'll text you both with the details. And Daphne, the dress is truly beautiful on you. You all look wonderful."

"We won't look as good as you will," Daphne promises. Camille smiles and, with a wary glance at Lyra, says a quick goodbye.

Camille's invitation settles the wild racing of my heart and the feeling of being under attack. It's still awkward being in this room when I'm so out of place, but I turn up my music so I can't hear the others. Lyra ignores me. And Kate gives me a sympathetic smile as the seamstress asks her to trade places with Daphne.

I wonder if Kate ever found out it was me who sent the picture of Gunnar that broke them up.

Maybe it wasn't the text—maybe they had issues and proof of Gunnar's betrayal was only the icing on the breakup cake.

Every time I see her, I want to apologize, even though I know it's not my fault.

It's not. It's Gunnar's fault. I was just the witness. The messenger, the bearer of bad news.

Lyra would hate me more if she knew, so Kate must not realize it was me.

I hope she never does.

As Daphne steps down to let Kate have her turn on the platform, I have hope that it's time to go, but Daphne doesn't make a move to change out of her dress. Instead, she studies her reflection in the mirror, turning this way and that, like she's trying to decide which side is her best one.

All of her sides are good, so sunshiny and cheerful. Beside her, I'm the darkness to her light, with a scowl in my dark-rimmed eyes.

I lean against the back wall and pretend I'm not trying to find the crack that marks the secret door. Not that it matters. My days of running through the passages of the castle are as much a thing of the past as the Viking raids across the Quebec border.

Except I know exactly where the crack in the wall is because I can *see* it—not two feet from where I'm standing.

The crack in the wall slowly widens.

The secret door to the secret passage opens while I'm standing watching it.

I don't know if I should run away or jump inside. That is until I see a pair of laughing blue eyes in the darkness.

"What are you doing?" I snap at Gunnar, who sticks his head out of the passage.

"Fancy a trip to Narnia?"

My breath catches and something inside... melts. But no. That can't be, because this is Gunnar, and just because I was caught in a haze of nostalgia does not mean anything is melting.

"Hey, bro," Lyra calls from across the room. "You're not supposed to be here."

"You don't see me." Gunnar waves at Daphne. "I thought your sister might need an extraction."

It takes a moment for me to realize Gunnar is talking about *me.*

"She probably does." Daphne is completely unbothered about doors in walls and her sister about to disappear into the darkness with a prince, as if such things happen every day. "I'll meet you at the car when I'm finished."

"You all look beautiful," Gunnar says in a loud whisper and grins at me.

With both dimples.

"But why?" I demand. *Why* is he here for *me*?

"You're not helping," Gunnar complains. "I'm trying to lead a successful rescue mission here, so get on board."

My mouth literally drops open. Rescue mission was something we played as children—running through the secret passages of the castle to see who needed escape from tutors or Mrs. Theissen or any chores. Once, Spencer led a team of Bo, Odin, and Gunnar through the walls to get me out of tea with the queen and my mother.

Maybe that's why I'm not the girly girl like Kate and Daphne—too much time spent with the princes and Spencer when I was younger.

"For who?" I manage.

"For *you*." He laughs and pushes the door open wider, enough for me to see that it's only him in the darkness. I thought maybe Spencer... but it's only Gunnar.

I'm through the door in an instant.

I was already caught up in the past when I arrived at the castle, but stepping into that passage is like jumping back into my twelve-year-old body.

It's the same, but very different.

For one, it's *cold* in here. Goosebumps rise under my sweater. The stone walls are like blocks of ice, cold to the touch. If I could see, I'm sure my breath would be a visible cloud.

But I can't see because it's a *dark* passage. There's not even an outline of light when Gunnar shuts the door. I can't see anything, including my hand in front in front of my face. I can't see Gunnar. I might have run wild through these paths as a kid, but the darkness has taken away any sense of direction.

"It's dark," I breathe, holding out my hands and turning in a circle, which doesn't help my confusion. It also leads me straight into Gunnar.

"Oof," he says as my hands slap into his chest. At least I think it's his chest. It's very solid. "What are you doing?"

"I'm trying to *see*."

"Let your eyes adjust."

"Where are the lights?" I hiss.

"Why are you whispering? They know we're in here."

"Do they know we're standing in the pitch black? Where are the lights?" I demand loudly.

I can hear the eye rolling in his tone. "It's a secret passage in a castle. When it was built back in the sixteen hundreds, there weren't fun things like electricity and nightlights."

"I don't need a nightlight." I need Gunnar to stop being so close to me, yet I don't want to be left in the dark. Even though we're standing in pitch blackness, I feel him right there, head and shoulders taller than me. He may be the shortest of the princes, but he's still got considerable inches on me.

He's close enough that his scent masks the old castle smell. Citrus and sea.

It's... not offensive.

"You sound like you need something though?" His hand closes on my wrist and I have no clue how he knew where to find my hand.

Oh, because my hand is still resting on his chest. I jerk it away, jerk myself away only to back into the wall, with Gunnar still holding my wrist like a leash.

"Scared, Stella?" Now he's laughing at me and I scowl into the darkness.

"No. Why would I be scared? Just because I can't see you, which gives you the perfect opportunity to lock me in here."

"Why would I want to do that?"

"Why would you want to do half the things you do?"

"Only half? You're beginning to think better of me."

"Don't flatter yourself."

Gunnar chuckles and it somehow warms the air. "You can trust me." And then he takes my hand.

His hand is warm. Long fingers fold over mine. And, oh my god, he's doing the *here's the church here's the steeple open the doors and here's all the people* reverse entwining of our fingers.

It's uncomfortably comfortable.

A flash of light blinds me as Gunnar turns on the flashlight on his phone. "It's been a long time since I've been in here. I thought I'd be okay finding my way in the dark."

"You're not going to get us lost, are you?"

I don't just hear the frown in his voice; no, I can now see it in the dim blue circle of light bouncing off the walls. "Anyone tell you you're a wee bit ungrateful? I just swooped in with a Mission:

Impossible move and got you out of dress duty, if you haven't noticed."

"Why?"

"Why what"

"Why did you pull me out of there?"

Gunnar looks down at me and my stomach twists at his expression of gentle...is it sympathy? Affection? It's not his smug, laughing-at-the-world face I usually see, but I can't read it. "You got roped into bringing Daphne and it's obvious this is the last place you want to be. Plus, you hate dress stuff, so being trapped in that room because you're worried Duncan will be outside can't be much fun."

"You—I—it's not because of Duncan," I stammer.

Gunnar gives me a knowing look. "This way, we can get you straight to your car without bumping into him until you're ready."

"I don't want to bump into him at all," I confess, surprising myself with my admission. "I didn't want to see him."

"He's your father. You have to talk to him."

"I really don't. I don't care whose father he is."

"He's yours."

This isn't our usual argumentative back and forth. Whatever Gunnar is feeling gentles his tone. And I'm raw, like an exposed wound, which lets him get past my defences.

"I don't need a reminder." I've spent years avoiding any discussion about my father, and now, it's happened twice in one day. Plus he was right there in the flesh.

"I know. But you're getting them anyway. I may not have father issues, but I've listened to Fenella enough to get that it's not fun. So c'mon; let's stop bickering and get you out of here."

Gunnar tugs my hand and starts off along the dark passage. The chill from the stone walls quickly seeps through me, except for my hand, which is warm because Gunnar is holding it.

I don't remember it being this cold—or this quiet. I can hear the thumping of my heart as I let Gunnar lead. The scuff of his shoes and the answering clump of my boots.

I hope he's going in the right direction.

He's probably not.

What if we end up on the top level of one of the turrets? Or down in the dungeons?

I don't want to go into the dungeons.

We used to play down there. In the cells, built to hold the most violent of the Vikings, which had to be pretty darn violent for Vikings, we had our clubhouse. Gunnar and Bo created a place where we could hide from the adults, stealing books and comics and pillows. Food from the kitchen for snacks, until mice found our stockpile and raided it. Cards and games—we played every type of game.

We played Truth or Dare.

We played it all the time—dared each other to jump into the cold water of the pond, demanded Kalle tell the truth about what happened with him and Marisa Bennett after baseball practice. But that day seemed different.

And Kalle wasn't there. Or Odin. It was me and Sophie, Lyra, Bo, Spencer, and Gunnar. There was kissing involved.

I'm not sure who came up with it or who dared whom first, but it was Gunnar who turned to me with a grin, mischievous and challenging. So of course I had to kiss him.

The touch of his lips against mine was a shock, but not a bad one.

Looking back, the kiss *was* a bad one because we were twelve and without a clue what we were doing. But I like to think it had potential if we had tried it again when we were older.

I thought about that over the years more than I like to admit. Not enough to do anything about it, just enough to keep me awake at night. Occasionally. Not much, because I don't think about it. Much.

"You okay back there?" Gunnar breaks into my thoughts. "You've gone quiet. It frightens me."

"Good. I can be quiet," I add a second later.

"I know that, but when you're quiet and we're walking in the dark, it makes everything quiet."

"We have light."

"I'm turning it off now. I've got my hand on the wall."

"Do you know where you're going?"

"Yes."

"Are you sure?"

"*Yes.*"

We turn to the right, and the floor slopes downward, which is a good sign. Gunnar is right; it is too quiet when we're not talking.

"You can talk," I offer.

"No, because if I say the wrong thing, you will undoubtedly rip my head off and leave it for the mice to find."

"I wouldn't do that."

The movement of his hand holding mine shifts like he's looking over his shoulder at me. "You sure about that?"

"I would never rip off your head because I wouldn't be able to find my way out."

He chuckles. "You'd end up in the dungeons for sure. We're on the west side now."

I nod my head even though Gunnar can't see me. "The queen's sitting room."

"The scene of the earlier rescue attempt. You know, you never thanked me for that."

"I thanked *Spencer* because it was his idea."

"Nah. Mine."

"You're trying to take credit for all the fun things we did as a kid?"

"You thought it was fun?"

He is not thinking of the Truth or Dare game because that would mean he's a mind reader. Gunnar Erickson might be many things, but he better not be able to read my mind. "I did not," I say in a prim voice.

"You don't even know what I'm referring to."

"I don't need to. None of it was fun."

"Are you arguing with me just for the sake of arguing?"

"I'm arguing because I'm right."

"No, now you're just being ornery. And I thought we were having a moment. We're here," he says, stopping so suddenly I bump into him.

Not much of a bump. "There are no moments," I mutter.

I can't make out what he says before a crack of light appears in the wall beside us, causing me to squint my eyes shut. "Ready to make your escape into Narnia?" Gunnar offers, tugging me by the hand. "Ladies first."

"You always said that when we were in danger of getting in trouble," I accuse, but I drop his hand and step into the opening. "Is there going to be—what is this?" I gasp, trying to push through heavy wool coats and puffy parkas.

It's like we're back in the wardrobe, only chock full of more—heavy, hard to push, possibly weighed-down-with-rocks more clothes. "Is this why you want me to go first?" With both arms, I shove and shift and find myself face to face with a heavy suit of insulated fabric with zippered pockets and reinforced panels. "Not that the king is going to be outside the closet but—"

My feet tangle with something and then I'm falling forward into the mass of material.

18

Gunnar

ONE MINUTE STELLA IS right in front of me, and then she's not. Instinctively, I reach out and haul her back, pulling her up. "I think that's my snowmobile suit," I say into her hair.

She's flush against my chest in the midst of the too-full closet, with both of my arms banded around her. I should let her go but—

"Or Bo's."

"Or a giant's." The insulated suit is heavy and unyielding and the legs tangle on the floor because the Erickson princes are taller than the average man and our clothes don't fit properly in normal closets. "You can let me go now. I'm not falling."

"But I think I might be." With the coats pressed against me, I'm off-balance and tighten my arms crossing her chest.

Her... chest.

One of my arms is wrapped around her waist, surprisingly slim under that baggy sweater, and the other is pressed against the fullness of her chest.

I should probably let her go.

With a huff, she pushes forward, both hands shoving, feet tripping and I have no choice but to move with her or let her go.

"I don't think you're helping," Stella manages as we break through.

Two steps free of the tangle and she shakes me off, like a dog forced into a sweater. "Sorry about that," I tell her like I hadn't been holding onto her like a barnacle, for no reason at all. "I think I might have—"

"Wasn't the first time." Stella turns and—

Is that a smile?

I stand gaping at the transformation of her face—lips curved into flushed cheeks, eyes bright. It doesn't matter that her hair is mussed and her sweater slips, baring a pale shoulder—Stella is beautiful when she smiles.

She always has been, but I haven't seen it in so long that I forgot what she looks like when she's not bad-tempered.

"What?" she snaps, and she's back to bad-tempered Stella. "Why are you looking at me like that?"

I give my head a shake. I must have imagined that. "Nothing," I mutter. "What do you mean, it wasn't the first time?"

She gives herself a little shake, same as I did but probably for different reasons. "It wasn't the first time you touched my..." She gestures to her chest area, her sweeping movement comprising the strike zone, from her shoulders to her knees.

"Do you want to say the word together?" I suggest. "*Breast*."

"I can say the word."

"You can rest assured I have never touched your breast area—"

—I mimic her gesture— "—before today. Not that I really touched anything today," I quickly add, even though the sensation of the soft swell has been burned into my hand.

"You have so."

"Are you arguing with me just for the sake of arguing?"

"I know if a hand has grazed my boob."

"Breast," I repeat. "You having problems with the correct names? And graze—not touch. There is a *big* difference."

"Not for a breast, there isn't."

"I was twelve. Why would I touch your breast?"

"You were twelve. Why wouldn't you, given the chance?"

She's got a point there. But still— "Are you saying you gave me a chance? It was consensual? That you may very well have wanted the graze? Let me know before I begin my very heartfelt apology for offending you."

Stella scowls. "You're mocking me."

I give her my best smile. "I would never mock you about this. Other things—definitely."

There's that curve of her lips. Bigger now. And I think, maybe...

"This is an inane conversation," she scoffs.

"Aren't they the best kind?"

"What, my breasts?"

I laugh. I can't help it and there's the hint of a very well may be another smile. "I fear for my life if I comment. No—inane conversations. We seem to be very good at them." She holds my gaze for a moment, then another. Just as I start to wonder if... Stella turns away. "Your car is outside," I say needlessly, pointing to the door.

"In the foyer of the castle?" she asks, reaching for the door.

For a moment, I'm tempted to stop her, to keep her here, in the closet, so we can continue this weird kind of intimacy that's going on.

But I don't, and a shriek greets Stella as she opens the door.

"What in the world!" a female voice cries and I hurry to follow Stella.

"Hello, Molly," I say as casually as I can after nearly frightening one of the maids to death by strolling out of a closet she never saw us enter. "Sorry about that."

Molly is one of the younger maids from Battle Harbour, brought in to help with the upcoming wedding. She stares between me and Stella. "How—how long have you been in that closet?"

I give her a wink. "Way too long for my liking."

Stella snorts. "You wish."

That brings things back to the normal level of scorn and derision between Stella and me but something seems off.

Like why am I reacting to a little close contact?

I lead her to the castle door, while Molly stares after us. Stella is Stella. Yes, I found her fascinating in my younger years. I listened to her go on and on about the places in the world she and Duncan wanted to visit, and the amazing things they would do. She would lecture us about how being royal meant responsibility and recite the Spider-Man quote about power so many times that Bo would yell at her whenever she started. Even as a young girl, she was intense and impressive with her strong beliefs.

She's still intense. And fascinating, but it's like she carved a chunk of herself out. Something about young Stella is missing in the present Stella, and it's irritating how much I want to find out what it is, and what happened to it.

If I focus on that, I won't think about how... good... it felt to have her in my arms.

The sun hangs low in the sky as we step out the castle door, the gravel crunching loudly under Stella's boots as we walk to her car parked off to the side.

"Those are more substantial than the boots I wear when I ride," I comment, just for the sake of breaking the silence as I gesture at Stella's feet.

"I like my boots."

"I didn't say I didn't like them."

"You always bring up things you don't like."

I hide my sigh. Just for a moment, I'd like to go back to when Stella smiled at me. "I've never once brought up anything I don't like about you," I tell her in a quiet voice. "The only thing I dislike is that we don't get along anymore."

She looks at me sharply, like I've insulted her. "What?"

"That was... almost nice," she manages, still looking at me like she expects my head to come flying off or something equally drastic.

I gently elbow her side. "Don't get used to it."

I'm rewarded by the curve of her lips, and this time she holds it for longer than expected. I wonder if smiling is difficult for her, like holding a five-minute plank.

I expect it must be by the way she sighs as the smile fades. "What a weird day," she admits suddenly.

"Because I was almost nice?"

She rolls her eyes. "That too. Just being here. Daphne."

"Your father."

Her face shutters as completely as if the portcullis slammed down. I could leave her here to stew in her father issues, but I don't want to.

It's odd that I don't want to. "What are you doing after you leave?" I ask instead of beating a retreat like I should.

Stella gives me a suspicious glare. "Why?"

I lift my hands. "Making conversation."

"Weird," she mutters. Then, "I'll go home, and Sophie will insist that I tell her every single detail."

"Will you tell her about the secret passage?"

She nods with a half-smile. "She used to be afraid to go through them."

"I remember. It's nice that you two are still so close."

"You're close to your brothers. Lyra."

I give a slow shake of my head. "We are, but not like when we were younger. My being away hasn't helped. Lyra is gone most of the time too. And Bo, living in his woods. But if I need them, they're always here."

I bite my tongue before I mention Spencer because I get the sense if I say anything about how close I am to her half-brother, Stella will shut down again.

"What are you doing after this? Your escort duty." There's only a touch of sneer in her voice.

"This isn't a duty. It's a... I'm not sure what it is."

"Makes two of us," she mutters.

"I might go for a ride," I say.

"Are you still racing?"

The fact Stella knows about my racing creates a little warmth in my chest. "I haven't raced bikes for a while. There's an F1 race in a couple of weeks that I might try to get into. Carrington is sometimes in need of a driver."

"That's Fenella's family?" I nod, but she doesn't give me a chance to respond before she continues with questions. "Why aren't you taking her to the wedding? It seems more logical."

"It's Odin's day. If I show up with Fenella, it'll be the Gunnar and Fen show."

"That's a little presumptuous. And conceited."

I shrug. "That's what happens. Doesn't mean I like it."

"So Daphne won't make the splash Fenella will?"

"It'll make a better splash. A nice clean cannonball instead of a bellyflop." Her lips twitch. "Was that almost a smile?"

"No."

"I think it might have been."

"You think wrong." She takes a deliberate step toward her car. "Your duty is complete. I'm at my car, so feel free to go play on your bike."

Don't be like this, I want to say, but that will only make things worse. "Like I said, it wasn't a duty. But Daphne should be out shortly."

"Like you know anything about trying on dresses."

"I thought we made it clear that I know more than you." I step away from her. "Your car, madam. I'll see if I can hurry along Daphne since you're so eager to get out of here."

With a curt nod, Stella turns and opens the car door.

I leave her huddled in her car and storm back to the castle. Why does she insist on being so abrasive, like a rash you keep coming back to itch? I knew she didn't want to stay with Daphne; I got her out of the castle without running into Duncan again, which I thought she'd want, but what did it get me?

A snappy tongue and a few moments that I'm not about to think twice about. Because thinking about holding her tiny hand cracked something inside of me, like back when I was racing dirt bikes and I'd come back with my bikes completely covered in mud.

Dad always insisted that I clean them and set me up behind the garage with a hose. The first burst of water did nothing, but if I held the stream against it, the mud would eventually flake off.

That's what holding her hand in the dark felt like—some of the mud is flaking off.

I need another run in the mud to cover the cracks.

19

Stella

THAT WAS... UNEXPECTED.

Strange. Odd. Not just spending that much time with Gunnar without wanting to maim him in some way, but delving into all the memories of my childhood.

The happy ones.

Usually, any thinking about my early years is after Duncan left, and it's rather on the sad side. But with Gunnar—

It's all very odd.

And he was... I won't say *charming* because that is the ultimate definition of him, just not my definition. I do not, nor I will ever, consider him a Prince Charming. He was... sweet. Considerate. And—dare I say—fun?

Except for that bit in the coats. I still haven't unpacked *those* emotions.

"Isn't he amazing?" Daphne cries as we drive away from the castle. She made her way to the car about fifteen minutes after Gunnar disappeared and just before I started to get seriously bored. I spent the time listening to Pink very loudly and wondering if Gunnar would show up on his bike before I can get away from the castle.

"Gunnar?" I demand, with more skepticism than is needed.

Daphne gives me an incredulous glance. "No, but he's great, too. *Daulton.*"

I imagine Cinderella would sound the same when she mentioned her own Prince Charming after the ball. But— "Daulton?" It's like she switches topics mid-sentence.

"Of, course. He's so wonderful. The way he came down to greet us—"

"I think that was part of his job."

"It's not. It's not like he's a butler. They don't have staff like that—butlers and footmen and ladies' maids. It's more of an office than a home."

"I know," I say but not as snappish because it's Daphne. "But I had no idea you did."

"Daulton tells me a lot about what it's like working there."

"Does he tell you what he does there? Because I have no idea."

"He helps with the public relations," she says, all very knowledgeable-like.

"I thought that was what Kate did."

"She's Odin's personal secretary, brought on after the mess of him being on The Suitorette."

I glance over with surprise. The way she said that— "Is that what *Daulton* says?"

"He doesn't think she's needed anymore. After all, none of the other princes have a personal secretary. Nor does Lyra."

I'd like to see someone try and organize Princess Lyra's life. "What does *Daulton* say about being married?" I ask.

"He doesn't consider himself married," Daphne says primly. "It's in name only."

I want to sigh at her naivety. "He's still named a husband. He took vows and—"

"Since when do you care about wedding vows?" she snaps.

Daphne *never* snaps. "I'm sorry?"

"You're the most anti-marriage woman I know. You won't go to the biggest wedding of the year because you don't believe in marriage."

I blink at the hostility in her voice. "That's not why I'm not going."

"Then why aren't you? You could have taken me as your plus one, and then I wouldn't need to go—" Daphne clamps her mouth closed like she's pretending to be a Sesame Street puppet.

"Go where? Go with Gunnar?"

"I'm happy to go with Gunnar to the wedding. But I could have just as easily gone with you."

"Because you really want to be at this wedding?" I ask skeptically.

"Stella, everyone who has a romantic bone in their body wants to go to this wedding. Prince Odin's love story with Lady Camille is like a fairy tale, so everyone wants to see them get their happy ever after."

I wouldn't go so far as to say fairy tale, but they are a good couple.

"I like Camille," I concede. "And Odin is... okay. That's not why I don't want to go. I don't want the fuss."

Daphne glances over with a confused expression. "You think there's going to be a fuss about *you*?"

"No," I say quickly. "Never mind."

"But why? No one knows you. You keep to yourself, you never go out… There wouldn't be any fuss if you were there. No one will even notice." Daphne says this with a bright smile like she's trying to reassure me.

I don't know what it does but it doesn't make me feel any better.

On the rest of the way home, I let Daphne gush about the dress, Lyra, even Daulton; anything that isn't about me and how no one would notice if I were there.

I don't care if no one noticed. I'd prefer it that way.

When I finally get home, Sophie is waiting for me.

"How was the dress?" she asks, dragging me to her room. Mom and Peter are having a pre-dinner cocktail and Daphne disappears to her room, phone in hand, probably already texting Daulton.

I have no energy to deal with what shouldn't be between those two.

"A dress," I tell her impatiently, sinking onto her bed. "Lyra was there and she said—Dad was there." The words tumble out of my mouth. I hadn't even planned on telling Sophie. I thought it would be better to keep it to myself in case it upset her.

"Wait, what?" Sophie's brown eyes are wide and eager. It pains me to see her obvious excitement to hear more. "Did you see him?"

I frown, confused by her reaction. "He came to talk to me when I was in the hall with Spencer and Gunnar."

"Spencer!" Sophie clasps her hands under her chin, her chin starting to tremble.

After seeing Spencer, I know exactly how she feels. I've missed having a big brother.

"I think you need to start from the beginning," Sophie adds, scooting across her bed so she's resting against the nest of pillows and childhood stuffed animals at the head of the bed.

I tell her about seeing Spencer and everything he said, and Lyra and everything she said. And when I mention our father—

"What was it like seeing him?" she demands.

"... Strange," I manage. I knead a stuffed llama, its softness matted by years of Sophie hugging it as she sleeps. "I—I wasn't expecting it."

"You were at the castle, so there was a good chance you'd bump into him," she points out.

"I didn't expect him to come and find me." I take a deep breath. "Soph, it seems...I don't know what to think." I can't form the words I want to say—that it seemed like he *missed* us.

How do I know that? Duncan gave us up for the king, and while that was done in medieval times, we are now firmly in the twenty-first century and the monarchy isn't that big of a thing.

"What did he say?" she whispers. Sophie has always had a softer heart than I do, always ready to forgive and concede. I'm the one who has made her hold firm to what we believe in.

What we believe in suddenly seems unsure, like walking on a frozen pond and not trusting the thickness of the ice.

I can't tell Sophie that. I need to be strong for her now. "He didn't say much," I report blithely. "Asked how I was, asked about you. He tried to say something about Mom, but stopped himself, which is a good thing. I didn't want to hear any excuses or blame."

"But Stella...there has to be more to it." Sophie leans forward, another stuffed animal in her hands.

"Like what?" I know there's more to it, but I don't think I want to hear it now. Or ever. But I never enjoy feeling stupid. "Are you saying Mom lied to us?"

The words hang frozen in the room with neither of us willing to touch them. "I'm saying she didn't tell us the whole truth," Sophie says finally, with more bravery that I can show. "We don't know his side of the story."

"Because he left," I snap. "He left us. Why should we give him the chance to explain? Do you want to forgive him? He'll just do it again—we'll let him in and he'll dump us."

"You don't know that."

"Do you know that he won't?"

"No." I hate the expression on my sister's face—hurt and disappointment, with a longing in her eyes that I understand, because I've shut down the same emotion in myself so many times over the years. "I've always thought it was something I did," Sophie confesses in a small voice. "I wasn't good enough. Not talented enough. Not—"

"That is a load of utter horse poop," I tell her vehemently. "You were perfect. If anybody, it was me. I was a miserable brat back then."

"No, you weren't. And even if you were, it wouldn't matter. Dad and Spencer leaving wasn't the fault of either of us. You know that, don't you?"

"Now I do." It's a hard admission to make. After Spencer left with our father, I was the oldest. I was the one left in charge of Sophie, and then Daphne. I had to be strong for them.

I still do.

"We should probably talk to Mom about this," Sophie says carefully. "Maybe it's time to get back into it. We're older now. We can understand things."

I shake my head. "You know what she's like whenever his name is mentioned." Sneery. Scornful. Angry.

"I feel like we're missing part of the puzzle."

I heave a sigh. "I know we are, but I don't know if it's a puzzle I want to solve."

"I do."

The admission is quiet, but firm. I'm not sure what to say. And luckily—or unluckily—I don't have to because Sophie changes the subject.

"How were things with Gunnar?"

"What about him? What things? There are no *things* with Gunnar."

Sophie gives me a strange look. "Gunnar and *Daphne*? The prince who is taking our sister to the ball."

"He's no prince."

"He kind of is."

"I mean, yes, he's a prince, but it's not like a prince of a man." Only, he kind of was today. Gunnar did the whole knight-in-shining-armour thing for me today and I'm at a complete loss at what to do about that.

So I decide to do nothing. Say nothing. Think nothing.

Only, thinking about Gunnar takes my mind off our father. But it also makes me very irritable.

20

Gunnar

I F I STAND AT one of the thin windows on the second floor, I can see Stella's car, but watching her makes me feel slightly stalkerish.

Still, I wait. And watch until Daphne appears and they drive out of sight.

And then I remain at the window, thinking about Stella.

Or trying *not* to think about Stella, because... Stella should not be thought about. At least not by me.

Stella hates me because I'm part of the royal family who stole her father, so I'll never be involved.

It makes sense why she hates me.

It doesn't make it any nicer though. Generally, people don't dislike me. I'm Gunnar—the fun prince. The happy prince. The travel-around-the-world prince, having adventures and trying new things.

Stella doesn't like me. And I don't like her.

So why was there a *zing* when I grabbed her hand in the tunnel?

And that is why I can't stop thinking of her. The way her lips curve up, how those silver eyes light up when—

"Who you looking at?"

The voice behind me makes me jump and I turn to see Lyra and Kate heading up the stairs. "Finished with the dresses?" I ask stepping away from the window.

My stomach no longer ties in knots when I see Kate, but it's still not as comfortable as I'd like it to be yet.

"Camille better have a darn good dress, or we're going to look better than her," Lyra says with her typical confidence.

"Odin won't like that one little bit," I warn. "I'd tone down the sparkle."

She flips her hair. "You should know, it's impossible to do that."

I grin at my little sister. "Still such a treat."

"Takes one to know one."

"Camille will look beautiful, much better than us," Kate says loyally, causing Lyra to give her a gentle slap on the arm.

"Hey! You're my friend first."

They laugh. It's nice to have Lyra home. Maybe she'll make it easier for Kate and me to reconnect, on a purely platonic friendship level.

If I'm being honest, I miss both of them.

"Stella gone?" Kate asks. I don't let my gaze flit back to the window, to where her car had been parked. Instead, I push away from the wall and prepare to leave the scene of my stalking.

"I suppose," I breeze.

"You whisked her away from the big, bad Duncan," Lyra says sourly. "You should know if she's still lurking."

"She doesn't lurk."

"No? She dresses like she'd lurk."

"Doesn't mean she lurks. And it's beneath you to make fun of what she looks like."

Lyra looks incredulously at Kate. "Are you hearing this? I think he's defending the woman who can't say a nice word about any-thing. She's not too happy about much, is she?"

"How would you know what she's happy about?"

Kate waves her hand between us. "Why are we fighting about Stella?"

"Is that the royal we?" Lyra asks with a laugh.

"We're not fighting about anything," I say at the same time. "And definitely not about Stella."

Kate studies me and it's so uncomfortable I have to look away. "Do you think Camille is finished with the wedding stuff?" I ask.

"You'd rather hang out with her than us?" Lyra clutches her chest. "Hurt."

"I have to finish up with Odin before I head out. I've got plans with Jackson...." Kate lets the name hang between us with a strange expression.

She isn't there yet and there's a flash of pain at the thought. I want us to be friends. Nothing more, just friends who can pass each other on the street with a few words. Who might share a drink if we're at the pub at the same time. Who can talk about what's going on in their lives.

Because of all the things I miss about Kate, the most is being her friend.

The facts are this: A picture was taken of me leaving Mabel Crow's house late at night, well past the socially accepted visiting hours, and sent anonymously to Kate.

Not exactly anonymously—there was a phone number attached but Kate never bothered to find out who it was from, nor ever told me the phone number no matter how many times I asked for it.

She didn't have to find out who it was from. The evidence was irrefutable; it was me coming out of Mabel's front door, usual backpack in hand. It had been ten thirty on a Thursday evening, the time of booty calls and I'll-stop-by-for-a-quick-drink. I had been twenty years old and known to do foolish things.

I let Kate believe the worst of me. I let her go.

A few months of silence and cold stares later, Kate had left for Canada without any explanation and I started country hopping and hanging with a different crowd.

"Jackson, huh?"

Lyra glares suspiciously at me. She may be my sister, and a princess of the royal house of Laandia, but when it comes to protecting her friends—namely Kate—she is a tiger. I can respect that, but it would be nice for her to be on my side at times.

Especially when I didn't do anything wrong.

"I'm glad things are going well with the two of you." I extend my olive branch to Kate and now it's up to her to accept it. "You and Jackson."

"Are you?" Lyra asks, eyebrows raised so high they almost disappear into her hairline. Kate looks at me with an unreadable expression.

And that hurts too, because once, I could read all of her expressions.

"Yes, I am happy. It's been a long time," I say to Lyra-the-bodyguard. "All I want is for Kate to be happy."

"Kate *is* happy."

"Kate is standing right here," Kate cuts in. "Thank you, Gunnar."

"I mean it. Everything that happened—"

"Was a long time ago," she finishes. "We were very young and different people then."

"Not very young," Lyra mutters.

"That's because you don't like the thought of pushing twenty-six." I nudge my sister. "You still want to be nineteen all over again."

"I don't." Lyra tosses her head, but it doesn't have the same effect since most of her hair has been cut off into a style that makes her look like Tinkerbell. "Nineteen wasn't fun. Twenty, on the other hand..." She nudges Kate and the gesture makes us laugh. "You were busy being studious at school and missed it all."

"I was having fun on my own," Kate protests.

This time the thought of Kate doing anything without me, when she should have been with me, doesn't rip apart my chest. It almost makes me *happy*. Like maybe I didn't ruin her life.

Like maybe my stepping away was for the best.

Maybe.

I head up the stairs. "I'll let the two of you reminisce about your Hot Girl phase while I go find the responsible princess of the castle and my girl, Bea Arthur."

"Camille is not a princess until next Saturday," Lyra reminds me. "And we are still very much part of our Hot Girl phase, *thankyouverymuch*."

"Of course you are, Princess Sister." I nod to Kate. "Have fun, whatever you do with Jackson tonight."

"Thanks, Gun." And she smiles, a real Kate smile. Plus, she calls me *Gun*, the only one to ever shorten my name like that. My family calls me Gunny or sometimes G, but Kate—Kate was the only one to call me Gun and make it sound like an endearment rather than a weapon of violence.

That makes me happy as I head up to Camille's room.

I've always enjoyed the company of women and have several platonic female friends. And some, like Fenella, have become friends after we broke up. When I'm not wooing a woman, I'm a safe bet. And I quite like my soon-to-be-sister-in-law. She's good for Odin.

"How did it go with Daphne and the dress?" I ask as I lounge on Camille's couch, Bea Arthur doing her best to climb up for a cuddle. "Stay down." I point my finger at the puppy. "Mommy doesn't like you up here."

Not yet a year old, Bea Arthur still doesn't look like any dog I've ever seen. Because she was a rescue dog—rescued by Stella's Catch a Pet shelter—it's difficult to tell what breed she is. When Odin brought her to Camille, I guessed the plump puppy might be part Labrador retriever and maybe German Shepard, but as she's grown older, she's lost some of her lankiness and become more compact, plus she's not as fluffy.

I have no idea what kind of dog she is, but as someone who always wanted a dog, I love her to pieces.

"Odin doesn't like her up there," Camille corrects, patting the seat beside me for the dog to jump up. Betty White, cocooned on Camille's other side, growls in protest. "We don't always tell him where you sleep, do we, Bea Arthur?"

The puppy leaps onto my lap and with a laugh, I crane my head away from the tongue determined to lick my face. "Tricky. If marriage is all about getting away with stuff, I'm going to be really good at it."

"It's a little more than that." Camille raises an eyebrow as Bea Arthur hops from cushion to cushion before settling beside Camille with an expectant look at me. "And it's not like you to even mention marriage, so is there something you want to tell me?"

I roll my eyes, rubbing behind Bea Arthur's ears. "How can I *not* mention marriage when the castle is full of preparations for the blessed event?"

"Are you complaining? You seemed to have gotten a nice bonus because of *my* wedding."

I glance around the dog to frown at Camille. "And what bonus would that be?"

"Daphne is very sweet," Camille says slyly. "I'm glad you invited her."

"Me too." It's the correct response, the automatic thing to say, but it doesn't quite feel truthful. But I'm not sure *why* it doesn't feel truthful.

"Do you like her?" Camille demands with more interest than she should have, considering it's a date-but-not-a-date. We're going as friends; which feels strange because we're not exactly friends.

"Everyone likes Daphne. But no, not like that." It's best to get that out in the open so Camille doesn't try to play matchmaker because I sense where this is headed.

"Because you like her sister."

"Sophie?" I ask with bewilderment.

"Stella."

I know Camille is frank and straight to the point but I also thought she was perceptive.

Apparently not. "No."

"No?"

"No. She hates me," I say a little more vehemently than I need to. "We fight like cats and dogs whenever we're in a ten-foot radius."

"I've never actually seen cats and dogs fighting, so I wonder now how bad it really is. I have seen seals fighting with each other so I imagine it would be similar."

It sounds an awful lot like Stella and me. Not that Stella and I are a thing. Nor will we ever be a thing because of the fighting.

"I'm sure it would be."

"Just because there are a few arguments between the two of you doesn't mean—"

"It's *always* arguments with me and Stella." I force a laugh. "I can't believe you'd think *anything* could *ever* be between us."

Camille studies me carefully as she strokes Betty White's head. "You seem pretty adamant about this."

"Because there is no *this*." I take a deep breath. "You've seen us together. If you don't remember, you felt the need to ask me to be nice to her, which you didn't have to do because I'm never not nice to her. *She's* got the problem with *me*. For whatever reason," I finish, lowering my voice to a mutter. "You should tell her to be nice to me."

"Maybe I will."

"No, don't." I shake my head to add more weight to my request. "It doesn't matter what she thinks of me."

"You sure?"

"Positive." I emphasize the *P*.

"Speaking of seals, are you still good to pop me over to Saint Pierre on Monday?" Camille leans back against the couch cushions and Bea Arthur blocks her from my sight. "I can book a flight if it's a problem."

I draw a shaky breath, happy to have the conversation move away from Stella. "My pilot's license and I are at your disposal, not to mention the family plane. We can leave whenever you like." I haven't had the opportunity to fly in a few months and I miss it. I've been looking forward to my little jaunt with Camille since she asked me about it.

Until—

"I invited Stella to join us," Camille says, still hiding behind Bea Arthur.

So that's where this was going. "Of course you did."

She peeks around the dog. "I thought if you spent time together, it might help you get along."

"Or it might result in Stella jumping from the plane mid-flight just to get away from me. Take your pick. It'll just mean one less guest at the wedding."

"It's not that bad." Camille laughs, but it's a little strained. "I thought she might enjoy it. And Daphne, too. There's enough room in the plane, isn't there?"

"As long as you leave your matchmaking hat at home. There is *no* room for that."

"I'm not matchmaking, I'm just... making friends."

"I can make my own friends, thank you."

"I meant for me."

Guilt rains down on me like a sudden spring storm. Camille grew up sheltered and protected and without many friends. Who am I to be protesting her decisions on who she wants to be her friend, or stand in the way of her being happy?

"It'll be fun to have them along," I tell her.

And I'm rewarded with a grateful smile. "I think it will be. And don't forget, you're helping Stella find that dog tomorrow."

I groan. I did forget.

"You promised," she reminds me. "You can't go back on your word."

I don't remember promising anything, but I did tell Stella I would help, since Stella is too stubborn to wait for the police to give their assistance.

Of course, I could insist some officer more accustomed to rescuing animals go with her, but I told her *I* would help.

And I will.

But I'm concerned by how much I'm looking forward to helping her.

21

Stella

I'M BEYOND SURPRISED WHEN Gunnar shows up at the door at exactly seven o'clock the next morning.

I'll repeat: Gunnar is at my door at seven o'clock the next morning.

With everything that happened yesterday at the castle and after, I thought he'd forget that he offered to help me look for the dog. More like demanded he be part of the rescue mission.

What is it about Gunnar and rescuing?

I thought he'd forget and had planned on going alone, but now he's here?

And for him to be on time? I would have bet my not-significant paycheck that punctuality was not his virtue.

"Good morning, Mrs. Luute," I hear him say from the front door.

"Prince Gunnar." Surprise coats Mom's voice. And her face, and even her body language. But she doesn't seem upset to see one of the princes at her door at this early hour.

I wonder when that changed. And why didn't I notice it?

Things might be different if she weren't fully made up for her yoga/coffee/gossip meeting with her friends.

Oh, my God—what is she going to tell them about this?

"I'll see if Daphne is awake," Mom says hesitantly.

"Oh, no need." Gunnar sounds hale and hearty and way too cheerful for this early hour. "I'm here for Stella this morning."

"Stella?" The way she says my name sounds like the crack of a whip.

"That's me," I echo. Mom whirls around to see me standing there with my lunch bag and bottle of water.

No coffee though, and I do regret that. It was a toss-up between sleep and caffeine and sleep won.

"Good morning, Stella."

I seriously didn't believe Gunnar would show up. And if he did, he would be so *perky* and polite. "Hey."

He didn't say anything about it yesterday when I left. I certainly wasn't about to on the off-chance he might consider a comment me *asking for help*, which I would never do. It's bad enough he's going to think I owe him for getting me out of the castle without bumping into Duncan.

The last thing I need is to have to show gratitude toward him.

"Ready to start the adventure?" Gunnar asks with a grin, dimples out to no doubt impress my mother.

Mom may be impressed by a prince, but not by her own daughter. "What are you doing?" she demands in a rude tone. "You have work. You need to be at the shelter."

"I'm going to see about a dog." I glance warily around my mother at Gunnar who is still standing there with his smile. "I don't need a ride."

Gunnar also looks around at my mother, who is still blocking the way. "Well, I'm here to give you one anyway."

"Please don't."

"What's that, you say?" he asks with his hand cupped around his ear. "Thank you so much, Prince Gunnar? Well, you're very welcome, Stella. Always happy to help."

I roll my eyes. The Gunnar I knew growing up was just as stubborn as I am, so other than running out the back door and jumping in my car, there's no way I'm getting out of here without his unwelcome assistance.

I seriously think about the back door. "Fine," I relent. "What are you so cheerful about anyway?"

"It's a beautiful morning. The sun is out, the birds are singing—"

"It's supposed to rain."

"Then we better get going."

Mom eventually steps aside so I can pass and allows me to *leave the house with Prince Gunnar.*

I may have passed into an alternate dimension.

"Stella?" It's clear Mom feels the same confusion I do.

"I'll explain later," I mutter, throwing her a wave. "Bye."

"Have a lovely day, Mrs. Luute," Gunnar calls as he follows me down the walk to the SUV waiting. He jumps ahead to open the rear door for me. "Is this what you picking me up looks like?" I ask with a knowing glance at the female behind the wheel.

"Safety first," he says, gesturing for me to get in. "Plus, Minka makes sure I leave early enough to stop for coffee." The scent of coffee hits me before I catch sight of the to-go cups waiting in the centre console between the seats. "I didn't think you'd have time for one."

"You thought right," I mutter, crawling into the far seat so Gunnar won't have to walk around the car.

"It's a talent." He settles beside me and taps the back of the driver's seat. "Good to go."

The SUV pulls away from the curb and I glance back to see my mother still staring after us. "So is freaking me out. Why are you being nice to me?"

"I thought I was always nice to you," Gunnar says in a hurt voice. A *fake* hurt voice.

"In that case, you thought wrong. You are not nice to me. I am not nice to you. It's what we do."

With perfect Gunnar timing, he hands me a to-go cup from Coffee for the Sole with a winning smile. "At least you admit it goes both ways. I was beginning to feel like the villain in this non-rom-com."

"What do you know about rom-coms?" I ask suspiciously.

"Surprisingly a lot, thanks to my sister and various female friends." I stare at him until he caves. "When I was younger and wanted to hang out with Lyra because she was with Kate, and I liked Kate, she would only let me if I did what they were doing, which was usually reading. And I always forgot my book, because I thought I could distract them with my presence, but my sister is a tough nut to crack and she would make me pick one of *her* books. Always romance, usually romantic comedy, but there was one book that was romantic fantasy and some of the love scenes were a little more R-rated than I thought Lyra should be reading, but I wasn't about to complain because she would have taken the book from me and—"

"Stop!" I hold up a hand. "I can't hear about you reading dirty books."

"Why not? There were Faeries, but they were called Fae and they could—"

I clap my hands over my ears, difficult to do when one is holding a cup of coffee. "*Nooo*. It's too early in the morning to hear about that."

Gunnar laughs.

I peel away my hands warily. "Seriously, why are you being nice to me?"

"I'm always nice to you."

"We've been through this, so *no*."

He meets my gaze for a long moment before turning to the window. "Honestly? It would make Camille happy if we got along."

I stare at his profile, noticing the faint scruff along his jawline. So the prince can get up early enough to pick up coffee but not enough to shave. I like it. Makes him more human.

I shouldn't like *anything* about him. "Huh. So Camille ordered you to be nice to me."

He turns back to me and I quickly avert my gaze. "I did not say that."

"It sounded like you did."

"I did not."

"You sound stuffy when you talk like that."

He sighs. "You're going to make this difficult for me, aren't you?"

I grin, my first happy moment of the day. "I like to try."

There's a snort of laughter from the front seat. "Hey, Gunny, I like her," the woman behind the wheel says.

"You would," Gunnar mutters, turning back to the window.

22

Gunnar

"YOU DON'T STRIKE ME as the country type." When I glance over, Stella points to the dashboard. "Sam Hunt. Country music. Is this your choice or your driver's?"

"Minka," I supply. "Minka Grace, this is Stella Laz. And we have playlists to listen to that we agree on."

"Your playlists that I tolerate," Minka corrects. "Since I technically work for you, you get the final say."

"And you choose country music?" Stella raises her eyebrows. "I would have pegged you for more... pop-y music. I recall you were big into boy bands at one time."

"*That* was a long time ago," I say quickly. "I like to think my tastes have matured since then."

"Sure they have." Stella's smirk mirrors Minka's.

"I'll have you know, we had the same musical upbringing," I point out. "Dads in bands?"

"I honestly don't know which of them was the coolest," Minka muses. "I've seen the concert footage and Stella, your dad was something else."

My gaze flies to Stella, wondering how she would take the praise for Duncan.

"I don't know which of them looked the more ridiculous with the big hair and leather pants," she drawls.

"It wasn't the best look," Minka agrees.

"Dad says his hair never recovered from all the product he used," I say.

"It would have been… interesting… to see them perform," Stella admits in a quiet voice.

"Get the band back together for the wedding," Minka suggests.

I laugh. "Good idea, but I doubt Camille would approve."

"Camille would be fine," Stella argues. "It's Odin who might go a little ballistic about the last-minute concert addition."

I shake my head. "It would be Mrs. Theissen who'd lose it and I would pay good money to see that. You like country music?" I ask her.

"I like everything. Music-wise," she adds, turning to stare out the window.

It doesn't take us long to get to the bottom of the cliff, helped by the four-wheel drive prowess of the car and Minka's excellent driving along the gravel beach.

Watching her drive always makes me want to get behind the wheel and drive *fast*. But I promised Dad I'd keep to the slow lane until the wedding.

Minka—not surprisingly—elects to stay by the car. "Looks clear," she says, staring upward. "And I'm a good enough shot to take out any threat. But don't trip and break anything. Because I'm not looking at getting beheaded by the king."

"I don't think Dad does much beheading these days," I tell her patiently.

"Vikings were more often to use ordeal by fire as a punishment instead of beheading," Stella puts in. "Or the 'blood-eagle' where they rip the lungs out of a person, possibly still alive."

Being a descendant of a Viking isn't all that special when I hear about stuff like that. "Pleasant. And you know this how?"

She gives me a face and shrugs then turns to study the hill. "I think we should look up there first." She points to a spot about a third of the way up where a few scraggly trees beside a bunch of rocks would provide excellent shelter for a scared dog.

"I concur." I sweep my arm. "After you."

Stella makes another face and sets off without a word. At least I turn to salute Minka, now positioned beside the front of the car with her coffee and gun at her hip.

Not that she would ever need it, but Dad insists our security be armed at all times. I've never not felt safe as a member of the royal family, but there's a first time for everything.

I take a deep breath; this far outside town, the air is clear and clean and smells of the ocean. It's been a while since I've enjoyed being outside in Laandia, and I don't stop my grin as I follow Stella up the hill.

I've been to countless places all over the world, and I've always thought Laandia most resembles the Scottish Highlands with the rocky hills and shrubs. I might be biased, but Laandia is more beautiful, especially on a morning like this with the sun playing shy behind thin clouds scudding across a blue-gray sky.

Gray days can be just as nice as the ones with a bright blue sky and warm sun beaming down.

Speaking of gray, today Stella has forgone her usual black for a sweater of the lighter shade. Her jeans are still black and surprisingly snug around her hips. Usually her pants are always baggy, almost shapeless, but today the fabric hugs her thighs and—

I whip my gaze away.

"How long has it been since you talked to Duncan? To your father?" I ask abruptly, mainly to get my attention off the way Stella's hips move in her jeans.

I've never seen her wearing snug jeans before. It's a good look for her.

Then I shake my head to stop the thought.

"That's very personal," Stella tosses over her shoulder.

"So is disappearing into a wall with me yesterday. You've no idea what Lyra had to say about that."

Stella is quiet for so long that I think she's ignoring me. I quicken my pace to walk beside her. "You said something yesterday about me wanting to travel," she begins, her gaze fixed on a point up the hill. "When my dad left us, I already had my suitcase packed. We were leaving for Paris in four days. Sophie wanted to go to the Louvre, and I...I just wanted a croissant. I don't know why—I thought they were so French. I was twelve, so what did I know?"

"Croissants are very French," I tell her. "The butter... French cows make better butter."

"I'm sure you would know that," she says, but there's no scorn in her tone. It almost sounds like... sadness. "Anyway," Stella continues. "He left, and my suitcase was still packed. I waited until the night before we were supposed to go to ask my mother—I had no idea what was going on. I honestly thought the trip was still on. Mom basically shut herself in her room after he left, and didn't say much to us. I'm sure she was trying to process."

I catch my breath, thinking of twelve-year-old Stella waiting with a packed suitcase. Her family had been ripped apart by Duncan leaving, and her mother couldn't be bothered to check in with her daughters?

I don't tell Stella that my father made a point of checking in with all of us several times a day after my mother died. And that was while he was running a kingdom. But hey—to each their own. "What did she say when you asked her?"

I only have to see how Stella's shoulders slump to know it wasn't a good response. "That there was no way we were going," she says flatly. "She said that if I wanted to go *anywhere*, it would have to be with my father, but I wasn't allowed to talk to him, so I was never going anywhere. And that was his fault."

"That's…" *Not fair*, I want to say, but I don't think Stella would appreciate that.

"Yeah," she says instead. "I've never been to Paris. Never been out of Laandia. And I could. I just… haven't."

The sadness in her voice is… It kind of breaks my heart. But again, I don't think Stella would appreciate any sympathy from me. She'd think I was pitying her, and I'm not. I… feel… for her. "Well, you're going to Saint Pierre, so that's something," I tell her.

"It is," she agrees. "And my father has nothing to do with it."

We walk in silence for a bit, scanning the shrubby rocks for a good place for puppies. Below us, the SUV is parked on the pebble-strewn beach, the constant whitecaps getting closer to the tires with each roll of the tide.

The only sound is the wind and screams of the gulls and the odd rock tumbling down the hill.

It's very peaceful here. I forgot how much.

"Where's your favourite place that you've been?" Stella asks suddenly.

"That's a tough one," I muse, thinking back to my travels. "There's been a lot of places."

"Yes, I know," she snaps, and I draw back like she's taking a swing at me. "I'm jealous of that," she adds awkwardly after a pause. "Which is why it makes me bad-tempered."

"Aww," I say. "Did Camille talk to you, too?"

"No. But if you're trying, it's the least I can do," she admits.

"Hey, maybe we'll end up as friends. Again."

"Don't push your luck," she grumbles without any conviction, which makes me laugh.

"We used to be friends," I remind her.

"We were," she agrees.

That's all that is said because then we hear the bark of a dog.

23

Stella

THE DOG IS HURTING and thin enough for me to see her ribs. Just the sight of her makes my heart hurt but I'm happy to see she doesn't look as bad as some of the dogs I get in the shelter. I don't want to guess on how long she's been on her own but I don't think it's longer than a few weeks.

But as I suspected, there are puppies involved. Mama Dog isn't letting us anywhere near them.

"What's the plan?" Gunnar asks. We've both tried to get close with soft words and soothing voices, but Mama Dog is not having it. She stands guard on a rock; beneath and behind there must be a hollow because we hear the pitiful cries of hungry puppies.

Slowly, keeping my eyes on Mama, I slip off my backpack. "I'm going to lure her away with some food while you check on the puppies."

"Good. What am I checking for?"

"How many, what shape they're in," I toss over my shoulder.

"Like, puppy shape?"

I roll my eyes. "If they're alive, mainly."

"Maybe you should look," Gunnar says quickly.

"Afraid of puppies?" I scoff.

"Dead ones, yes!"

I take a deep breath. "Okay. Here's some food." I pass over a Ziploc bag wrapped in a towel.

"What is it?"

"Maybe you don't want to know," I tell him slowly.

"What is it?" Gunnar all but shrieks.

I laugh. "Raw sirloin steak. It won't hurt you."

"That was mean," he mutters. "I was still thinking puppies."

"Yep." I giggle and the sound has Gunnar whipping his head around.

"Did you just *giggle*?"

I stiffen, the smile vanishing. "I may have made a laugh-like noise. There was no giggle."

"There so was! I've never heard that noise come from you, not even when you were a kid."

I raise my chin. "And you never will again."

"Don't count on it. I will make it my life's work to make you giggle again."

I make a face, only to have Gunnar laugh louder. The dog barks again. "Are we doing this?"

"We are doing this." He unwraps the towel and tosses it over to me. "In case you need to cover someone up." And then he reaches into the bag without a flinch. "C'mere, pup. Feel like a snack?"

"Move her away," I remind him.

Gunnar walks backward, holding out a chunk of steak and slowly, the smell is too much for the poor, hungry dog, who follows for a few feet, and then stops.

Her attention is completely on what Gunnar is holding, and as he tosses one of the chunks onto the ground, she's there in a flash to gobble it up.

I'm just as quick, leaning over the rock to find three puppies mewling like kittens. "Their eyes are still closed," I cry.

"What does that mean?"

"They're only a week or so old. I have to take them. They'll die up here."

"Is that really a good idea?" Gunnar is still feeding the dog, who has moved closer to him. "You don't have anything to carry them."

"I have a bag."

"Your knapsack?"

"No, a bag." I pull a cotton tote from my backpack.

"What do we do with her?"

Gunnar has already emptied half the bag of steak, Mama Dog now at his feet. She looks pathetically hungry but not like she's about to eat his face. She even sniffs the back of his hand. "We'll try and take her too."

"In the SUV? Minka's gonna love that..."

Somehow, it works.

Gunnar manages to lure Mama Dog down the hill to the car, while I carefully place the puppies into my bag and hold it against my chest as I try and keep my distance as to not distract the mother. Once we get to the car, Minka is surprisingly on board with the idea, especially when she sees the puppies. She also has the idea of putting Mama Dog in the backseat with Gunnar and me to sit up front with the puppies.

Somehow, Gunnar manages to get the mother in the car.

"I think you might be the new dog whisperer," I tell him. He carefully strokes under Mama Dog's chin as she cowers on the floor at his feet.

"She's good, she's okay," he soothes, over and over again. "Everything is going to be okay. We're going somewhere safe, for you and your babies."

"I have never been party to kidnapping dogs before," Minka tells me, sounding a little too excited at the thought.

I have to ask. "Have you kidnapped... other... things before?"

She grins. "You might not want to know the answer to that."

24

Gunnar

NOT GOING TO LIE—THE dog and I are pretty good friends by the time we get back to Stella's shelter.

She finishes the steak and as we reach the streets of Battle Harbour, Stella passes me a wrapped sandwich to feed to her. "Is this your lunch?"

"She needs it more than I do."

I look warily at the beeswax paper it's wrapped in. "Is it safe for her to eat? I mean, is it dog-friendly food?"

"Aren't you Mr. Concern? It's ham and cheese with butter, so yes, all very dog-friendly."

"That's good," I mutter, unwrapping the sandwich, the dog watching my every move with big, pleading eyes. "Take it easy," I tell her. "Don't want you to get sick from eating too fast." I meet Minka's incredulous gaze in the rearview mirror. "What?" I shrug. "I'm invested."

"You're invested in something," I think I hear her mutter.

Stella called Ajax and they're ready when we pull up, holding a harness leash and a box for the puppies. "I don't think she's been on her own for long," I say as I manage to get her into the harness. "She's letting me put this on her."

"That's a good thing. Still, be careful."

"Aww, it sounds like you care." I meet her gaze with a smirk, only to have her stick her tongue out at me. I laugh.

Is this possible? I'm having *fun* with Stella Laz?

I watch her with the puppies as we settle the little family into the biggest crate in the shelter, complete with a thick dog bed and water bowl. There's room for Stella to deposit the puppies on the bedding while Mama Dog drinks, keeping one eye on me outside the cage as she laps up the water. "She was thirsty."

"It's good we got to her in time," Stella says ominously. "I can't believe someone could just let her go off in her condition without doing anything to find her."

"How do you know they didn't?"

"People talk. Someone would have said something to us if there was even a hint of a search for a dog. Because we find them. No one wanted Mama Dog to be found." Stella's expression is more anger than sadness, but my heart is breaking for the dog.

"She's safe now," I say more to the dog than Stella. "You'll take better care of her than her owners ever would."

"I will." Stella backs out of the cage, giving Mama Dog as wide a berth as she can.

"What happens now?" I ask as Stella gets to her feet.

"I take care of her," she says, looking at the dog with a soft smile. "We all take care of her. I think she'll be okay. We got to her in time."

The dog finishes the water and sniffs her way to where the puppies are mewling as they cuddle into each other. I'm glad when she settles around them, letting her still-blind babies find their way to nurse. "I'm really glad."

"Thank you."

I look down at Stella and try not to smirk because saying the words seems to cause her great difficulty. "Thank you for your help," she adds through gritted teeth. "I… appreciate it."

My smile widens. "Can you say that again? Didn't quite catch it."

"Don't be annoying," she snaps.

"But it's so much fun to annoy you."

"And you're very good at it."

On the other side of the crate, Ajax watches us with wide eyes. "I'm impressed the two of you made it back in one piece," they say.

"Mama Dog is too sweet and scared to be a danger," I say with a confidence I don't have. I lured a stray, possibly feral, mother dog away from her babies with a bit of steak. At any moment, she could have turned on me, thinking I'd make a better meal.

And Stella does this all the time.

What is she thinking?

"I meant the two of you being in danger from each other." Ajax laughs, pulling me away from darker thoughts.

"Nah, I think I'm growing on her," I tell them. "But you've got to name one of the puppies after me."

"Not on your life," Stella mutters, which makes me laugh.

Stella has made me laugh quite a few times today and I think some of them were even intentional.

I'm distracted by the sound of footsteps upstairs. "What's up there?" I ask Ajax.

"Cats. Lennie is up there with them now."

"You have cats?"

"Catch a *Pet*," Stella emphasizes, giving the puppies a last concerned glance before moving on to another cage. They decided to keep the other dogs penned or caged until Mama Dog is more settled with her puppies. "Cats are pets too."

"Can I go up?"

"You like cats now?" Stella meets my eagerness with the usual coolness back in her voice.

"Who doesn't like cats?"

She looks annoyed but before I can open my mouth to make it worse, she relents. "Just knock before you open the door and watch out no one escapes."

"No escaping. Got it." And then I'm off to find some cats.

The door at the top of the stairs is closed and I do what I'm told, only I don't wait until it's opened before I slide inside. "Hello?"

"Hello?" comes an answering voice and a *parade* of cats.

Big cats, little cats, black and tabby, some winding through my legs, others hovering on the sidelines to watch. A few hiss, and a skinny gray one pops onto two legs and stretches up to my knee, digging claws into my jeans.

"Hello, kitty cats," I sing, crouching. Immediately, my hands are full of fur babies demanding my attention.

Who says cats are anti-social?

"Prince Gunnar?"

Glancing up, I notice an older man with long graying hair and missing an arm stands before me, with a massive fluffy white cat tucked under his arm.

"Hi. Sorry to burst in." I stand and automatically hold out my hand, which I quickly drop because of the missing arm and the fact the other one is busy holding the cat, who mirrors Stella's usual expression when she sees me. "Ajax and Stella gave me the okay to pop up."

He nods, studying me with a curious smile. "Always like visitors. Should I bow or something?"

A few cats continue to circle but most are quick to go back to their business. "It'd be weird if you did. You're Lennie?"

"Leonard Tak, Your Highness."

"Just Gunnar. Leonard…" Now it's my turn to study him because the name rings more than a few bells. "The surfer?"

He gives a tight nod. "Used to be. I've given up the waves to help care for the cats."

"That could be more dangerous than the waves around here." I point to the cat under his arm. "He doesn't look friendly."

"Her. Snowball'll gut you if you give her a chance." Lennie juts his chin proudly. "Named her myself, after Lady Camille."

I laugh, sending more cats scurrying away from me. "She'll love that."

"She is appreciated around these parts," Lennie says, stepping back to let me enter.

"She'll like hearing that, too." I brace myself for questions about her, but none are coming. Maybe Camille has already met Lennie from her visits into town.

I have no idea who Camille may know in town since I haven't been around much.

"What brings you up to see the cats?" Lennie asks. "Either you want one, or you're a friend of Stella and Ajax."

"Uh… neither?" Are we friends? After today, I'm not sure.

I'm not comfortable being not sure. "I mean, Stella and I are friendly when she's not biting my head off."

He laughs but the cats don't run away. "Her bark is worse than her bite. Bite's pretty bad though." He sets the white cat down and it blinks at me with vibrant green eyes. "I'd watch out. She has notions about the castle."

"Tell me about it," I mutter. I take a step toward Snowball, but her hiss has me backing away to find a friendlier recipient for my attention.

Unlike downstairs, the floor is still separated into rooms, sparsely furnished with a few tables and chairs. There are cages and soft beds to sleep on every surface, and carpeted cat trees line the windows.

Fans move the air around and windows are only open a crack, so there is a faint haze of cat fur. Anyone with allergies would be wheezing in a second. But still—cats.

Cats everywhere. I pick up a tiny tortoiseshell for a cuddle and scratch the back of a gray tabby. A huge orange one looks bored but swipes at my arm from his perch on one of the cat trees when I walk by.

I want to take them all home.

"I knew your mother."

Lennie's casual comment stops me cold. I've had so many of the townsfolk stop me to tell me about my mother and it's always bittersweet. I appreciate knowing a little more about her, but it doesn't stop the hurt being reminded that she's gone.

But Lennie being here is a surprise because with Stella's obvious disapproval, why would she want a pro-royal working here? "Does Stella know?"

He chuckles. "If she bothered to ask. I taught your mother to swim. Surf. I cried at her funeral."

I swallow the sudden lump in my throat. "You're not the only one."

"She was a good woman," Lennie says in a gruff voice.

"She was the best," I agree.

"She'd be proud of you."

This—I'm caught off guard and, to my embarrassment, my eyes begin to sting. My mother... I turn away to blink back the threat of tears.

"She'd want you to do more."

I whirl around to face Lennie. "Excuse me?"

"The travelling you do; helping out in other parts of the world," Lennie says in his rough-as-sandpaper voice. "I follow you a little closer than most. I see you. I see who you are and who you could be."

"And just who do you think I could be?" I ask in an icy voice.

"A force to be reckoned with," he says, oblivious to the fact he's crossing a line. "You and Stella—now that would be a royal couple who would make waves."

I scoff, hackles lowered at the mention of her name. Is this some sort of matchmaking? "Me and Stella would cause more destruction than a tidal wave."

Lennie's face creases into a smile. "I don't know about that. She let you up here—alone. She doesn't do that."

I turn back to the cat, not wanting to talk about Stella, but not wanting to stop. "She's a little busy with the puppies we brought in."

"She let you help? That's also a good sign."

"A sign for what? She didn't have much choice." I continue to wander, petting as many cats as I can, conscious of both Lennie and Snowball watching me.

"I knew her father."

The bombshells keep coming, but this has me turning to find out more. "Again— does Stella know this?"

"Again—if she bothered to ask. These notions she has about you folk up the hill give her a bit of tunnel vision. It's not healthy."

Considering my chest should have holes from all the barbs she's thrown at me, I can't disagree.

"It would be good if you could help her with those notions."

I scoff again at the thought. "I value my self-respect too much. It's not easy to help Stella."

"You're here, aren't you?"

I turn the interrogation back to Lennie. "How do you know Duncan?"

Lennie stoops beside a litter box in the corner of one of the rooms and scoops a few pieces of poop into a bucket beside it. "They like clean litter boxes," he tells me. "I knew your father as well, back in the day. I worked as a roadie for every one of their shows."

"Really?" My reply is quick and delighted. My father is amazing in so many ways but it's his years as a founding member of Kräftig that fascinate me. The band's music, is loud and chaotic, perfect for Dad.

Lennie finishes the litter box and moves on to the next one before he stands and answers. "Your father could drink more than any man I've ever met," he chuckles. I've heard people talk about my father for my whole life, and I can tell when they like him.

There is real affection in Lennie's voice, and the sound of it warms me to him, despite his comments about Stella. "Duncan was a close second."

"They had a lot of good years together."

"I hope they're still having them."

"You should come up and see them," I suggest. "They'd love that, talking about old times." I'd like that, if I could be a fly on the wall when it happened.

Lennie gives a rueful smile. "I'd like nothing better, but I've stayed away over the years because of the friendship I shared with your mother. And… you don't know…"

There's a flash that I'm going to hear about something I don't want to hear about. "What don't I know?"

"I was in the other car when she had the accident."

The accident that killed her.

It's as if a white film covers my eyes. It's not anger, because everything about the accident proves that it was Mom who was at fault, but rather a blankness that helps me withstand conversations like this.

There hasn't been one in a while.

"I didn't know that."

"It's how I lost my arm." There's no anger in Lennie's voice. No resignation. He's just as casual as if we were talking about the weather.

How does one do that?

"I tried to save her but…" Lennie swallows, and right there, I can see it. I can tell this is a man who is haunted by that day just as much as my family is.

Maybe more.

"Thank you." I reach out and grasp his shoulder, and he flinches under my touch. "Thank you."

"Stella gave me a job when no one else would."

"But it wasn't your fault."

"Tell that to the town who worshipped your mother."

"Stella doesn't know this?"

"This she knows. We've never talked about it, but she knows."

Why would she hire the man involved in the accident that killed her mother's best friend? Just one more thing about Stella Laz that I don't understand.

"I should be going," I tell him. "Thanks for the tour... and the talk. I'll tell Dad and Duncan that I met you. I think you should come up to the castle sometime."

"I'll let them decide that. It's good to meet you, Prince Gunnar."

"Just Gunnar."

Lennie frowns. "You need to remember that you are an important member of the royal family, even though you do your best to forget it. Like I said, your mother would be proud of you, but she'd want you to do more. Take your place in the family."

His cryptic words ring in my ears as I make my way downstairs, but they pop right out when I see who is standing with Stella over the puppy pen.

25

Stella

"**J**ONATHAN."

I don't hear Gunnar come down the stairs until he speaks in a voice that's so cold I almost don't recognize it.

"Your Highness." Jonathan flicks his gaze to Gunnar, disapproval clear in the lines of his face.

I glance between them—Officer Jonathan McKibbon, who acts as the animal control officer as well as keeping the peace in Battle Harbour, and Gunnar. His black jeans are covered in flecks of dirt and white cat hair. Jonathan is immaculate in his uniform; just starting his shift and, finally, responding to my calls about the dog.

I get frustrated that the police don't give the strays around town the priority I do, but Jonathan has always been helpful in tracking them down. It just sometimes takes a while. But there's no way for Gunnar to know that, or be resentful of the fact.

And then the connection hits me—Jonathan is Kate's older brother; Kate as in, "Gunnar and Kate scandal."

Not really a scandal, but rather an ill-fated love affair.

With cheating, on Gunnar's side, documented by me. Even though no one knows that.

I frown as Gunnar shifts his gaze from Jonathan to the puppies snuffling into the blankets. "They settling in okay?" Gunnar asks, his tone still icy in the warmth of the room.

"I think so. I'm not sure if she'll be strong enough to nurse, so I might have to try a bottle for them. I thought I'd give her the day before I step in."

"That sounds fun," he says, sounding anything but. His blue eyes stray to Jonathan without a hint of the smile I've become used to.

"What wouldn't have been fun is if the dog had gone after you." Jonathan's frown deepens. I'm surprised because a moment before Gunnar showed up, he was all smiles.

Jonathan is usually always all smiles with me. We have our dislike of the castle in common, plus I've had a secret crush on him for years.

Not that I would ever do anything about it, but he's nice-looking and... well, I never said I lived as a nun.

"We had it under control," I assure Jonathan.

"*You* did. What does *he* know about rescuing dogs?" He flicks a scornful gaze in Gunnar's direction. I've given Gunnar the exact same look too many times to count, but it irritates me when Jonathan does it.

"It's fine, Jonathan. And clearly, we couldn't wait for you." I move away from the cage because the puppies have either given up or have full bellies. Either way, the three of them are asleep, nestled up to their mother, who watches us with wary eyes.

"Next time, you wait. I don't want anything to happen to you."

Three days ago, Jonathan's words might have set off a chain reaction in my chest. If he doesn't want anything to happen to me, that might mean he cares what happens to me, which might mean—

I won't go any further because no chain reaction is happening. Instead of sounding sweet and possibly romantic, it irritates me.

I don't show any of that in my expression though.

Gunnar meets my gaze and quickly looks away. "If the pups are okay, I think I'll take off," he says uneasily.

I have never heard Gunnar sound uneasy.

"Good idea," Jonathan says, fixing Gunnar with his stare.

Gunnar stiffens, and I hold my breath, waiting for the outburst, but none comes. I shouldn't be surprised—Gunnar is a prince, after all, and must be used to dealing with hostility. Still, he doesn't deserve it in here. "Thank you again for helping me," I tell him. The words come a lot easier this time.

"Anytime." He takes a last look at the sleeping puppies and heads for the door. "Let me know if I can do anything else to help."

"She doesn't need your help," Jonathan calls after him.

"I can answer for myself," I snap, strangely gratified by the smirk on Gunnar's face.

"Yes, she certainly can. Officer." He gives an almost imperceptible nod. "Ajax—always a pleasure. And Stella..."

His expression softens the tiniest bit and I get the feeling there's more he wants to say.

But no. With another nod, he's gone.

"What are you doing with him?" Jonathan demands as soon as the door shuts after Gunnar.

"He wanted to help." All the adrenaline from finding Mama Dog and getting her and the puppies safely back here suddenly drains out of me, leaving me as exhausted as if I pulled a double shift at the shelter. It's not even noon and already I wish I was done for the day.

I wonder if I can sneak out to *Coffee for the Sole* for an early break. I left the remains of my coffee in the SUV.

"Why?"

What is with Jonathan? "Gunnar was here with Camille—Lady Camille—when we got the call about the dog..." I trail off with a shake of my head. "Why am I explaining this to you?"

Jonathan moves closer and Ajax is still watching us like a Wimbledon match. "Because we're friends. I help you here."

"Yes, but extra help isn't bad."

"It is when it's Gunnar." Even the way Jonathan says his name is angry.

I take a deep breath. "Look, I know you've got a problem with him because of your sister—"

"You've got your problems with him, too. With the entire family."

Do I? Spending the morning with Gunnar, and after what went down yesterday at the castle has me seeing him in a different light.

Who knows what colour of light that's going to be, but I don't think I need to stay angry with Gunnar. The realization shifts my balance and I grasp the cage to hold on to something solid, that isn't changing with every moment— "I don't know," I admit.

Jonathan gapes as if he can read the thoughts racing through my mind. "What are you talking about? Everyone knows you hate the castle, so seeing him here with you—"

"Is none of your business," I finish. "It's no one's business."

"What's going on with you?" Jonathon demands.

I shrug. "Nothing, other than I have a lot of work to do since my morning was spent searching the cliffs, which was actually your job."

Five minutes later, Jonathan is gone, leaving a wide-eyed Ajax staring at me. "Stop looking at me like that," I grouse.

"You..." They hesitate for a long moment before blurting out: "You like him."

"You need to stop saying that!" I cry loud enough to startle the dogs.

"But I've never said it before," Ajax protests.

For the next two nights, I stay at the shelter to take care of the puppies, feeding them baby formula from a bottle and having the vet come to check on the mother. On the third day after we brought them off the cliff, the puppies opened their eyes, Mama Dog was back with a full belly to nurse them, and I went home for a full ten hours of sleep. I left a Sabrina Carpenter mix on—not my usual style, but Ajax will approve.

"Stella?" Mom calls when I finally get home.

"It's me."

She meets me in the hallway as I take off my boots. "Are you finished with those dogs?"

Maybe it's the lack of sleep but something in my mother's tone irks me. "I'm not finished with those dogs, but they're safe and comfortable and well-fed for the first time in their lives. That is my job."

She sniffs and I'm not sure if it's the usual disappointed-in-my-daughter-sniff, or that I kind of smell. "Do you think you might have overdone it this time? You haven't been home since you disappeared with Prince Gunnar."

"I was at the shelter—"

"So you say," she cuts in. Disappointing daughter sniff then. "How do you think your sister feels about that?"

At that moment, Sophie wanders into the hall, digging her hand into a bag of potato chips. "How do you feel about that?" I ask her with bewilderment.

Chip crumbs sprinkle the floor. "Huh?"

"Not her." Mom shakes her head. "Daphne."

"What about Daphne?" Sophie asks slowly.

"Is she okay?" I demand.

"She's devastated!"

I meet Sophie's equally confused gaze. "Why?"

Our mother throws her hands out. "Because she's going to the biggest event this country has ever seen and her sister is trying to steal her boyfriend!"

I laugh. I have to because if my mother is serious then there's something terribly wrong here. "What are you talking about?"

"Gunnar isn't Daphne's boyfriend, Mom," Sophie tells her in a patient voice.

"He could be if *you* stayed out of things," Mom spits at me.

I don't believe what I'm hearing. "What are you talking about?"

"You spent an entire day with him. He's calling all the time, to talk to you, not Daphne."

"He doesn't call anyone." I turn to Sophie for help.

"There's nothing between Daphne and Gunnar," Sophie tries again.

"Have you asked her how she feels about this?"

I slowly hang up my jacket and collect my thoughts. Who is this woman? For years, any member of the royal family as well as those who worked there have been persona non grata in this house. And now, Prince Gunnar is an acceptable companion?

But not for me. It's fine for *Daphne* to hang out with him, but not me.

As what my mother is saying sinks in, the ball of hurt grows in my chest. I've always loved Daphne like a true sister, but Signe Luute is *my* mother, not Daphne's. Daphne has her own mother encouraging her, supporting and fighting her battles.

I don't seem to have that today.

"Do you even know what's going on with Daphne?" I ask in a low voice, enunciating each and every word. "There is absolutely nothing between her and Gunnar other than he needs someone to look good on his arm and she did him a favour by agreeing to go to the wedding with him. Daphne doesn't like Gunnar because she's in love with Daulton Drake. That's who she wants to be with and pushing her toward Gunnar isn't going to make that go away."

"Well, it certainly won't if you're in the way," Mom says in a cool voice. "Step aside so Daphne might have a chance with the prince. That was the plan, wasn't it, before you decided to hijack it?"

My mother has her moments when she's not that nice to me. I acknowledge that; I accept it, and I move on because she's my mother and I love her. But this time, her words feel like my chest is a dartboard and she keeps trying for the bullseye.

"I'm not hijacking anything, because there's nothing there," I whisper since I've lost any strength in my voice. "I'll talk to Daphne tomorrow when we're in Saint Pierre. I need some sleep now."

Mom steps in front of me. Conversation clearly not over. "You can't talk to her in front of Lady Camille when she's one of Lady Camille's bridesmaids," Mom says in a tone full of contempt.

I shake my head as I push past her, but then I stop. "I don't understand. Are you suggesting Daphne and Gunnar should be a couple?"

"Why not?"

Sophie widens her eyes at me and I know she's telling me not to get into it. But no—conversations of the last few days have bottled up and it's a good time to unclog that drain.

"Why not? Why not? Because for the last fourteen years, you have had nothing good to say about the princes and the king and anyone who spends more than two hours in the castle. What happened? What changed things?"

Another sniff. "It would be beneficial for Peter, as mayor, to have a connection with the castle. It's been difficult for him. Establishing a social relationship would be helpful."

"Daphne and Gunnar, then. You want to use Daphne to get Peter points with the castle. Does she know this? Does *Peter*?"

"Daphne understands what her father needs for his political career."

"So you hate the castle when it's convenient for you?"

She averts her gaze. "I don't hate the castle."

"You do, you have for years. That's really selfish, Mom." It's a lot more things, but I can't say them. I can't even think them, because this is my mother.

"How dare you?" she cries.

Sophie moves, standing shoulder to shoulder with me. "How dare *you*?" she accuses with more fire in her voice than I've ever heard. "You robbed us of our father."

"You made your own choice."

"We were kids," I say sadly. "You were our mother. We didn't know we had a choice."

Mom tries to brush it away like she always does when confronted. Any hint of an opinion other than hers was brushed under the dining room table like last night's crumbs. "Come and set the table. We're not talking about this. You can help me finish dinner."

Sophie offers me the bag of potato chips, and I take one. "We're not hungry," I say flatly. And then I go to my room.

26

Gunnar

I DIDN'T CALL A meeting of the brothers but I didn't *not* call one. I texted the bro chat on Sunday afternoon and said I felt like a beer.

They came.

"And we're here because...?" Kalle begins after frothy pints are poured and passed around. I drink deep—Dad's special IPA is something else—and for a moment there, it feels like another competition. Eyes wide over the rim, I check glass levels as I keep swallowing.

Bo is the only one who has ever been able to get through an entire pint in one go, but I think I might have a chance after these last few days.

It actually hasn't been all bad. The last day was okay, maybe, but the time spent with Stella was...

I'm not sure what I think it was.

Odin slams his glass onto the bar, now two-thirds empty. "Enough. I'm not doing this. It's not even four o'clock in the afternoon."

Kalle sets his down beside Odin's like he's measuring the level, and he totally is. I slam mine down, gasping a little. Beat them both.

But not Bo.

His glass is empty when he finally sets it down, nudging it forward for a refill.

If you know the history of our family, then it's clear we're of Viking descent. But there are certain characteristics of my brothers that scream they're descended from Erik the Red—Odin and his swords, Kalle being the toughest man I've ever come across, and Bo and beer.

If Dad hadn't already gone into the microbrewery business, I bet that would have been Bo's thing. But we don't copy each other, just compete in our own special way.

"Why are we here again?" Kalle repeats as he refills Bo's glass from behind the bar. There's no sign of Edie, so Kalle mans the bar on his own.

"I felt like a beer."

"With your brothers?" Odin raises an eyebrow. I wonder if he knows how much he looks like Dad when he does that.

"What's wrong with my brothers?" I demand like Odin offended me when the truth is I'd rather hang with them than someone with the talent of taking my every word and twisting it against me.

I haven't seen Stella in two days and I can't seem to get her out of my head.

I replay walking with her on the cliffs, the fierce protectiveness on her face when we found the puppies. The way her tiny hand felt in mine in the passage.

It's the feel of her hand that's stopped me from visiting Mama Dog because I know Stella has been staying there to look after them. I know she's at the shelter and it would be easy for me to stop by. I'd have the best excuse.

I shouldn't want to stop by the shelter because I shouldn't want to see Stella. Dog or no dog.

Hence the text to the bro chat because I'm *thisclose* to going to the shelter. And since Stella is part of the group I'm flying to Saint Pierre tomorrow, if I went to see her tonight, that would only make things weird.

Things are strange enough between us without any added weirdness.

"Nothing, they're awesome," Spencer says, dropping his man-purse on the stool beside me. "What'd I miss?"

"Bo had a beer."

"Starting a little early, are we?"

"Call it a pre-wedding celebration." Bo looks at Odin with his eyebrow raised. "Or maybe helping a brother with some liquid courage."

"I don't need courage," Odin protests. "I need things to slow down. There's too much going on. I'm marrying Camille in less than a week, but I haven't seen her for more than twenty minutes in days."

"Aw, you miss her." Kalle may tease, but we all know he's happy for Odin.

We're all happy for Odin.

He is truly the best of us. Odin takes the responsibility of being part of a royal family more seriously than any of us. He knows his duty and sticks with it, unlike me, who rides on the coattails of being a prince rather than doing anything princely.

Why can I hear Stella's voice in my head saying the exact same thing?

I drain the rest of my beer to get rid of the voice.

Odin is a true prince. He'd do anything for the kingdom, is protective and loyal; smart with important thoughts. He decided it was the right time to be married and, thanks to Camille being the one he thought would be the best fit, is the first of us to fall truly in love.

Except for Bo, but we don't talk about that.

"Yes. I miss my bride-to-be," Odin says defensively. "What about it?" Kalle laughs and reaches across the bar to slap Odin's shoulder as he continues— "But we're not here to talk about me or the wedding, because I can't wait for the thing to be over. I have no idea why I went along with such a spectacle."

"Because you had no choice," Spencer soothes. "If that's what Camille wants—"

"She didn't, that's the thing. She would have been happy if we got married on a beach somewhere."

"No, she wouldn't," I correct.

Odin's shoulders slump. "No, you're right. But all this would have been much smaller if we'd done it back in February."

"You had that choice," Spencer points out.

Odin shakes his head. "We were only just falling for each other. I wanted to make sure it was real for her before we took that step."

"And for you, too," Kalle says quietly.

"I knew from the beginning she was the one. But these extra few months have been good for us. We're solid."

I lean my head on Odin's thick arm and bat my eyelashes at him. "You *wuuuve* each other."

My brother, the best among us, squares his shoulders. "I do. I love her. I love Camille," he announces to the bottle over the bar with a serious expression.

"Did that make you feel better saying it out loud?" Bo drawls in a teasing voice.

"Doesn't matter how long it took you to say it, all that matters is that you do," I tell him. "Besides, this gives Mrs. Theissen more time to plan the party."

"Your dad really wanted an excuse for a party," Spencer puts in.

A groan passes from man to man. "He could have used the excuse of having all of us home," I say. "He didn't have to make O be the centre of attention. Or Camille— because you know she *loves* that." I roll my eyes, thinking back to the night I brought Camille here and helped her drink too much screech so she could show off her moves on the dance floor. "Or maybe she secretly does."

"She deserves to have all the attention," Odin says in a proud voice.

"She does," Spencer agrees. "And don't think Lyra didn't try to get the king to have a party for her."

"Letting her have a party is different than having a party for her," Bo argues. "We had to put up with enough of her 'get-togethers with friends' growing up. That girl should not be allowed to socialize with more than three people at a time."

"She could probably take down most governments with just three if they're the right ones," Kalle says with a shiver.

"You mean the wrong ones." Odin laughs. "Where is she, anyway?"

"She's not part of the bro-chat."

"That's seriously what you call this? Dude, think of a better name." Kalle shakes his head at me.

I honestly never thought of inviting Lyra, and the realization irks me so much that I pull out my phone. "She's gone," Spencer says in a low voice, guessing my intentions. "She went to St. Johns for the weekend and she's not back yet."

"Shopping? I would have gone with her." It might have been a nice distraction.

Spencer shakes his head as he reaches for his beer. "I think there's a guy."

"There's always a guy," Bo says with resignation. Lyra is our little sister—perfectly able to take care of herself, but usually deserving our worry and concern.

"I wish she'd settle down, so we'd have someone to look after her," Odin frets.

I laugh. "Do you not know our sister? She doesn't need looking after. She's capable of taking over the world on her own."

"That's what I'm afraid of. Sometimes she needs to be reined in—"

"And you think a man is going to do that?" Bo interrupts, and they all laugh with me.

"Camille better not hear you being all misogynist-like." Kalle nods at Odin. "It's not a good look."

"I am not misogynist," Odin argues. "I'm an older brother worried about our sister's actions affecting the kingdom."

Silence greets his words. And then—more laughter.

"Dude—Lyra has fun, but she cleans up her messes," I tell him. "She always has. You don't have to worry about her, or the kingdom."

"Someone has to," Odin mutters into his glass.

This has the potential to go dark, very fast. Or go someplace where I can't get to pull it back to tell them what I brought them here to share. "Look, the kingdom is just fine and no one needs to worry about anything with Duncan on the ball."

"Dad is definitely on the ball," Spencer agrees with a glance between Kalle and Odin.

Odin cares too much. Kalle doesn't care enough. It's been like that since Odin was born nineteen months after the heir to the throne.

"I don't wanna talk about that," I say loudly. "But I do have something to talk about."

"About what's going on with you and my sister?" Spencer asks with a raised eyebrow.

"No, and nothing. Told you that already."

"But you spent the other day with her, finding that dog and helping in the shelter. You're heading to Saint Pierre with them tomorrow. Then there was the rescue mission through the passage." Spencer looks expectantly at me. "That's a lot of time spent with a person when there's nothing going on."

I shake my head. "You know *way* too much about what goes on in this town. But hey—did you know that Lennie works at the shelter with Stella?"

"Lennie is..." Odin begins but Bo quiets him with one word. "Mom."

"Lennie Tak," Spencer offers.

"He's still in town?" Odin asks.

"He comes in sometimes," Kalle admits. "I never know what to say."

"Our brother speechless?" I tease. "Imagine that."

"What did you say to him?" Bo wants to know.

"I told him Dad would love to see him. And Duncan. They were friends once. He was their roadie. He was with them through all of it. "

"I think that's why Dad feels so guilty," Kalle says.

"He shouldn't. It wasn't his fault. It wasn't anyone's fault."

"Lyra doesn't think that," Bo says in his quiet way.

"That's why Dad hasn't reached out," Kalle adds. "For Lyra's sake."

"He's like that," Odin says.

For a moment, the usual dread sweeps over me—what will happen when Dad goes. Dies. Leaves this world. As someone who has already lost his mother, it's a real fear. I could be an orphan tomorrow. Dad's big heart could stop beating because of too much cholesterol; there could be an assassination attempt.

Both scenarios are unlikely.

But here's what could be: an icy road. A moment of distraction. Two cars, minding their own business as their passengers laugh, love and live, without knowing that their lives will change in an instant when one car crosses the centre line.

It takes several mouthfuls of beer to push down the lump in my throat.

Our little group has gotten quiet but the rest of the pub has not.

There's a group of fishermen getting rowdy at a table in the back before they head out to open water tomorrow. Silas, Jem and Leodie from Coffee for the Sole laugh together at the bar beside us. There's trash-talking at the pool table as Mabel Crow readies her shot.

None of us have said a word to Mabel, or even met her eye. It's better that way.

"I want to do more around here," I tell my brothers, breaking the silence between us. "I want to be a part of things."

"Because of Lennie?" Odin asks with confusion.

"Because... I think it's time."

Odin looks at Kalle, and Kalle turns to Spencer. Bo keeps his gaze on his pint of beer, and Spencer studies me.

"I think it's been time for a while," he says. "What were you thinking of?"

My brothers aren't active members of the royal family like other monarchies, but they have their duties. Odin more than any of us, but Bo and Kalle have roles to play.

Dad has pretty much let Lyra and me off the hook.

He's let me play traveller and race car driver and playboy—at least that's how it seems to the world thanks to the media. But I've never taken an interest in what it takes to run a kingdom, to put your people's needs and wants before yours. To focus on making Laandia one of the best places in the world to live.

I'm not biased about that—it's on a list. Number six best place to live.

I've been selfish and lazy and while this isn't a self-browbeating, it's time for me to step up.

"What can I do?" I ask Spencer. He's really the best one to ask, next to Duncan and Dad. Odin doesn't need the responsibility of finding me a role, not when he does so much. And Kalle and Bo would have no idea of where to start.

"Really," I add. "You know my skill set, which is nothing. I like fast cars, travelling and having fun. None of which helps run a kingdom."

"And that's what you want to do?" Spencer asks skeptically. "Help run the kingdom?"

Some of Stella's words float back, the biting comments, the sharp retorts that prove she doesn't think much of me.

I don't like people not thinking much of me. Because it reinforces the times that I don't think much of myself.

I'm the fly-by-the-seat-of-my-pants prince. I'm the fun-loving one of the family; the one who is cheerful and happy and makes others feel good.

I've never been the serious type who can do things.

Maybe I want to be that.

"I do," I say with as much seriousness as I can muster.

"I think we can find something for you that falls within your skill set," Spencer says with a smile and a glance at Odin. "There's lots of room at the table."

"And I think you'd fit in fine," Kalle says.

27

Stella

MONDAY MORNING, CAMILLE SENDS a car for us. Early.

I'm always surprised that Daphne isn't a morning person; there is no smile and she slouches in the seat, attention on her phone as her finger flicks the screen in a never-ending scroll. My headphones are in, with ABBA my morning music of choice, but I keep it low in case Daphne wants to talk.

Or if I do.

I'm excited and I just can't hide it. "What do you think it's like in Saint Pierre?" I ask Daphne as we near the airport, only one of three in the entire country of Laandia.

I know this even though I've never been to any of them. I've never been out of Laandia and the thought of getting on a plane and flying out of the country has me vibrating like an electric toothbrush.

"I have no idea," she says without looking up from her phone. As well as not being a morning person, Daphne isn't that punctual, and making sure she was ready to go before the car arrived meant I never had time to make a coffee.

It's not too big of a deal for me but I think Daphne needs a jolt of caffeine. "Google it," she adds.

"I'm not about to Google a country when we'll be there in a few hours. Not that Saint Pierre is a country. It's an archipelago. It's part of France."

"Are we supposed to speak French there?" she demands. "Because I don't know French."

"Camille didn't say, but I'm sure we're fine with English."

"Are you sure?"

I'm not sure because I've never been to Saint Pierre. I've never been anywhere, and that's part of the problem. The slight trembling in my hands is from nerves as well as excitement. "No," I admit. "I have no idea what to expect."

"Because you've never been out of Laandia." There's a tinge of scorn in Daphne's tone, recognizable only because I, too, have used that same tone.

But never toward her. I turn to the window as Daphne continues to scroll. "No. I haven't."

The car passes the terminal. There are only twelve commercial flights a day, so it's quiet. It's a pretty small country.

I'm going to be on one of those flights leaving the country. And I'm going by myself. Not with my father.

I'm done waiting for him to take me anywhere.

"Where are we going?" I ask the driver as we leave the terminal—the way out of the country—behind.

"Private airstrip," he replies. "His Royal Highness keeps his plane there."

"Which Royal Highness?" I demand.

"What are you doing here?" I demand when I get out of the car to find Gunnar standing beside a small plane, his knapsack slung over a shoulder and his grin fixed on his face.

No dimples. I know it's not his full smile because I'm here and he doesn't know what to expect from me.

Because he knows I'm friends with Jonathan? Or just because of me?

"I could ask you the same thing, except I know—Camille invited you, and so you're along for the ride." Gunnar spreads his arms wide. "You think it might be the same reason for me? I'm doing her a favour too by giving you all a ride."

"*You're* giving us a ride?" I scoff. "In what? One of those crazy sleds you made when you thought going over that jump would make you fly?"

Gunnar sweeps his arm behind him with a smirk. "Welcome to Air Gunnar."

I close my eyes. "Of course you're a pilot."

"I knew he was a pilot," Daphne says with her sunny smile. Oh, to be given the gift to instantly wake up when you see someone you're not related to. "Morning, Your—"

"Just Gunnar," he says. "If I'm going to be dancing all night with you this weekend, at least you should call me by my given name. You do like to dance, don't you?"

"Of course."

"Great. I knew I picked the right partner." With a sideways glance at me, he steps back. "I'll check the plane and we're good to go. Wheels up in ten."

"What, does he think we're on a mission or something?" I grumble, angry at myself for not being able to look away as Gunnar walks around the plane.

He's wearing cargo shorts, which don't have the same impact as jeans, but I can't deny his calves are... very nice calves. Bunches of muscles tapering down into ankles...

Since when have I noticed ankles?

Luckily, Camille hurries over with her tiny dog in her arms, distracting me from more internal monologue about Gunnar's appendages. "Good morning," she says with a smile. "Before you ask, I'm not bringing Bea Arthur because she hasn't learned how to behave on a plane."

"And Betty White has?" I extend my hand for her to sniff. The little dog deems me acceptable and nudges my hand to pet her.

"She's an old hat at flying."

I wonder if I will be.

I've never been on a plane before.

It's not something I'm proud of, especially when my childhood dream was to travel the world, exactly what Gunnar has been doing.

The irony is not lost on me.

And my plans for school in Canada or even America fizzled out as well. It's not that I'm not happy in Laandia, but I do regret not making the most of the opportunities when they were given to me. I wasn't given too many, but I could have gone to school somewhere other than King's College in the neighbouring town of Pleasant Bay.

I could have stopped waiting and I could have left.

Instead, my first time in a plane, and leaving Laandia, is with Gunnar.

Because Gunnar is our pilot—or maybe despite it—Daphne shows the first sign of apprehension about the flight. She's been out of Laandia nine times, and yet she's nervous. I've never been anywhere and I'm more excited than scared.

It's not a competition, but score one for me.

Because of this, both she and Camille are content to sit together in the cramped backseat, leaving me in the co-pilot's seat beside Gunnar.

He hands out headsets and makes sure we're buckled in properly as I study the instrument panel and the screens before me.

Not that I'm going to be doing any co-piloting, even with the yoke in front of me. I touch it tentatively, jerking back as Gunnar takes that moment to start the engine.

Propellers begin to spin. Things start to vibrate more than I am. "I didn't know you were flying," I say to Gunnar.

His hands move confidently across the panel. "Do you have a problem with flying?"

"I don't know," I admit. "I don't think so."

He meets my gaze with a frank stare. "Do you have a problem with me?"

After the escape from the castle and helping with Mama Dog, I should give Gunnar a break. But fourteen years of listening to how the castle is hard to get past.

As of this morning, I'm finished with listening to what other people think of the castle.

"You're doing a lot of thinking for a simple question," Gunnar interrupts my thoughts.

I wave my hand across the dashboard with the dials and gauges that wouldn't look out of place in a sci-fi movie. "You know what all of this does?"

"I do."

"And you've flown a lot?"

"What do you mean by a lot?"

"I mean, is this your first time flying a plane?"

Gunnar chuckles. "No, Stella, this is not my first time flying a plane. I know exactly what I'm doing. Do you?"

I don't. I really don't.

I point to a flashing red light. "What does that do?"

"That tells me how high we are."

I point to a switch. "And that?"

"You really don't trust me, do you?"

I take a deep breath. "Of course I trust you, Your Highness."

"Where did that come from?"

"To remind myself that you're a prince of Laandia and I can't say exactly what I think."

Gunnar laughs. "You are the only person who says exactly what they think around me."

"Do you have a problem with that?"

Before Gunnar can answer, the little plane begins to move and we start the slow taxi to the runway.

"I don't," he finally says. When I glance over at him, Gunnar is smiling at me.

Two dimples.

"I've started to like it," he admits.

I don't know if it's the words or the smile or the increase of the vibrations as we start down the runway, but there's a warmth in my chest that hasn't been there in a very long time.

"I don't, either," I tell him as the plane speeds up. I clutch my harness and fight to keep my eyes open so I can see it all.

"Don't what?"

"Have a problem with you," I say loudly over the engine. We're going very fast, getting closer to the end of the runway. I know the scientifics, that the wheels will lift off the ground as the speed increases but it seems so impossible.

So amazing.

"Good." Gunnar gives me a flash of a smile and I respond with a hollow scream as the wheels of the plane leave the ground.

28

Gunnar

I T'S BEEN TOO LONG since I've flown.

I know I have an unheard-of amount of independence for a royal son, but flying always gives me a rush of freedom. There's nothing else like it.

And to have Stella here beside me for her first flight...

I feel like I'm twelve and doing some inane prank to get her attention. But I'm no longer twelve, and all of Stella's attention is focused out the window at the receding ground below.

I peek at her profile, smiling at her open-mouthed expression.

"It's amazing," Stella cries with delight, staring at the patchwork of forests and hills, rivers and lakes, and lonely roads snaking through the green and gray, and I puff with pride as if I'd laid it all out for her.

As we fly over Battle Harbour, I angle the plane slightly. "What are you doing?" Stella gasps, fingers tightening on her harness.

"You can see the town better this way," I offer.

I love flying.

I'm like Maverick in Top Gun—I have a need for speed, and until I got my hands on a plane, the car racing, boats, dirt bikes had never been enough.

The first time I was up in a small plane was when I was thirteen and demanded to be able to fly it. But as demanding and slightly obnoxious as I was, I wasn't entitled enough to expect to have full control. When I was sixteen, I signed up for lessons.

Duncan was the first person I took up after I had my pilot's license.

I will never tell Stella that.

But as much as I love flying, being one with the clouds, the sense of adventure mixed with the peacefulness of being in the sky, it's even better when I get to see Stella's reaction. I never expected that—either the joy on her face or the pleasure I get from seeing her so happy.

"You know who would love this view?" Stella cranes in her seat to look at Daphne. "Your father."

"Yeah," Daphne says.

That's all she says. "He loves the town," Stella says to cover Daphne's lack of enthusiasm. "He has drone pictures of it in his office, maps of the area."

"I'll take him up one day."

Stella looks at me suspiciously. "Just like that?"

"Why wouldn't it be just like that?"

"Well, because you don't know him."

"He'd like to go up in a plane. I have a plane and my pilot's license. Why wouldn't I take him up? And he's the mayor—of course I know him. You make me sound like a monster," I add. "The way you're so surprised when I want to help someone."

Is that guilt that flashes across her face? "You're not a monster," she mutters so quietly that if I wasn't looking at her, I would have missed it.

"I know that. I just wish you'd believe it too."

Two spots of colour dot her cheeks before she turns away.

The wind picks up when we near the coast of Newfoundland. It's not bad—at first. My hands are steady on the yoke, the instruments aren't going crazy, and Camille and Stella are happily chatting over the headset.

And the radio crackles as the air traffic control from Gander reaches out.

"Gunnar?" Stella asks in a low voice.

I hold up a finger. "All good." Thankfully, only I can hear what they're saying: that the wind has picked up, and do we want to land in Newfoundland?

"Negative," I say into the radio. "We'll continue on our planned route." But I tighten my grip on the yoke, gaze flitting between the horizon and the instruments.

"What's wrong?" Stella demands. There's a line slashed into her forehead and her smile has vanished, her lips tight and worried.

"Absolutely nothing," I tell her. "Only that it's windy out."

"Is windy bad?"

"Not always." I check the screen to make sure I'm close, then dip the wing. "Camille," I call. "Look down."

There's no response. "Quidi Vidi Lake," I tell her. "In St. John's. Where you—"

"First met Odin," she finishes. I don't have to turn around to hear the smile in her voice.

Stella touches my leg. When I look over, she's pretending to wipe beneath her eyes and gestures back to Camille.

I smile and focus on the sky.

Stella is quiet after that, watching the clouds as we fly above them. I kind of miss her chatter and inane questions.

But before long, I drop down to prepare for landing. The wind has picked up more than I expected and it's good Stella stopped talking because I don't need the distraction.

She's always been a distraction for me but never one I appreciated.

Do I appreciate it now? Do I really like spending time with her?

Another glance over at her to see the awe on her face as I ready for landing makes me think that maybe I do like to be around her.

Weird.

Gusts push the little plane, and it takes all my concentration to get us on the ground.

The girls don't notice the force of the wind, which is probably a good thing.

"We might have to adjust our departure," I mention to Camille after I taxi over to the tiny terminal. "That wind picked up quicker than I expected. There's a storm coming in, maybe sooner than they say."

"Will we be able to see the animals?" Stella asks.

"Let's go there first," Camille suggests. "Then I can show you around Saint Pierre."

The prefect has a car waiting at the airport for us and I meet the girls there after I've made arrangements for the plane.

"Have you ever been here before?" Daphne asks as I settle in the backseat beside her.

"Once," I tell her. "I was pretty young. And I don't remember why I came."

"It was during one of the rounds of negotiations for the fishing," Camille explains. "Your father brought you, Bo, and Lyra to make friends with me. I think I was seven."

"Were we best friends?"

"No, but I think that was more my fault than anything. I didn't play well with others back then."

"That's still how it is for Stella," I say with a teasing glance at Stella on the other side of Daphne. "She doesn't play well with others."

To my surprise, Stella sticks out her tongue at me rather than giving a sharp-tongued comeback. I take it as a win for me.

29

Stella

BEING IN SAINT PIERRE is like another world.

In truth, it's not much different than Battle Harbour—narrow streets, colourful homes, the screech of sea birds and boats dotting the ocean.

But it's a different country.

And I want to see *everything*.

From my reading, I discovered that Saint Pierre isn't an actual island but an archipelago, which is made up of little islands. And it's not just Saint Pierre—the animal rescue centre is on Miquelon.

Seems like most of the people live on Saint Pierre and the animals hang out on Miquelon.

I know which place I would be happier in.

Gunnar flies into the tiny airport at Miquelon and we spend the morning at SealSave, tucked into a lagoon facing the Atlantic Ocean. Camille escorts us around with a smile reminiscent of a parent bragging about their child. She should be proud; the centre is an amazing setup and I can see why the sea lions don't want to leave.

Gunnar *loves* it. I had no idea he was so into animals; not that I wanted to know that about him. Or cared, really. But it's a surprise, a different side of him.

Daphne takes lovely pictures of us and the animals. More of us.

Lots of selfies.

She certainly dressed for it; wearing a summer dress the colour of butter, once again my sister looks like a literal ray of sunshine. Her long, golden legs sweep out from the short skirt, finishing in platform sandals, and the dress cinches in at the waist to showcase her curvy figure.

Friends or more than friends, Gunnar certainly seems to appreciate her effort.

I wore cut-off denim shorts and an oversized sweatshirt with the sleeves falling over my hands, plus my boots. Daphne looks like she should be walking the boardwalk eating ice cream whereas I could be mistaken for one of the employees who muck out the walrus pen.

Not that I'm comparing, and if I were, why would it matter? I'm not out to impress anyone but myself.

I've never been outdoorsy, never been one for hiking or exploring like Gunnar.

He is in his element here.

"It's like Laandia a bit, reminds me of the Highlands of Scotland, only it's not as high," he says, standing straight and tall, with his hands on his hips and his customary backpack slung over his shoulder as he looks around.

For a moment I let myself admire the view. For just one little moment.

There's a reason Gunnar was named one of People magazine's sexiest royals. His black polo shirt makes his arms look... arm-ly. Like arms, but nicer. Nice arms.

I need to stop looking at Gunnar altogether.

But it's difficult when he sticks to my side like the dribble of honey on the side of a cup of tea.

There's so much more to look at besides Gunnar and I drink it all in. There are so many birds—and Camille knows the names of all of them. Ducks, doves, and pigeons are easily recognizable, as are the cormorants and herons that are found in Laandia. Camille points out something called an American coot, as well as terns and plovers and sandpipers. We see a heron poised to catch his lunch and an osprey swoop down to pluck a fish from the water.

There's a pelican at the end of the pier.

I've never seen so many seagulls, but I don't find them annoying here, unlike at the docks at home with their constant theft of French fries. There are so many puffins, and I've always found them adorable.

Camille shows Gunnar and me how they feed the birds. Daphne documents it all with her phone and misses a sea eagle coming in to land on a nearby tree.

"That's a Steller's sea eagle," Camille tells us, squinting to make sure she's recognized it correctly.

"You've got good eyes," I say.

"I think we should rename it Stella's sea eagle," Gunnar suggests, tossing seeds for the ducks.

"We can't rename a bird," I protest, mainly to offset the spark of warmth in my chest at Gunnar's words. "Some guy named Steller found it and he should get credit for it."

"You don't think you deserve credit?"

"I didn't find the bird."

"You found the puppies," he points out. "That was pretty cool."

Why is he being like this?

I don't know how to deal with Gunnar when he's being nice to me. Technically, he's usually nice; it's me who gets the digs in and he reacts. But if he's all smiling and happy, how can I say anything to change that?

Why does the Laandian prince have to have such a great smile? Seriously, Gunnar's is toothpaste-commercial-worthy. And his lips? If the man wore lipstick, he'd make a fortune modelling for MAC.

Why am I obsessing over his lips?

Why now?

After the birds, we visit the seal colony and it's by far my favourite part. The mammals lounge on the rocks and on the wet sand, and they move faster than I expected. They sound like barking dogs, a noise that sends Daphne backing away with her hands at her ears.

"They're just like dogs. I love them," I tell Camille.

"I thought you might." She smiles widely.

She takes us into the centre and we meet Miquel and Benoit who run things now that she's spending most of her time in Laandia. There are injured birds, a few baby seals that were rescued from a shark attack that killed six others, and a walrus who, Miquel explains, has been hanging around for years and just doesn't seem to want to leave.

"It's amazing," I say later, staring out the window of the plane as Gunnar takes off for the short hop to Saint Pierre. It's late afternoon, and we've been here longer than expected. I'd stay here until dark, but Daphne and Gunnar both want to visit the town before we head to the prefect's house for dinner.

The wind hasn't let up and the sky remains ominous, enough that Gunnar looks worried as he lands, a quick twenty-minute flight across the thirty or so kilometres that separate the islands.

I find that I don't like it when Gunnar looks worried.

30

Gunnar

THE TOWN IN SAINT Pierre reminds me of home. It's a marine town, but a little different and I wonder if it's the French influence. I might have been here before, but I don't remember any of it, so I'm as eager to wander around as Stella was to see the seals.

I find myself walking with her more and more, making little comments to both annoy her and see if I can get her to laugh.

It's important to me that Stella has a good time, like Odin escorting some high-ranking diplomat around the castle. But it's more, because it's Stella.

And I really don't know why I feel that way.

It begins to rain as we finish the tour. Once we scrambled into the car Camille ordered, I didn't have to tell Camille anything. "We're not flying back home tonight, are we?" she asks.

I shake my head. "We're right on the ocean here and storms can be a little more intense. I think we'd be fine, but the weather can change too quickly to make it a good idea. I think we should let it blow itself out and head back first thing in the morning."

"Is that a problem?" Camille asks Stella and Daphne, who shakes her head but doesn't look up from her phone.

"I have to make sure Lennie can help Ajax in the morning, but it shouldn't be a problem," Stella says.

I'm glad she didn't challenge me on flying home; I might have tried it just to prove a point.

We pull up to the prefect's house on the edge of town, a grandiose, two-story brick box that looks out of place among the basic wooden homes. An older woman, with gray hair tucked tightly in a knot at the back of her head and a warm smile greets us at the door. "Lady Camille," she exclaims, opening her arms.

When Camille first came to the castle, she was chilly and prickly, a lot like Stella. Seeing the prefect's house reinforced what Odin had let slip out once or twice—that there hadn't been a lot of affection or warmth in Camille's life.

I know my big brother feels some guilt for that; if he had pursued their friendship when they first met at the gala at Quidi Vidi Lake all those years ago, he might have helped Camille feel loved rather than left behind.

I had told him to stop worrying—Camille is who she is because of how she was raised, and he loves her that way. They have the rest of their life together for him to make her feel seen and appreciated. So far, he's off to a good start.

Knowing all of this, it makes me very happy to see the welcome my soon-to-be-sister-in-law gets from this woman.

Madame Carol.

Camille introduces us and while there are no hugs, it's still a friendly welcome. In fact, I'd put money on hugs when we leave tomorrow. Madame Carol shows us to our rooms; the girls take the time to freshen up but my empty stomach has me heading back down in search of the really good smells.

"Prince Gunnar." Carol doesn't seem surprised when I show up in the kitchen. "It's been a day."

The kitchen is half the size of the one in the castle and much more modern, with glass-fronted cupboards and shining stainless-steel appliances. Carol hovers over the stove, wooden spoon in her hand. "It has been a long one," I agree, taking the stool at the island she motions to.

"I meant it's been a day since I last saw you."

She has an accent but it's hard to place it. I hear a hint of French with a twist of Newfoundland and something else. It could be the Saint Pierre sound. "You were here back then?" I ask.

"That I was. I've been here for a good long time." She rests the spoon on a plate and turns to me. "I suppose you're looking for something to eat?"

"It's been a long day," I say with my most winning smile. Carol smirks, reminiscent of the way Stella smirks at me, and busies herself getting a plate of cheese and crackers for me.

"There's enough to share with the others," she warns as she pushes the plate toward me. "But first—how is my Camille making out in Laandia? She seems quite fond of you."

"She's said that?" I'm surprised at how good that makes me feel. "I'm quite fond of her too."

"Is she happy?"

There's no hesitation in my voice. "Yes. She's really happy with Odin. Maybe, at the beginning, some of Laandia didn't welcome her with open arms, but she's won over everybody by now. And we—the family—just adore her."

"Good." Carol smiles. "Good. I miss her but I want her to be happy, and if she can be happier there, then we will figure things out so she can run Saint Pierre from there."

"But she won't take over for years. The prefect... Where is the prefect?"

"Paris." The way she says it more than suggests there's more that she's not telling. But before I can ask, Carol nudges the plate closer. "Go. Find the others. Dinner won't be too much longer."

I know when I'm being dismissed. Taking the plate and a beer that Carol unearths for me, I head back upstairs to find the others.

Stella is easy to locate. She's standing on a balcony on the second floor, staring off into the water. "Do you think we can see whales from here?" she asks as a greeting.

I set down the plate on a small table and heap a piece of Brie onto a cracker. "If whales are swimming by, I'm sure you'll see them."

"What's that supposed to mean?" The wariness is back in Stella's voice, and I sigh as I pop the cracker into my mouth.

"Relax," I tell her when my mouth is empty. "I meant that as a compliment. That you always manage to get what you want. In a good way." I motion to the snack before helping myself to another cracker.

Stella reluctantly takes a wedge of gouda. "No, I don't."

"You wanted to save the world, one dog at a time, and look what you're doing," I begin. "I know how you've been making Battle Harbour more conscientious about waste and recycling and damage to the environment. You drive my father crazy with your protests about sustainable fishing. You make a difference, Stella.

You have to see that. With you and Camille joining forces, who knows what you'll be able to accomplish."

I think that was a lot of nice things. Compliments, even. But Stella stays silent even as I watch the way her lips move as she chews her food.

I'm watching her *chew*. That's so weird. "You don't agree?" I finally ask so I can stop staring.

"Sure, but..." She hesitates, staring off into the waves. Can she tell that I can't stop looking at her profile, tracing the line of her nose with my eyes? Her top lip is a bit fuller than her bottom, her chin slightly pointed. Her cheekbones are high and sharp like Duncan's but— "I wanted to see the world," she bursts out.

I spread an arm. "This is the world. You're seeing this."

"More. I wanted to travel. You know. You remember my maps. I wanted to do what you do."

"Race cars and try to break the sound barrier?"

She gives a gentle *hmph*. "I don't think you'll get that fast."

"No, but it's fun trying."

I go for the joke. I keep it good-natured, just like Stella says I do. But I don't have to, not with her.

We stand at the railing, staring into the distance. The sky is purplish-blue with fat clouds hovering along the horizon. Waves rock the boats anchored in the harbour and the screams of seagulls cut through the quiet.

It smells of... cinnamon. And flowers from the gardens below.

"It's going to storm," Stella says finally.

"Pink sky this morning. Pink sky at night—"

"Sailors delight. Pink sky in the morning," Stella recites the rhyme that every child born within sight of the sea knows by heart.

"Sailors take warning," I finish. "It'll blow over by morning. We'll be fine to fly home by then."

"I trust you. As a pilot," she adds hastily. "I mean, sure, I guess I trust you as not-a-pilot but—"

"I want to do what you do," I interrupt.

She frowns, the sun hitting her face just right to bring about a pinkish glow. I can't take my eyes off her, and I'm really glad she's still looking at the water. "What do I do?"

"Save the world."

"You can do that. You can do whatever you want. You're a *prince*."

"A prince who will never wear a crown. And I'm fine with it. Kalle and Odin can fight it out between them."

"Do you think Kalle will step down?"

"I have no clue. I think deep down he wants to, but they've all got this thing called duty. Responsibility to the crown. Even Bo. Everyone but me. I don't have a duty. I don't have a role."

For a moment, I regret opening my mouth, because Stella is going to shoot me down and her words are always like the sharpest of needles, pricking me over and over and leaving little drops of blood. But then—

"It must be hard, growing up in your family."

"I—" I glance at her incredulously. "Sometimes."

Stella laughs quietly and sways toward me, brushing my arm with her shoulder. Standing like this with her makes me realize how small she is. Duncan is as tall as I am, but I could easily tuck Stella under my arm. "You thought I was going to say something mean, didn't you?" she asks.

She stays propped up against me and I try not to look concerned as I stare down at the top of her head. The scent of cinnamon is stronger. This behaviour seems almost affectionate, and while I'm not complaining, it's not usual Stella behaviour. "Well, that's what usually happens, isn't it?"

"I guess. This didn't seem the place for it."

"What does this seem the place for?"

We're alone on the balcony, Camille and Daphne somewhere in the house. I've been alone with Stella before, but it's never felt like this—like we're caught in a bubble that's shrinking and pushing us together.

It's not a bad thing.

It might be a good thing. Or not, if Stella decides to smack me in the face.

But I think it might be a very good thing because as Stella tips her face up, I find myself leaning down. Her lips part slightly and they're so close...

I'm not sure who is about to kiss whom, but it sort of seems like it's about to happen and the thought both terrifies me and—

Just as my mouth grazes her nose, heading to those lips, with a quick inhale, Stella pulls away.

Pulls right away; turns her head, turning her body so that she's facing the door. "You can't make a move on me here."

I have trouble catching my breath. "What gives you the idea I was making a move on you?"

She laughs again, but this time there's a note of bitterness in it. "It's what you do."

My heart plummets the two stories to the ground. "I don't. Not always. I haven't made a move on Daphne."

"Good. Don't. Although my mother would disagree. Daphne is in love with someone totally unsuitable and my mother wants her to transfer her affections to you," Stella rattles off, seemingly unconcerned about what almost happened.

What did happen? Did we almost... kiss?

"She thinks if you were to fall in love with her, everything would be perfect. Instant happily ever after for all," Stella continues and I finally focus on what she's saying. Her mother matchmaking me and Daphne?

"I—I see. I don't understand."

"You should definitely not fall in love with her."

I take a step away from Stella in the hope that distance might help clear my head because if I almost kissed her, that means—

I'm not exactly sure what that means.

"I have no plans to fall in love with Daphne," I say instead of giving in to the questions racing around my mind. "I had no plans to fall in love with anyone, but..."

The *but* hangs between us and I don't know if I should take it back or push forward. Stella turns to me, her eyes silvery, her face soft. I push forward. "I had fun with you today."

What am I *saying*?

"Me too." It's barely a whisper, but I hear her. Her cheeks flush and I know this time it's not the sun hitting her in just the right spot.

"I've had a lot of fun with you lately."

Stella's gaze flicks from my eyes to my mouth, and I see it. I see the expression on her face change like she's wondering the same thing I am—

If I lean forward, a little farther down, and press my lips against hers, so pink and soft…

How can her mouth look so soft when her words can be so sharp?

I don't mind the sharpness when she's calling me out on something. When I deserve it.

Not now. *Don't say anything now.*

I tilt forward, just a bit and that's all it takes.

Stella pushes off from the railing and steps away to the door. "I need to find Camille," she says in a rush.

"O-kay." Disappointment floods me. And embarrassment. Getting shot down before you get to shoot your shot is never a good thing for the ego. And when it happens twice—?

"I think maybe—" She stops, a foot before the door leading to the hallway. "I think you can do whatever you want," she says carefully. "In your family. Your father is a good man. A good king. And a great father, because he cares about all of you enough to give you the space to make your own decisions. He let you go away for years without having to be a prince because that's what you needed to find yourself. It can't be easy belonging to your family."

"You said that."

"I believe it. Spencer always said that when we would feel jealous of all the things you got to experience. And you could go on for years, playing at travelling and seeing the world and having fun, but if you don't want that, all you have to do is tell them. Decide what you want, who you want to be. If you want to be a prince, tell them. They'll help you find your duty, and give you responsibilities. You can save the world easier from the castle than I can from down below."

And then she's gone.

"I did tell them," I say into the empty space.

31

Stella

I FIND CAMILLE ON the second floor, giving Daphne a tour.

I wish I had to search through other floors to find them to get me further away from Gunnar and that *look* on his face. Because there's a serious argument between my head and other parts of my anatomy going on and I need to be far away from him.

Was he really about to kiss me? And why are those other body parts telling me it would be a *good* idea? A great idea. An idea that would be much better than any whale sighting in the Atlantic.

This is so not me.

"Everything okay?" Camille asks with a frown when I catch up to them in the hall. Can she sense the internal screaming match going on in my head?

Kiss him.

Nooo!

What does it matter? You've kissed him before.

It does matter because this is a different Gunnar—he's man-sized now and wears jeans that fit like that, *and with a mouth that I might enjoy getting to know better.*

You want to kiss him.

"Fine," I chirp, wide-eyed and breathing heavily in my haste to resolve the discussion inside my head that is in the process of messing me up.

Gunnar? Kissable?

"Were you with Gunnar?" Daphne also wears a frown, as well as one of Camille's sweaters over her dress. The mottled gray wool cardigan looks like something someone on a post-apocalyptic world would wear.

The grays and browns and beiges of Camille's wardrobe when she first arrived in Laandia have slowly been replaced with colours.

Colours suit her.

"No," I snap. "I mean, yes, but he was just giving me some cheese."

The frowns deepen. "Cheese is good," Camille says.

"Not when you don't want any cheese." But what if I do want... cheese? I don't even want to think about it. "He's—I was looking for whales."

"It's the right season for whale-watching, but mornings are usually better. Maybe if we fly low enough over the water you can see some."

"Isn't that dangerous?" Daphne asks. "Looking for whales from a plane?"

"We won't be that close," Camille says kindly.

She's been so kind to my sister. Is she hoping for a match between her and Gunnar like my mother is?

What would they think if they had seen what almost happened?

Nothing almost happened.

Prince Gunnar was *not* about to kiss me, because—why? Why would he want that? Why would I?

I don't. That's why I didn't. Not that he was going to.

I take a deep breath and tune back to what Camille and Daphne are saying. They're not actually saying anything, just looking at me strangely. "What are you guys up to?"

"Camille was showing me around," Daphne says. "It's a beautiful home."

Something twists in Camille's expression as she walks to the next door in the hall. "This the prefect's office." She swings open the door and I push past Daphne to get inside, to have more walls between me and Gunnar, still outside on the big balcony.

And then I look around. If a room could be grim and unsmiling, it would be this one. Cold, even with the west-facing windows and fireplace. Everything is dark gray or brown with heavy furniture and strange artwork on the walls. There are no bookshelves or papers out of place on the desk big enough to host a sit-down dinner for six around it.

"It will be mine when I take over as prefect," Camille tells us.

I really hope she gets a new interior designer.

And I can't tell from her tone if she's looking forward to that—to taking over as prefect for Saint Pierre.

From my research, I know the archipelago is under the formal jurisdiction of the French government but is overseen by the prefect of Saint Pierre, who has a certain amount of autonomy. Camille will take over that role after her father passes or steps down.

It can't be good for her mental health to look forward to a job she'll get in the event of her father dying. Same as Prince Kalle, but the whole country knows he doesn't want to be king.

"And your father's not here?" Daphne asks, looking around with ill-disguised alarm at the décor.

Camille hovers at the door. "No, the prefect is in Paris. In meetings."

"Why do you call him the prefect?" I ask before I catch myself. "I've never heard you refer to him as your father. Are things—I'm sorry," I say as her expression changes again. "That's none of my business."

"It's okay."

"No, it's not. I have my own father issues and it's not always easy to talk about them."

"It's not a father issue." Camille holds her breath for a moment. "He's not my father."

I didn't see that coming. "Oh. He's—"

"What do you mean, he's not your father?" Daphne demands with an uncommon lack of subtlety. "Who is your father?"

"I'm not actually sure," Camille says in a careful voice. "My mother—she didn't marry Lord Arnaud for love. She needed to be married to become prefect of Saint Pierre, same as me, so she found a suitable man, one who really wanted to be prefect."

"I don't understand—she had to be married?"

"It's an old, archaic French rule that says the prefect must be married in order to take authority and become a representative of the French government." She shakes her head. "Gotta love the French."

"I like the French," Daphne says.

"But not archaic French rules that leave a woman beholden to her husband," I point out.

Camille shrugs. "That's how it was and still is. My mother felt a duty to Saint Pierre and met and married Lord Arnaud to become prefect."

How it still is... Camille's alleged six engagements are starting to make sense. "Did you—that's why you and Odin...?"

"It was an arranged marriage," she confirms before a smile of pure happiness creases her face. "But not anymore."

"You were going to marry him so you can be prefect?" Daphne asks incredulously. "When you didn't love him?"

"It was complicated," Camille assures her.

"But she loves him now," I cut in.

"I do. Very much." Her smile says it all, makes *me* smile at the sight of it. Prince Odin and Lady Camille might have started out as an arranged pair, but it's clear that they will be getting married as two people in love.

"I don't understand." Daphne looks between us. "I've heard your love story. You were in love when you were younger, and when he was sent home from The Suitorette, you got back together."

Camille shifts nervously. "That's what we told the press, yes. We didn't want people to know that—"

"You lied."

"Daphne," I murmur, surprised at her outburst because Daphne doesn't burst at anything. "You don't know the whole story."

"No one does," Daphne says with a frown. "And I don't like the thought of my prince—You think that's okay? To get married when you're not in love?"

"It wasn't my first choice, but it was necessary. There are a lot of marriages like that," Camille tells her.

"Is that why you pushed back the wedding?" It makes sense now. When it was announced, only days before their planned wedding, that they would postpone the ceremony until June, the country flew into an uproar thinking the relationship of one of their princes was in danger. But maybe the relationship wasn't ready for marriage yet.

All I knew was that there was more to Camille's story than the castle was letting on, especially about her alleged six engagements.

Now that we're friendly, I can't wait to ask her about that, but not in front of Daphne because she's acting a little strange about it.

Camille nods in response to my question. "It was so we could have more time to get to know each other. Again. Because people change a lot in ten years. I think it helped." Another smile spreads over her face. "Because now, mine is a love match instead of an arranged marriage, and I'm so happy about that."

"So is all of Laandia," I point out with a grin.

"This happened to your mother, too?" Daphne queries. "She was supposed to marry a man she didn't love?"

"She had to marry him," Camille explains, sounding both wary and weary of the personal questions. "And they were—I have no idea what they were. But I do know she fell in love with another man while she was married. He was a fisherman, and he loved her very much, from what I heard. And she got pregnant with me.

Lord Arnaud knew but didn't say anything and raised me as his own. But my mother died before she could tell me the truth. I found out but there was no way to ask her anything about him. So—" She raises her hands in surrender. "I don't know who my father is, but it's not Lord Arnaud."

"Ah." There's not a lot to say to that, nor does it seem like Camille wants to. Daphne opens her mouth, but I put a hand on her arm. "That's sad."

"There's a lot of sad stories," Camille says briskly. "Why don't we go see if Madam Carol has dinner ready?"

Topic closed.

32

Gunnar

EVEN THOUGH I'M TEMPTED to chase after Stella, I don't. I'm not the chasing type.

Anymore.

Because I chased Kate for almost a year before she agreed to go out with me. She was Lyra's best friend and a constant presence in the castle. And I wanted her as my girlfriend, even when no one thought it was a good idea.

Considering how it ended, maybe I should have listened to them.

I can't believe I almost kissed Stella. Would everyone—my brothers, Lyra—think that was a bad idea too?

Maybe, considering her stepsister is my date for the wedding.

Right now, I wished I never asked Daphne for that favour.

When I come in from the balcony, plate with only crumbs and a cheese rind left in my hand, I hear female voices down the hall.

I go the other way.

The house is laid out in a square with a wide centre staircase, so I make my way around to the stairs without passing the room the girls are in, and head back down to the kitchen.

Madame Carol is back at the stove and greets me with a wide smile. "Not as hollow a stomach, now?" she asks, gesturing to the empty plate.

"All better now." Wiping her hands on a towel, Carol comes and takes the plate from me. "That smells incredible."

"Fish pie. And it's almost ready."

"Can I...?" Do anything, I want to ask, but I stop myself with the realization that I know nothing about helping in the kitchen. I don't spend much time in kitchens.

So why do I feel so comfortable in this one?

"You can open these for me," Carol says, motioning to the bottles of wine on the counter.

Three bottles for the four of us.

This might be a more enjoyable evening than I even expected, especially when I notice one of the bottles is a Barolo with a hint of dust.

"Seeing as the lord isn't with us, and that Lady Camille never brings friends around, I took the liberty of visiting the wine cellar. Hope you know what to do with those." She smiles again and I'm struck by the difference between her and Mrs. Theissen, who manages everything castle-related. Mrs. T would never find us wine.

In fact, she's been known to lock the wine cellar on occasion.

"Corkscrew, please?" I hold out my hand and prepare to be entertained.

Or entertain.

The girls soon join us and I get the sense Camille has spent a lot of time in here with Madame Carol.

There's a strange vibe as we take seats at the harvest table. As well as not spending much time in kitchens, I've also never eaten in one. I decide not to mention this tidbit, so as not to give Stella any more ammunition.

At first, I think it's Stella, that our moment on the balcony made it awkward. She takes the seat across from me rather than beside me and quickly holds her glass out to be filled.

And then I realize the vibe is coming from Daphne.

She sits beside me. Her phone isn't at the table but she's as preoccupied as if she were scrolling through social posts. Stella's words come back to me—Daphne is in love with someone but Stella's mother wants her to be in love with me.

Does Daphne know about the ulterior motives? Does she have other reasons for going to the wedding with me?

Camille is quiet for the first half of the meal, watching both Daphne and Stella with an almost nervous air.

And then, halfway through, Stella leans over to whisper something to her that has Camille relaxing.

Everything is fine after that.

Everything is great.

Madame Carol made a fish pie with a crust so flaky and delicious I can almost taste the pound of butter in the mix. She serves it with a salad of simple greens, but dessert is the crowning achievement—chocolate torte.

Camille insists that Madame Carol eats with us, and as the second bottle is opened, she starts to tell stories of Camille's childhood.

I can't imagine Mrs. Theissen ever being so funny.

Daphne doesn't eat dessert. I have such a sweet tooth that I never understand people who don't. Daphne could be full from dinner, or watching her weight, or allergic to cacao beans, but she gives none of those reasons. She only says *no, thank you* with a dismissive sniff that borders on rude.

Madame Carol doesn't say anything, but I catch the glance she gives to Camille.

Daphne also doesn't drink much of the wine, but I'm fine with that since it leaves more for the rest of us.

Despite the tension coming from Daphne, it's a fun evening. I laugh, eat good food, drink excellent wine. But the whole time, I'm conscious of Stella across from me, sleeves pushed up and smiling with those lips I wanted to kiss.

I still do, especially when she smiles.

I've read enough of Lyra's romance novels to know opposites attract and enemies do turn into lovers, but it's never happened to me. People like me. I attract people with similar interests—at least I did.

I have no idea if Stella is interested or attracted or anything but in loathe of me. She has never given any indication that she feels... well, anything.

But then, as I refill her glass, her silvery eyes meet mine and it's not her usual direct gaze. Instead, the gaze seems shy, almost timid; and Stella is never timid.

She's never looked at me with longing before, either.

I don't know if the lump in my belly is hope or fear, or possibly bad fish, but I gulp back an extra glass of wine to get rid of it.

After dinner, we sit around the table for some time. It's fun to find out more about Camille, and it's clear that she wants to spend more time with Madame Carol. But eventually, the older woman shoos us away so she can clean up and go to bed.

Camille takes us to a sitting room with a fireplace already lit to take away the chill in the air. One wall is taken up with book-shelves, and a stereo is in the corner of the room, complete with turn table and CD player.

"I spent a lot of time in here when I was growing up," Camille says, selecting a CD from a case. "And a lot of my music was retro."

She slots in the CD and "Wannabe" by the Spice Girls bursts into the room.

To my amazement, both Camille and Stella jump into an im-promptu dance party that lasts several songs until Camille collaps-es into a chair, laughing.

I'm happy to make myself comfortable on the couch with the bottle of wine.

"I love the records." Stella fingers through the stacks, long hair escaping from her bun and a glow of happiness on her face. "My mother got rid of most of mine years ago."

I wonder if music was as much a part of Stella's life as it was mine. It may have been years since Dad was in the band, and he's gone on to other interests, but there was always music at the castle. It was never a quiet place and the best was when he would break into song at the most random of times.

Was it like that for Stella too? Or when Duncan left, did he take the music away? I want to ask her. I want to talk to her about this and other things. Our fathers are as close as brothers, and once there had been a time it could have gone that way with us.

Not close like brothers, but *close*. Who knows what could have developed between us?

"I think I'll go to bed," Daphne says, pulling me away from my thoughts, which have become a little drunken from the wine. She stands awkwardly at the door, the sole person at the party not having a good time.

I should have made sure she was having a good time. Because I am the party prince.

"Stay for a bit," Stella urges, but Daphne shakes her head.

"It's been a long day. And I can find my own way," she adds when Camille offers to show her to her room. "Good night."

She smiles and quickly disappears. So much for making sure everyone has a good time.

"I think maybe..." Camile begins with a worried glance at the door.

"I have no clue what she thinks," Stella finishes. "But I'll talk to her tomorrow."

"What'd I miss?" I demand with concern.

"Camille told the true story of how she and Odin got together and Daphne seemed a little put out," Stella explains as she returns to the records.

"I just hope..."

I meet Camille's eyes and I know what she's thinking. That she and Odin have been so careful to cultivate their story of long-lost love and shared pasts, and if Daphne were to mention the truth—

"No," I decide. "You don't need to worry about it." I lower my voice, but Stella is still fixated on the shelves. "She's too nice to say anything."

"I think so too, but—"

"Look!" Stella interrupts, pulling a record off the shelf. "Oh, I loved this record." She holds it up so I can see the cover.

Not that I recognize it. "No clue who or what that is."

"Anne Murray. Canadian national treasure." The scorn is back in her voice, and it makes me smile, especially when she hugs the album to her chest. "How could you not know that?"

"If you say so. Play it," I suggest. "If you're cool with that," I add to Camille. "And if you know how to use a record player."

"Of course I know how to use a record player," Stella scoffs. The vinyl is out and set on the turntable before I can finish my mouthful of wine.

"It was my mother's," Camille says in a soft voice. "There was this one song..."

"This one?" Stella gently places the arm on the vinyl, and after a few scratchy seconds, a woman's voice follows.

And Stella starts to sing.

And oh—her voice.

Soft, with a touch of rasp like Miley Cyrus. I recognize the song and Stella's sound doesn't quite match it—a little higher and not as soothing, but the words sound amazing. She could make an excellent cover of it.

And watching her sing, swaying back and forth and able to catch a glimpse of this expression on her face...I can see Stella on the stage. I *want* to see Stella on a stage.

"Oh, my goodness, your voice," Camille cries, standing trans-fixed as Stella stands with her back to Camille like she's singing to the wall of books and records.

"What?" Stella cuts off, whirling around like she's done some-thing wrong.

"Don't stop, it's beautiful," she begs. "I've got chills. And I'm changing our wedding song to this."

"You can't do that," Stella protests with an embarrassed laugh.

"I can do whatever I want because I'm the one getting married. You convinced me. I forgot I loved this song so much because I stopped listening to it after my mother…" She swallows and presses her lips together. "Listening to her—you—being here. It has to be our song."

"Odin will understand," I tell her, getting up to throw an arm around Camille's shoulder. I know exactly how she feels. We've always had the losing-our-mothers card to draw us together but maybe it's stronger than I thought.

"You used to sing when you were younger," I say to Stella, transfixed by this hidden side of her.

"I still do, but never in front of people," she admits shyly. "It's not my thing."

"You need to make it *our* thing. Start from the beginning," I order. Because I can't ask Stella, I step back and hold my hand out to Camille with a low bow. "Can I have this dance?" I sing along to the chorus. I don't have the voice Stella does but Camille smiles and takes my hand.

The song starts from the beginning, and with my hand gently on her back, I guide Camille around the room as Stella sings, one song moving into the next. It's been a long time since I've danced like this, a slow waltz around the furniture, and while Camille stumbles more than a few times, she lets me lead her in the dance.

"You've got some moves," Camille compliments as Stella starts the third song, having found the lyrics on the sleeve inside the cover.

"I should hope so."

After Mom died, we all did our best to take care of Lyra. It was easier focusing on our little sister rather than our own grief.

Kalle provided the alcohol for her and the means to drink it without getting caught. Odin took her for walks, tried to get her to talk, and when that didn't work, let her beat the stuffing out of him with his swords. Bo really took one for the team and let Lyra paint his nails while suffering with all kinds of face masks.

I danced with her.

With Mrs. Theissen's help, I arranged for a dancing instructor to come to the castle three times a week for the entire summer after Mom died. We did ballroom dancing. Lyra took hip hop, jazz, and basic ballet and I was her partner in all of them.

So I do have some moves.

I hope Stella notices.

33

Stella

I'M NOT SURE WHAT feels stranger: singing in front of people or watching Gunnar dance with Camille.

He moves so gracefully across the floor. It doesn't surprise me—dancing well should be a princely thing to do. And Camille is a good partner for him.

I wouldn't be a good partner.

It wouldn't be a princely thing to dance with me.

I stop after the fourth song, not because I don't want to continue, but because I'm feeling emotions I don't want to deal with, especially not after the wine I've drank.

Things seem on edge with Gunnar and me after what happened on the balcony and I'm not sure if I want to tip over that edge yet. And I don't want the wine to make my decision for me.

Those three bottles we drank have made me sing and feel. I should stop drinking.

I lift the arm off the record. "That's it for me."

"Your voice is amazing," Camille cries.

I snap my mouth shut. "I don't sing anymore." I flash to singing lessons, arranged by my father over my mother's protests because he said I had talent. I used to think it was what he was most proud of, and I embraced it—when he was there. We would sing duets, with him playing his old acoustic guitar.

Like he knows what I'm thinking, Gunnar leans back against the couch. "You and Dunc used to sing. Remember that?"

I remember everything I did with my father but I'm not about to tell Gunnar that. "No."

"What happened with you and your father?" Camille asks, blunt as a sledgehammer.

I slide the album back onto the shelf. "He stopped being my father."

"Stella. How can you say that?" Gunnar's voice has more remorse than accusation, but I don't want to hear either.

"Because it's the truth. He picked your father—all of you—over his family. When that happened, he stopped being my father."

"He didn't pick us."

"He moved out of our home into the castle. That's him picking you."

"He only moved in with us after your mother told him to get out."

I turn to glare at Gunnar. "She never told him to do anything."

Gunnar lifts his hands. "I don't want to get you upset and I'm not saying you're not telling the truth, but do you know the whole story?"

"Do you?" I snap. I pick up my glass of wine with a shaky hand and drain it. I see the sadness in Duncan's expression, hear the scorn in Lyra's voice. Even Sophie seems to know more than I do. To want to know more.

Why haven't I wanted to know?

It's not like me to blindly follow someone but that's exactly what I've been doing. I took everything my mother said as gospel and I didn't question a thing.

That's not like me, but why has it taken me this long to snap out of it?

"No, but I heard Duncan's side of it," he says. "And I hate to say, it's a lot different than what you think it is."

Again, Gunnar seems to read my mind as he lifts the bottle and offers it to me. So much for not drinking more—I nod and he gives me a generous pour. Camille perches on the arm of a chair, leaving a wide expanse of couch for me to sit on.

Beside Gunnar.

There is a cushion between us, but it's not a big cushion. And maybe it's the very nice wine I've had, but I don't think I'd mind if it was a bit smaller.

"What did he say to you?" I ask reluctantly.

"Nothing to me, but Lyra..." He smirks. I'm so glad he finds this amusing. "She was furious when Duncan left your mom. Said it wasn't fair to Sophie—and you. Or for Spencer to lose his sisters."

"Duncan left my mom," I repeat with a sneer. "You just said it."

"Yes, but *why*? That's what you need to know."

I give my glass of wine a dirty look meant for Gunnar. Why does he have to be *right*? It's annoying.

"Were Lyra and your sister friends?" Camille asks, caught up in Lyra stories, as a way to get to know her soon-to-be sister-in-law.

"Best friends," Gunnar supplies. "When they were little, the three of them were inseparable. Sophie, and Lyra, and Kate."

"Kate never said anything about that," Camille muses.

And I almost forgot about it. My sister and I lost our father and our brother when our parents split up, but Sophie lost her best friend. And I lost...

I glance sideways at Gunnar, but thankfully he doesn't notice.

"She's never understood what happened between them," Gunnar continues. "One day they were running wild through the castle dungeons and the next, Sophie wasn't allowed to step foot inside. And then she wasn't allowed to see Lyra. Because Kate was always with Lyra, she never saw Sophie."

"She could have made the effort," I say stiffly.

"She was ten. You don't know how to make an effort when you're ten."

"What did Lyra say?" I ask, jolted at the resurfaced memory of my sister's crumpled face when our mother refused to let her see her friends.

"She yelled at Duncan one night. Little Lyra marched up to Duncan and told him it wasn't fair to Spencer to lose his sisters like she lost her friend, so he had to make it better."

Camille smiles. "I don't know her very well, but that sounds like Lyra."

"Duncan got down on his knees on the floor, because he's so tall, and told Lyra that, no, it wasn't fair. He said he wanted nothing more than to make it better but he was no Harry Potter, and he didn't know magic. Lyra was really into Harry Potter back then," Gunnar adds.

I smile sadly. "So was Sophie."

"Duncan said—and I remember this—it was hard when someone stopped liking you. That you can be with someone and love them, but if they stop liking you, then there's nothing you can do about it."

"He said my mother stopped liking him? That's how he explained it?"

"To a ten-year-old."

"Did he mention that she may have stopped liking him because she never saw him because he was at the castle all the time?"

"Lyra actually accused him of that." Gunnar laughs.

"This isn't funny."

"No, it's not," Gunnar agrees, his face smoothing into seriousness. "But the memory of Lyra stomping her foot and telling Duncan he was mean was. She said exactly that—that your mom must have stopped liking him because he lived here. Duncan told us he wanted to be at home with you and Sophie, but he wasn't allowed. He said he was at the castle with Spencer because he didn't have anywhere else to go."

"That doesn't prove anything."

"It kind of proves that your mother was the one who asked him to leave."

I stare into my glass of wine like the answers are there.

They're not. To find out what happened between my parents, I'm going to have to ask them the tough questions. Both of them.

It's time. Past time.

I can feel Gunnar's eyes on me but I don't look up. "I think that's enough of the heavy stuff," he suggests. "How about a game?"

"We might have Monopoly upstairs," Camille says.

"I was thinking something different."

I give him a quick glare. "Not Truth or Dare."

I'm not being dared to kiss him again. It's one thing that I'm sitting beside him, quite another for him to repeat his move from earlier—the one where he was about to kiss me.

I know he was. Only I don't know what to do about it now.

For a casual evening hanging out with friends, there are a lot of heavy thoughts swirling in my mind tonight. I do not need to dwell on almost-kissing-me Gunnar.

He makes it very difficult though, with his smiles and his dimples and the close proximity on the couch—he could bounce over a cushion and be sitting leg to leg with me.

He's not going to do that, though, is he?

It's bad enough I can smell the Gunnar scent from here. I hate that it's a nice Gunnar scent.

He chuckles, and I really hope he can't read my mind, even though I suspect he's remembering that game as much as I am right now. "Aw, you're no fun. How about Never Have I Ever?"

"I don't understand." Camille reaches for the wine bottle.

"Let me explain." Gunnar doesn't seem as affected by the closeness as I seem to be, so I inch closer to make him notice. And then I change my mind and lean away from him. "Like, I would say— 'Never have I ever kissed a woman', and then of course I would drink because I've kissed a few women in my time. But if you've kissed a woman, then you get to drink."

He looks expectantly at us.

"Wouldn't it be easier to ask if we've ever kissed a girl before? Since that's what you're trying to find out?" I demand.

"What's the fun in that?"

"I want to go first." Camille slides down the arm of the chair and ends up sprawled with her legs dangling over the other arm.

"Never am I ever going on a plane. Never." She pauses. "I think I said that wrong."

"Never have I ever flown in a plane," Gunnar corrects. "Drink for that one, Stella."

I've been in a plane. I can now say I've been to another country and that makes me happy. "I can drink because I've been in a plane!" I take a big gulp of wine.

"Maybe we shouldn't drink wine for this," Gunnar mutters.

"No, we should because it's my father's wine and he never lets me touch it." Camille takes a mouthful for emphasis. "Your turn, Stella."

"What about me?" Gunnar complains.

"You'll ask something inappropriate," I point out. "Never have I ever been in love."

I don't know why I ask that, or why I hold my breath waiting for Gunnar to take a drink.

He doesn't. Camille does, but both mine and Gunnar's glasses remain untouched.

"Nope," he says.

"You've never been in love before?" Camille asks with surprise. "You're lying."

"Hey, I like to drink wine. And I don't lie."

"But Kate?"

"Okay, maybe," he relents. "But that was a long time ago and it would be different if I was in love now."

"Of course it would be. Every time you fall in love it's different," I say.

"You sound like you know what you're talking about, and yet I noticed you didn't take a drink," he points out.

"I just know."

"Because you know everything?"

"I thought you were supposed to be nice to me," I cry before remembering that it was Camille who made the request. But a look at Camille and how she's trying to aim the remote control at the stereo suggests she's not paying attention to me and Gunnar.

"Okay, new one," I say. "Never have I ever lied. But I guess you could just lie about that."

"Are you trying to call me a liar?"

"If the shoe fits."

The way Gunnar stares at me, like he's got one last turn at Wordle and doesn't have a clue, is disconcerting. Also, it makes me feel guilty, something I rarely feel about Gunnar.

"I'll tell you one time when I lied," he finally says. "Something no one knows about."

Camille leans forward and rubs her hands together. "And that's the purpose of the game, isn't it?"

"What did you lie about?" I demand, feeling the first flicker of vindication that Gunnar is about to prove me right, as well as the faint disappointment that he's going to prove me right.

To be truthful, it's more than a little disappointment.

"When I was with Kate—remember?"

"I don't remember because I didn't know you then, thanks to your brother for blowing me off ten years ago. Oops!" Camille slaps a hand across her mouth and giggles. "Maybe I shouldn't say that out loud."

"He did blow you off, so it's not like *you* told a lie," I assure her. "You lied to Kate?"

I should be offended on behalf of Kate, like I was when I sent her the picture of Gunnar with Mabel, but the disappointment lies heavy instead.

"I never lied to Kate." Gunnar holds up a finger as if he's correcting me. "I let her believe that something happened with me and Mabel Crow, and it never did."

I force myself to blink. Then again. Why is he talking about this now? "But there was a picture of you at her house," I say slowly.

"It was a picture of me standing on her front steps, taken by someone who clearly had no idea what I was doing there and just wanted to make trouble."

I hold my breath but he doesn't continue. He doesn't know it's me who saw him and took the picture. That it was me who didn't know why he was there but jumped to the assumption that he was cheating on his girlfriend.

A very bad feeling starts in the pit of my belly and starts to spread. "Why were you there then?" I manage.

"I can't tell you that, but it had nothing to do with Mabel," Gunnar says. "And that's the truth."

"Why wouldn't you tell her nothing happened?" Camille wants to know. "Kate told me the story. That's what broke you two up."

Gunnar takes a long time to answer. "I hated hurting her," he says finally. "Seriously, that was the worst thing ever. But staying quiet about why I was there meant that I could protect someone, and I felt that was more important than my relationship with Kate."

"That's not fair to Kate," I tell him.

"No, but she never really gave me a chance to explain, either. She didn't ask me about it, but went ahead and accused me because she chose to believe what the picture was trying to say. I don't think that was very fair to me, and it showed me that our relationship wasn't all that I thought."

The sick feeling inside me spreads, not only because of the familiar guilt of being the reason they broke up, but because Kate's story sounds too much like my own.

I accused and refused to listen.

"I don't think I want to play this game anymore," I say.

34

Gunnar

I DON'T UNDERSTAND WHY Stella runs.

One minute, she was smiling and happy—I think she was happy—and *singing*. Stella sang and I know that was a big thing for her. I know the wine helped, but there's more.

She was comfortable. She was happy.

And that makes me happier than I could have imagined.

This thing with Stella—and yes, it is a thing because I admit I was about to kiss her on the balcony—confuses me. But maybe it shouldn't. Maybe I should just run with it, because that's worked for me in the past.

I need to stop overthinking because clearly, Stella is doing that enough for the both of us.

She ran when I tried to kiss her, and that should tell me something, like she's not ready for it.

I'll wait.

But I don't get why she ran now.

Was it something I said? Talking about Kate?

Or is she just tired? Maybe it's as simple as that because Camille seems ready to call it a night too. I take the wine bottles and glasses back to the kitchen while she turns the lights off and activates the security system.

That in itself is a novelty to me because the castle doesn't have a security system. And there's always someone awake after I come home to turn the lights off.

Little things like that bring it home that growing up as a prince is different.

Up in the guest room that Madame Carol assigned me, I take a few moments to look around. It's a simple room—bed, desk, dresser, armchair in the corner—decorated with quality in mind, but it's tired. The colours and styles might have been popular twenty or thirty years ago, and confirms what I already knew: there weren't a lot of visitors here when Camille was growing up.

I'm glad we came. I'm glad we stayed over because I feel like we were a breath of fresh air for this house.

I've moved to the window, staring at the lights of the town, when the knock sounds at the door.

It's so quiet that for a moment, I think I've imagined it. But she knocks again and I lunge for the door because somehow, I know it's Stella.

"Forget to say goodnight before you ran off?" I open the door with the smile that gets me into trouble more than it gets me out of it.

Stella stands far enough away from the door as if she knocked and then took a step back, so I lean against the doorjamb to be closer.

"No." Still frowning, still dressed in her shorts and sloppy sweater; so wherever my male mind went at the sound of a late-night knock, this gives me a kick back to reality.

"Can I help you with something then?" A bigger smile because this means that maybe…

"No," she says automatically.

Now she has me frowning. "Then why are you here?"

Stella takes a deep breath. Whatever this is, it must be good if she needs deep-breath preparation.

She started singing on a whim; she took a deep breath to talk to me.

"Yes, I need something," she manages, "but not *that*."

"What's *that*?"

"That." She motions between us. "*This.*"

My heart soars like the first time I took off in a plane but since Stella looks so miserable at the thought, I feign confusion just to get a rise out of her. "I don't understand."

She huffs with frustration until she notices my smirk. "You!"

My grin widens. "Yes, me. Waiting patiently to find out what I can help you with."

Stella's shoulders slump and she rubs the hem of her sweater with clearly nervous fingers. "I need to tell you something."

"I'm waiting with bated breath."

Maybe I'm wrong; maybe this *thing* is going somewhere. Maybe this late-night knock on the door is what my male mind jumped to. Maybe—

"I broke up you and Kate."

I pull my wandering mind back and focus. "Excuse me?"

"I'm the one who saw you with Mabel Crow that night. I took the picture and sent it to Kate."

This is not what I expected. I'm not even sure what it means, or how to respond.

It was Stella? She refused to speak to me for years, and when I had finally gotten over that and found something with Kate, she took it upon herself to ruin it? Why would she do that? That doesn't sound like—

It kind of *does* sound like Stella.

"Why?" I finally ask.

"Because I'm mean. And nasty, and I wanted to hurt you." Her voice, so beautiful when she sang, rings hollow with anger now, so I know she's telling the truth.

Wow. "No, you're not," I tell her instead of giving voice to my inner thoughts.

"I did want to hurt you," she argues.

"Because you were hurt," I explain. "By your father, and you took it out on me because you blame us for taking Duncan from you." The reasoning is clear to me, which tempers the anger that should have spouted.

I should be furious, but I'm not.

Stella blinks, clearly not expecting *that*. "But I broke you up. You loved her."

"I told you that I didn't know if I was in love with her."

"But you cared about her."

"I did. I do. But I cared about you, too, Stella." I shrug a shoulder. "Maybe I still do."

"That doesn't make it okay."

"No, but it helps me understand why you might have done it."

"Still—"

"Do you want me to be upset with you? Do I think it was a crappy thing to do? Yes, I do. But I took a risk going to Mabel's that night. If it hadn't been you, someone else would have seen me and splashed it around town."

"There was no one else around!"

I laugh because Stella seems so earnest. And angry that her admission isn't bringing the response that she expected. "You keep trying to argue with me."

"But I did something wrong."

"And you clearly feel a great deal of guilt and remorse, or you wouldn't be here, outside my bedroom door in the middle of the night."

Stella's gaze flicks to my mouth before dropping to the ground. I didn't imagine that—she looked at my mouth, which you do when you want to kiss someone.

I take that as a win but know now it's not the time for the smile of satisfaction.

"It's not that late," she mutters.

"You're outside my room," I remind her. "I was about to go to bed. I need some sleep before I fly you all back home, and here you are, keeping me awake."

"I'm sorry," Stella bleats, taking a big step back. "I thought I needed to—"

"Stella." I reach for her hand and catch her fingers in mine. "I'm messing with you. Joking."

"You don't joke with me," she protests.

"I banter. Argue. Why can't I joke?"

But Stella's expression pulls me back into seriousness. "Gunnar. Just tell me you hate me and get it over with."

"But I don't," I admit. "And while I would have a different reaction if you'd told me this years ago, Kate and I broke up a long time ago and you just heard me say that this was for the best. Thank you for telling me, because I've always wondered. But as for hating you..." I tug her closer. "Lately, I've been thinking maybe it's the opposite."

"The opposite of hate is indifference." Stella stumbles a step toward me.

"Is it? I thought that was love," I say in a low voice, leaning closer.

"Why can't it be hate, too?" she whispers.

I huff out a laugh. "You really need to stop arguing with me."

"You won't like it if I do," she stammers.

"Do you mean I won't like you?"

"Why would you?"

We stand a foot apart in the hall, her fingers still in mine. If we both lean forward, we could meet in the middle. Or I could take a step—

She could take a step—

I study Stella's face: the flashing silver-gray eyes that are more greenish when she laughs. I made her smile today. I listened while she sang. I stood there while she confessed her crime, and I'm *still* here, holding her hand.

But I don't think she'll take that step toward me. She might not mind if I do, but it should be her.

It needs to be her. I was ready to shoot my shot earlier, so it's her turn next.

"Do you want a list of reasons why I would like you?" I counter. "I'm happy to tell you, but I really don't think you'd hear me tonight even if I told you." I bring her hand to my mouth and softly kiss one of her knuckles before I drop it. "There's a lot going on in that head of yours tonight. Come see me when you're ready to listen."

"I don't—what?" Confusion mars her pretty face, along with what might be fear.

"Good night, Stella. I'm not angry with you for the part you played in Kate and me breaking up. It was a long time ago, and I've moved past it. You should too." I smile ruefully. "You should move past a lot of things."

I take a long step back into the bedroom and gently close the door. "Goodnight."

35

Stella

I DO NOT LIKE apologizing.

Especially when the person takes it as calmly as Gunnar. I tell him I caused the break up with the love of his life and he still looks at me like he wants to kiss me.

What?

Why?

How can he want that? Want me?

And why do I want the same thing?

36

Gunnar

IT'S A QUIET FLIGHT home.

Stella sits beside me but there's none of her questions that peppered the trip to Saint Pierre. Instead, she stays silent.

I bet it takes a lot out of her to be quiet, especially with me.

I catch her looking at me more than a few times and can't help but wonder what's going on in her head.

I could have kissed her last night. I think she would have let me, but the memory of her walking away when we were on the balcony sticks to me like gum on the bottom of the shoe. I could have kissed her, and she would have let me, but I didn't know how she'd feel about it today.

Stella isn't a late-night kiss type of girl. She's a morning type when the sun shines and turns everything golden. She's a late afternoon, with the hint of coffee on her breath and her hair mussed from playing with the dogs.

She's one to kiss all the time, at least that's how I feel this morning. And, to be honest, I've been feeling that way for a long time.

It's an awkward trip back to Battle Harbour, at least for me, seeing as I'm doing all the heavy thinking about Stella with her sitting so close beside me in the cockpit.

"Thank you for that," Camille says after Minka picked us up at the airport and we dropped Stella off at the shelter, and Daphne at home so she can change before she has to go to work. "I hope it wasn't too horrible."

"It wasn't horrible at all." Even if it had been, I would never confess it to Camille. Unlike Stella, I don't say all the bad things that pop into my mind. There's no point.

But yesterday wasn't horrible at all.

"You seem to have called a truce with Stella."

The image of us on the balcony sweeps through my mind, of me leaning in and her moving away. Saying that it sweeps into my mind is a lie—it hasn't left. Last thing I thought about before I fell asleep, first thing I thought about when I woke up this morning.

Am I wrong about Stella? Does this go both ways? There's something about Stella; she twists me into knots for the fun of it.

"Yeah." Because there's nothing else to say to Camille about it. I need to speak to Stella first, but the ball is in her court.

"You're getting along with Daphne," Camille presses on. Maybe she's going somewhere with this.

I think I know where she's going with this.

"A troll would get along with Daphne. Doesn't mean I'm falling in love with her."

"I didn't expect you would."

I lift an eyebrow. "Really?"

"She's a lovely girl, but there's not... much... there. Is there? Am I not seeing the whole Daphne?" The Daphne who was quiet and off last night had vanished this morning, back to smiles and scrolling on her phone.

I shrug ruefully. "I have no idea about the whole Daphne. Nor am I in much of a hurry to find out. I think she'll be a great addition to your wedding party though."

"I should have made the time to make more friends," Camille says in a small voice.

"Hey! None of that." I turn in the seat to face her, alarmed at the sadness on her face. "You've been a little busy organizing a wedding. As well as Odin's life."

"It's never been easy for me to make friends," she admits. "Even when I had the opportunity, which wasn't often, I'd always mess it up."

"You haven't messed this up."

"This?"

I point between us. "You and me. We're friends."

"Really?" Camille's smile is the sun pushing its way from behind a cloud and it transforms her face. Not that I paid much attention to her physical attributes—ours is a platonic friendship only—but I can't deny Camille is a beautiful woman. It's not a traditional beauty but it's there. And when she smiles like that, it's hard not to think of her as an incredible-looking person.

"Of course! You didn't think we were friends?"

"I don't know what to think. I thought you were just really friendly. Or bored. Or that Odin asked you to babysit me."

I laugh out loud. "While I would do that for O if he asked, he didn't. Just between you and me, I think he's a little jealous of me getting so much of your time. But this goes above and beyond simple babysitting, don't you think? This isn't a ten-bucks-an-hour job here."

"Is that how much babysitters make?"

"I hope it's more. I have no idea. I've never had a job." I turn to her in bewilderment. "I've never had a job. I'm twenty-six years old and I've never had a job."

Just saying that out loud makes me feel so... *lazy*.

"I've never had a job either. At least not one that pays me."

"How can you say that? You run SealSave. You run Saint Pierre, or at least you're going to."

"I really hope I get paid for that," she says primly.

"Me too. But back to the friends issue—we're friends. In fact, next to Fenella, you've become one of my best friends. So get used to me being around and dropping in at the prefect's house for Madame Carol to feed me."

"Okay." There's that smile again. "Okay."

"I even would have been your bridesmaid if you wanted. Brides-man, we could call it."

"But that would have messed up the numbers."

"Numbers aren't that important, you know?"

Camille rolls her eyes. "They are to Mrs. Theissen."

"That is true." We share a knowing look. "But at least you got Daphne, who will be a perfect bridesmaid and behave herself all night long. And maybe even keep me in line."

"I don't expect you to be kept in line," she says with a smile.

"Good, because I don't know how to do that. This is my big brother's wedding, the first for the castle. I think we're all ready to have a good time."

"Is this going to be like when you took me to Kalle's pub and got me drunk?"

"I don't recall getting you drunk," I pick my words carefully and try to hide my grin. "But I did make some helpful suggestions on how you could go about doing that."

"Screech is a helpful suggestion?" Camille laughs. "I seriously hope any other suggestions you may have go over a bit better. I had such a headache the next morning."

"Yes, and his name is Odin," I tease and Camille leans against me as she laughs.

I wonder if it will ever be this easy with Stella.

I'd like it if it was.

37

Stella

I DON'T SEE GUNNAR at all after we get home from Saint Pierre.

Not that I was hoping to. Or expecting to, but I just thought... maybe. I thought he might stop in to see Mama Dog and the puppies. Or I'd bump into him at Coffee for the Sole. Or...

Despite what he said, Gunnar might really hate me for taking the picture and I'll never talk to him again. After thinking it over, he might resent me for ending his relationship and hate me forever.

The thought is... distressing. I hate to say it, but I don't want to never talk to Gunnar again. And I don't want him to hate me. Now that I'm over my... my whatever it was I felt for him, I really don't want Gunnar to start hating me.

At least not until I figure out what this new thing I feel for him is.

I spend most of the time that week with the dogs, doing my best to think of ways not to be distressed.

Do you want a list of reasons why I would like you? Come see me when you're ready to listen.

Is that Gunnar trying to be cryptic? And what am I supposed to do if I want the list? Pull up at the castle door and demand for Gunnar to tell me why he likes me?

Hard no.

The day of the wedding rehearsal, I meet Sophie at Coffee for the Sole as usual. Daphne has the day off; she's currently at Tips and Toes, the salon in town, getting her nails done. Then she's off to get her brows and armpits waxed, according to Sophie.

Her facial was this morning.

There's a lot of work that goes into being a bridesmaid.

I glance at my bitten nails and don't want to think about the state of my armpits.

"Have you seen Gunnar since you've been back?" Sophie asks, pushing the plate with the pretzel across the little table. The town is busy with the influx of people and paparazzi here for the wedding, and most of them seem to have discovered Silas's coffee. The queue stretches all the way outside and Sophie was only able to snag one of the tiny two-seat tables by the door.

"Why would I want to see Gunnar?" I snap, breaking off a piece of the salty pastry.

"Because... oh, are we repressing everything that happened now?"

"I'm not repressing anything," I tell her a little too vehemently.

"You're not admitting it."

"I shouldn't have said anything to you." But I did. Of course I did. I came home and told Sophie all about the trip, about Gunnar flying and the seals and the drinking game. I told her I sang and confessed to breaking up Gunnar and Kate—which she didn't know about either—and that I thought Gunnar was about to kiss me.

I didn't tell her about how I felt about that because I didn't know myself.

I didn't need to tell her anyway, because Sophie went on a bit of a tangent and started spouting out all these *what ifs*. I tuned her out because I was having a problem with all my own *what ifs* and didn't want to add hers to my pile.

"You should always say something to me! But in this case, you should also say something to Gunnar."

I look at her with confused eyes. "And what, pray tell, should I say to Gunnar?"

"Get over here and try and kiss me again!" Sophie cries with delight. I hunch my shoulders and try to hush her.

Silas looks over with a raised eyebrow at Sophie's outburst.

"If I wanted to kiss him, I wouldn't need to wait for him to make a move," I tell her, hoping for a modicum of dignity.

Though I think I lost that when I admitted it had been a mistake to walk away from him. But it's over. Done with. "We're not talking about that anymore."

"There's still the wedding tomorrow. You could be there, looking gorgeous. He'll be there, and we all know what he looks like in a tuxedo. Hot AF."

"Did you honestly just say Prince Gunnar was hot AF? Using the letters, not the words?"

"Well, he is. And it doesn't seem right saying *as...*" She mouths the F-word because we were brought up never to say it.

"But *you* can't think that if *I* think that."

"I can so think that! I just can't act on it, and I never would. Not that Gunnar would be my type. He's too nice. I'd go for someone like Kalle." She smiles dreamily at the window as if Kalle, serving beer at his pub across the square, could see her.

"You've always liked the grumpy guys."

"It's because I'm little Miss Merry Sunshine," Sophie says in a grumpy voice.

"You are nicer than even Daphne," I point out. "If you got together with someone like Gunnar, that would be an overload of cheerfulness."

"Exactly. It would be too much. Opposites attract is always the best trope. Like you and Gunnar."

"We are not a trope."

"What are you then?"

"We're nothing." I make a slashing motion with my hand for emphasis.

"That's quite the protest of something you're not anything of."

I look up to see Silas collecting mugs from the next table. "Are you going to the wedding tomorrow?" I ask him, thinking it would be nice to see a friendly face there.

If I go. I still haven't decided if I want to be there. Or if anyone wants me there.

"I don't know," Silas says slowly. "I got invited and I really like Camille, but..."

"No one to go with?" I guess.

"I know lots of people who are going but—"

"Take me!" Sophie practically bounces on the seat. "I don't have an invite and I really, really want to go."

"I was going to suggest we go together," I protest.

Sophie points her finger at me with a stern expression. "You are not going with Silas. Or anyone. You are taking Ajax, and you are leaving yourself wide open for anything to happen."

"Nothing is going to happen," I say into my coffee.

"Don't be too sure about that," Sophie argues. "Because—Dad."

I groan. "Soph, I don't have the bandwidth to deal with that right now."

"No," Sophie whispers, her gaze fixed to a spot behind me. "*Dad.*"

Heads turn in the coffeeshop.

Jem, standing at the frother, stares at the door until Leodie nudges her. She's staring wide-eyed as well, and even Silas—cheerful, easygoing Silas—looks affected, like he's about to break into a sweeping bow.

Duncan Laz is not royalty, but he looks like he should be, even more than King Magnus. He also still looks like he belongs on the cover of a romance novel, with the windblown hair and a jaw that looks like it was carved out of stone.

"What are you doing here?" I blurt as he approaches our table.

"Hello," Duncan says, looking awkwardly between Sophie and me. "I was planning on coming to the house tonight, but decided that might make your mother uncomfortable. And then Gunnar told me you'd be here around this time, so I thought..."

"Thought what?" I snap.

"We could talk."

Before I can take another bite at those words, Sophie lifts her cup. "Best coffee around. Can I get you one?"

"I haven't had coffee in years. The doctor told me—well, never mind that."

"What did the doctor say?"

Duncan—I'm not referring to him as Dad, not yet—seems surprised at my question. "Just that it wasn't the best for me. I am getting up there in years. Sixty-seven last month."

My father is on the cusp of seventy, and I had no idea. Or maybe I did and I didn't think. Or maybe—

"Thank you for the card," he says to Sophie, and my head spins toward her so fast I'm afraid it might break off.

"It's time we fix this," Sophie says without an ounce of contrition. "Can I get you a tea? Or they have nice lemonade."

"That sounds great." He smiles so warmly at her that it's like a battering ram against the high walls around my heart.

Sophie leaves before I can rip her head off because I don't like my walls battered. It's better they stay intact. "I didn't know you were that old. I mean, not that it's old but—" I fumble. "Never mind."

"It only feels that old in the mornings. I run in the morning and it gets tougher to start every year."

He runs. There is so much about this man that I don't know. I study him, trying not to seem like I'm staring. His thick hair falls to his shoulders, the strands a handsome silver. My father is a very attractive man and seems to get better with age, the lines on his face adding character, like layers in a painting. His silvery-green eyes—

He has my eyes.

I guess I have his. Sophie has always bemoaned her brown eyes, telling me I got the better eyes of the two of us, and I never considered where they came from.

From the man sitting across from me.

Duncan clears his throat and I whip my attention from his features to the dregs of coffee growing cold in my cup. "I understand you've been spending time with Gunnar."

"Is that a problem?" I'm quick to ask.

Is that a sigh? "Nothing is a problem, Stella, as long as you're happy. Are you happy?"

I narrow my eyes at him. "What kind of question is that? You haven't spoken to me in years, and the first thing you want to know is if I'm happy?"

He studies me with the same intent that I'm looking at him with. "Seems logical to me since that's all I've ever wanted for you."

"I've kind of been a chaperone for Daphne," I concede reluctantly, not wanting to get into the question of my happiness. "Her and Gunnar—"

"Are going to the wedding together," he finishes. "Why the chaperone? Gunnar is harmless."

I don't consider Gunnar harmless, but I let that one go.

"You used to be good friends with him," he adds.

"That was a long time ago."

"Sometimes it seems like a long time," Duncan says in a heavy voice. "And sometimes it feels like yesterday."

He sounds... sad. And I have no idea what to do with that.

Thankfully, Sophie takes that opportunity to slide back into her chair, setting a green tea lemonade in front of Duncan and a second coffee before me. "I thought you might need a refill," she says with an apologetic note in her voice.

"You thought right."

"Stell," she sighs. "Let's just hear him out."

"Easy for you to say since you're already sending him cards," I hiss.

"Only because you're so pig-headed and won't give him a chance when he clearly deserves it," she snaps back.

I suck in my breath; when Duncan laughs, I turn to him with fury. "Sorry, sorry," he says, hands raised. "You get the pig-headedness from me. Mag always says—"

"Thank you so much," I tell him sarcastically.

His shoulders slump. "Look, I'll just say what I came here to say and leave you in peace. It's about your mother."

I open my mouth, but Sophie lays her hand on mine and nods at him.

Duncan clears his throat. "When I left... I think she and I remember things differently."

"How do you remember it, then?" My voice is suddenly rough, hoarse, and I sip my coffee to break up the lump that has taken up residence in my throat.

"I've always been a hard worker," Duncan begins. "Working for the king was no different. Mag kept telling me to go home. 'You've got a young wife, babies,' he'd say. 'Get out of here.' But I found things to keep me occupied, things that needed to be addressed and finished because Magnus has a lot going on. Plus, your mother was often angry with me when I was home. She was so young and all she wanted to do was go out and have fun. Sometimes we'd leave the two of you with the castle nannies and I'd take her to St. John's, or Halifax, just to give her a change of scenery. I'm not sure if she wanted me home or just someone to do things with. She was, well, I think she was bored and looked to me to entertain her, but I couldn't do that all the time. She had friends, but she wasn't really close to them."

"She really isn't close to many people," Sophie says apologetically.

"She was good friends with the queen."

I remember the visits to the castle where Mom would drink tea with the queen and Sophie and I were left with the princes and Lyra. Those were fun times, but looking back, Mom never really seemed happy when we came home. There would be comments about the queen, not nice comments, and a tone in her voice that made me wonder how they were friends when it seemed Mom didn't like Queen Selene all that much.

"I don't think she was," I say. "I think she was jealous of the her."

From the expression on Duncan's face, I know I'm right.

"I'm not going to bring up things about your mother," he says diplomatically. "But it became obvious that I couldn't make her happy. She didn't want me to work at the castle, but she wanted to be seen as part of the inner circle."

"And when you left, she lost that."

Duncan shrugs. "I'm not sure what she expected would happen. Magnus and I have been friends since we were boys, and Signe—your mother—"

"Isn't always a very nice person," Sophie finishes. "I figured that out when she married Peter."

"So you're saying, that this—" —I point between Duncan and us— "—that this is *her* fault."

"Pretty much," he says with a rueful shrug.

Duncan sit and talks to us for an hour. He's careful not to say anything disparaging about Mom but enough to show that the rift between us was truly one of her making. I'm not sure if it was revenge or petty jealousy, but it was my mother's fault that we had no relationship with our father.

Just like Gunnar and Lyra, and even Sophie, implied. I was too stubborn and refused to see the truth.

With Duncan there, Sophie also takes the opportunity to share our worries about Daphne and Daulton. It's news to him and he doesn't seem happy about it. He promises to talk to Daulton, and from the tone of his voice, I doubt it will be a friendly discussion.

"Did you know all that?" I demand of Sophie after Duncan leaves. There are no hugs but I like to think I dropped some of the North Pole iciness when I said goodbye.

It's not perfect, but it's a start.

"That it wasn't really his fault? I've been piecing it together over the last couple of years."

"Why didn't you say anything to me?" I demand.

Sophie tilts her head and gives a knowing smile. "Would you have listened?"

"Probably not." I sigh ruefully. "I'd better get back to work. I didn't mean to be here this long."

"I texted Ajax when I got your drink and told them you might be a while."

I shake my head. "You surprise me sometimes."

"With my generous consideration and general awesomeness?"

"Because you've let me be a jerk about him for years."

"You weren't ready to hear what really happened."

Her words echo in my mind and her voice becomes Gunnar's. He knew what was going on in my head, that I wasn't ready for more.

That I wasn't ready to admit more.

Am I now?

"I think I am now," I tell her. "Ready, that is. Lately, I've been feeling—"

"Because of Gunnar," Sophie interrupts.

"This is *not* about Gunnar," I lie, more to myself than to my sister.

"It so is about Gunnar. You've figured out that you've been wrong about him, so that started you thinking about what else you've been wrong about."

"That surprises me too. That you're so smart."

She gives a happy sigh. "Finally, someone who appreciates my brilliance."

"I wonder if your brilliance can help me with a problem I have." She motions expectantly. "I need a dress for the wedding tomorrow."

Sophie's smile is brighter than the summer sun. "I already have the perfect dress for you."

38

Gunnar

"THIS WOULD BE A lot more fun if we did this after dinner," I grumble to Bo standing beside me at the front of the church. "And a couple of bottles of Dad's mead."

It's the third time we've run through the ceremony and Mrs. Theissen wears a frown as Lyra gallops down the aisle like a horse to join Edie, who tries not to laugh.

"I need a shot of whatever Lyra's got going on," Bo says under his breath.

"How hard is it to get married?" I wonder. "You walk in, say some stuff, do some kissing, and that's it. Odin seems like he's got the hang of it."

If getting the hang of it means he looks like he's about to be sent off to a penal colony for life imprisonment, then sure, he's got the hang of it.

"He looks scared," Kalle leans across Bo to point out.

"Is something going on with him and Camille?"

Kalle shakes his head. "They're as sickly sweet as ever. No, I think it's just this... thing."

"It's a big thing," Bo admits. "I'd be scared too."

"Especially since if it were you up there, you'd have to talk to a lot of people," I tease. "You do know you're going to have to talk to people tomorrow, right?"

"I'm fine with talking to people," he mutters.

Kalle looks between Bo and me. "Only when you want to."

"It's for O, so it's all good."

We glance over to Odin who shifts uneasily, never taking his eyes off the back of the church.

Our brother Odin is getting married tomorrow.

The first prince of Laandia to have the big church wedding, with invitations going far and wide and hotels in Battle Harbour have been booked solid for weeks.

Odin and Camille have gone for traditional, conversative, and with as much pomp and circumstance as Mrs. Theissen could give them.

And right now, neither of them looks very happy about that.

Is this the type of wedding I would want?

Bo nudges me as Daphne appears at the back of the church. "Your girl."

"She is not my girl," I whisper.

"I think she knows it too," Kalle hisses. "I saw her cozying up to Daulton before we started this."

"Daulton, as in married Daulton?" I watch Daphne glide down the aisle with more concern than I did the first and second times. Is that who Stella was talking about—*Daphne is in love with someone totally unsuitable*—when she warned me not to fall for her?

"I don't think he's still married. I haven't heard anything about a wife," Bo says.

"And how would you hear about a wife deep in the forest where you hide out?" Kalle teases, and I choke back a laugh. Not because it was a particularly good tease, but utter boredom has brought out my punchy side.

Daphne is almost at the end of the aisle in her simple yellow sundress, never taking her eyes off Odin at the front.

Which means she never glances at me. Not that I would want her to look at me, especially if she were looking with love-struck eyes, but no man wants to be completely ignored by a woman as pretty as Daphne.

And she does look pretty. Golden hair, yellow dress, her skin glowing with good health and June sunshine—she's the complete opposite of Stella.

Stella, with her multi-coloured hair and pale skin, all-black wardrobe and clunky shoes, tattoos dotting her shoulders.

I never asked about the tattoos.

I never asked if she changed her mind about coming to the wedding. She didn't give Camille an answer the other day, but an evasive response is different than a yes.

It's surprising how much I'd like her to come tomorrow.

It also makes no sense. Daphne is my date; I will be the perfect escort and dance when I'm instructed to and when the music moves me.

The music would definitely move Stella. Her voice still haunts me, rich and husky and—

I blow out my breath and Mrs. Theissen scowls at me.

Either Stella is giving me trouble or I get in trouble when I think about her.

"Is Stella coming tomorrow?" Bo asks in a low voice.

How does he know—? "I have no idea."

"I thought you've been hanging out with her?"

"I might have been, but I still have no idea what goes on in her mind."

"What's going on between the two of you?"

"What makes you think *anything* is going on with us?" I demand, forgetting to lower my voice.

"Prince Gunnar," Mrs. Theissen reprimands with her famous frown.

Daphne sweeps by, a questioning expression on her face. I should never have invited her. I should have made Camille pick someone, or bow out entirely. Having Daphne here makes me think of Stella and I still don't know *why* I think of Stella...

"I've always thought she was pretty cool," Bo whispers.

"Me too," I confess without thinking.

And there lies the problem.

Kate, as Camille's maid of honour, makes her way down the aisle, smiling at everyone. I'm happy to acknowledge I feel nothing for her when she glances at me, other than friendship and a desire for her to be happy.

Is that because of Stella too?

"Here she comes," Kalle hisses.

For a moment, all I can think is *Stella* and then I realize it's Camille at the back of the church, looking scared and tired and—

Camille's gaze meets Odin's and they both transform with smiles of love and happiness in their eyes. It's like Camille has a rope around her middle and Odin is slowly pulling her to him, but she's good with it. She wants to go to him.

Now they look happy.

They've been through a lot to get here, the eve of their wedding, and being a royal family, I'm sure there will be more challenges in store for them. But in this moment, their worlds have aligned to give them this—joy. Happiness.

Love.

This is the type of marriage I want.

39

Stella

Turns out Sophie bought me a dress for the wedding weeks ago.

"I hoped you'd change your mind, if only for Ajax's sake," she tells me as I model the dress—black, hitting just below my knees, fitted but not tight with a modest asymmetrical neckline and sheer sleeves.

It's exactly what I would have bought for myself, if I'd gone shopping three days ago.

I crane my head to see the back view in the full-length mirror. The mirror came with the house and it's a little warped, but we use it to play with the puppies. It's cute when they bark at their reflection. One of the videos I took went viral and all six in the litter were adopted in days.

I had no desire to talk to my mother, so after meeting with Duncan, I went straight back to the shelter to finish my shift and Sophie met me here with the dress.

"They were very excited when I told them I was going," I admit, smiling at the memory of six-foot-tall Ajax jumping up and down in the middle of a pen of just as excitable puppies.

"I knew you'd change your mind," Sophie says.

"You just said you *hoped*."

"Yes, well, you've been spending enough time with Gunnar lately that I thought you'd be so furious with him that you'd want to show up to spite him."

I make a face at my sister. "That makes no sense."

"It totally does, if you really think about it. You stopped talking about travelling to spite Dad. Duncan. Only it backfired because he had no idea you were doing that. Gunnar would assume you'd never go because you hate him, so you'd go. Perfect Stella logic."

I hate to admit she's right. And I'm also not going to admit that, for once, I'd like to wear a little colour to the wedding.

"I don't hate him," I say instead. "Gunnar."

"It was a toss-up between him and Dad. Duncan. What should we call him?"

I used to call him Daddy, but that was when I was twelve. "Lord Laz," I suggest with a sarcastic twist.

"But I thought you—"

"I listened. Looking at it, he's probably right. Mom can be—"

"Mom," Sophie finishes.

"But that doesn't mean we can repair the lack of relationship of fourteen years in an afternoon over coffee. Which he doesn't even drink. Did you know that? We know nothing about him."

"Yes, but it's a start. And we can learn."

I don't know what to say to that. I don't know what to say about any of this. Along with the very confusing thoughts of Gunnar running through my head, I now have to figure out what kind of relationship I'd like with my father. *If* I want a relationship with him.

I'm leaning toward thinking that I might.

But nothing needs to be decided tonight.

"I might dye my hair." I pull a thick hank over my shoulder. The green is still vibrant, but the purple is fading. There are some pink strands throughout, but it could use a touch-up.

"Same colours?"

"I thought maybe... brown." I meet Sophie's gaze in the mirror, shift to her hair pulled back into customary ponytail. Her hair is a rich, deep brown with a hint of red. Mahogany hair, someone called it. My natural colour is the same, even though it's been years since I let the dye grow out.

It's the same colour as Duncan's hair, before he went silver.

Sophie smiles. "Maybe we can cut some of it too. Why don't you get changed and we'll go get a box of dye? And grab some fish and chips, and a bottle of wine?"

I nod my head as I turn to take off the dress. "Nail polish," I mutter. "I need to paint my nails."

"Your toes, too." Sophie grins happily at me. "This is going to be fun!"

"For you maybe," I grumble.

But I'm looking forward to the new me.

40

Gunnar

WEDDING DAY DAWNS BRIGHT and sunny—and early.

Earlier than it needs to be, thanks to the rude awakening I get.

Unlike Stella's knock in Saint Pierre, I hear this one right away because it's a steady *thump thump* on the heavy door of my bedroom.

The *thump thump* vibrates in my head as well, thanks to too much mead and wine and the bottle of Screech I shared with Lyra and Bo after the rehearsal dinner.

"They're not getting married until four," I grumble as I stumble to the door. "It's not nearly four yet. Why did you—Kate?"

Kate stands at the door, dressed for work rather than wedding in black pants and a short-sleeved blouse. She's also wearing an expression more suitable to bad news than the happy event of the wedding.

"What's wrong?" I demand, holding the door open for her. I'm fully awake now and Kate stalks into my room.

A year ago, this would have made my day.

But now— "There's a thing in the papers," she practically growls.

I shut the door behind her. "What kind of thing?"

"An article about Camille." Kate meets my gaze for the first time, her eyes full of anger and disappointment and resolve. "And her father."

"The one that's not her father?" Camille had told me that tidbit weeks ago when we had a heart-to-heart about losing mothers, so I know all about the prefect not being Camille's biological father. And I know that not too many people know about it.

"That one. Also, the article seems to have some information about how Camille and O first got together." Kate blows a frustrated raspberry. "The arranged marriage idea."

"Oh, man." Neither Odin nor Camille wanted to tell the world that their union started as an arranged marriage that would benefit both of them; for Odin, it would lessen the humiliation of being sent home from The Suitorette, and for Camille, being married would allow her to take over as prefect for Saint Pierre. "No one knew about that. I mean, we did." I spread my arms to encompass the castle. "But no one else."

Except... they did.

Stella's words when we were in Saint Pierre flash. *"Camille told the true story of how her and Odin got together and she seemed a little put out."*

What else did Camille say to Stella?

Only—Stella wouldn't say anything. She *couldn't*.

Except that she did take the picture that broke up me and Kate. The two things are not connected, but sending an anonymous picture and talking to a reporter are both secretive. And spiteful.

But... *no*.

I can't even get my head around the possibility that Stella might do that. She's not the same person now. And Camille is not me, and Stella wouldn't hurt someone she considered a friend. "Stella wouldn't say anything that would hurt a friend," I tell Kate.

Except for Stella once considered *me* a friend, and look what she did.

"She wouldn't," I repeat, more for myself than for Kate.

Kate nods, ready to spin or slay or do whatever she does for my brother. "Something was said when you went to Saint Pierre?"

"Yeah, but I don't know how much. And Stella wouldn't," I say fiercely before my heart sinks. I rub the back of my neck. "But Daphne—"

That makes more sense. Even with her usual sunny personality, something was *off* with Daphne while we were in Saint Pierre.

I quickly throw on some clothes while Kate meets Jackson at the door to fill him in. All the bridesmaids slept at the castle last night, and when Kate and Jackson follow me to the guest room where Daphne was staying, we find it empty.

All of Daphne's things are gone, the bed not slept in.

"There's something going on with her and Daulton," I say to Kate.

"It's easier for me to do my job when people tell me things," she snaps, hurrying up the stairs to the suite Daulton was given for his use when he started working for the castle.

Daulton is nowhere to be found.

"It doesn't take a genius to figure out they're in this together." Jackson's mouth thins into a tight line. He came with Camille from Saint Pierre and his dedication can never be questioned.

"No, and there's nothing we can do about the article. It's coming out tomorrow and there's nothing we can do to stop it," Kate frets. "It's going to spoil everything for them."

"We can't tell her," Jackson decides as we head to Duncan's wing to marshal the troops and figure out how to stop this from ruining the wedding.

"We can't keep it from them," Kate argues, practically flying down the hall in her flat shoes.

I've heard they were dating, but right now I can't see it.

"Camille will be devastated that someone she put her trust in—" Jackson throws a dirty look over his shoulder, which stops me short.

"You think *I* did this?" I call after them.

"You brought Daphne into this situation," he says over his shoulder, his voice as cool as the Arctic wind.

"Yes, but I wouldn't... I wouldn't ever..." I stammer, guilt souring my stomach even more than last night's festivities. I hurry after them. "I didn't think."

"That seems to be a common occurrence for you, doesn't it?"

"Jackson," Kate chides him. "It's not helping."

"Let me help," I beg, overtaking both of them with my long legs, and turning to walk backward before them. "I can help."

"There's nothing to *do*," Kate hisses with frustration. "The article will come out. We can't stop it. We can't stop the press from saying what they want, regardless how much it hurts Camille and Odin."

"No, but we can distract them," I say. "Like announcing an engagement when the episode of Odin being sent home aired did."

Kate stops suddenly. "What can distract the press?"

"Me," I say grimly.

Thankfully, my phone was still in the pocket of my jeans, and before we get to Duncan's office, I've called Fenella and convinced her to get on the first flight to Laandia she can find.

"Odin thought me showing up at the wedding with Fenella would take the spotlight away from Camille," I explain, standing before Duncan. "Let's hope he's right."

"It might work," Duncan muses. "Good idea, Gunny."

"So you think they'll fill the papers with pictures of the two of you with no room for the article about Camille and Odin lying about their marriage?" Jackson demands, so protective of Camille and still not convinced. "Not to mention that the prefect, who is walking Camille down the aisle, isn't really her father?"

"It will definitely distract," Kate concedes. "I saw the attention the two of you got when you were dating. Even when you weren't dating."

"Kept track of me, did you?" I ask before I can stop myself. "Sorry," I mutter. "But I do need to talk to you about that. Us. Old us."

Kate rolls her eyes. "Now really isn't the time, Gun."

"No, it's not." Spencer enters just in time, already fully dressed in his usual suit. "Has there been a confirmation about the story from anyone here?"

Kate and Jackson both shake their heads. "I don't think so," Kate says. "But they're still running it. They think Daphne's a credible source."

"But it's her word against ours. If we can find someone to deny it..." I trail off, my gaze meeting Spencer's.

"She wouldn't," he says with a rueful shake of his head.

"She might. For Camille."

Kate looks between us. "Are we talking about Stella?"

"She was there."

"This is her sister we're talking about," Jackson cuts in. "And from what I've heard, she has no love for the castle."

Duncan clears his throat. "That may have changed. At least," he says with an un-Duncan-like wistful tone in his voice, "I hope it has."

"I'll go find out," I announce.

41

Stella

I'M GOING TO A royal wedding.

Once we got the dogs settled for the night, Ajax joined Sophie to help with my transformation.

Sophie cut *ten* inches of my hair. She loosened it from the bun I had it pulled up in, grabbed a handful and just *cut it off* with the sharpest scissors we had at the shelter.

This was after half a bottle of wine, so in hindsight, it might not have been the best idea. Thankfully, Ajax had stylist talents that I never knew about and fixed the damage, and this morning, the choppy blunt cut has morphed into easy waves falling just past my shoulders.

"I never knew you had so much hair," Sophie kept saying. "And the colour..."

The mermaid shades are gone, leaving me with a similar reddish-brown colour as Sophie. With my face clear of makeup, it's like a new person smiles back from the mirror.

I like it.

Ajax also painted my toenails while Sophie did her best with my fingernails. We drank another of bottle of wine and stayed at the shelter with Ajax for the night and talked about our father.

We talked a lot about him—memories and regrets and what we missed about him.

I cried. I cried a lot about a lot of things, thanks to the wine, but when I finally fell asleep, I felt like I found clarity. I finally accepted the truth about what I want in my life, and what I need.

I want my father in my life again.

And Gunnar?

Early this morning, I leave Ajax to take care of the puppies while I run home with Sophie for a quick shower and to hang up my dress. I'm not looking forward to seeing my mother—since our talk with Duncan yesterday, neither Sophie nor I know what to expect from her. Or what to say.

A conversation will be had, but I have other things on my mind today.

Like what I'm going to say to Gunnar.

If I'm going to the wedding with my new short hair and the dress Sophie got for me, I'll see him.

Come and see me when you're ready to listen.

I think I'm ready to hear what Gunnar has to say.

42

Gunnar

As Minka drives me into Battle Harbour to Stella's house, part of me wishes Daphne will be there but the other part—the rational, there's-too-much-going-on-to-really-enjoy-giving-her-a-piece-of-my-mind hopes I don't lay eyes on her.

Because how could she do that to Camille? And on the eve of her wedding?

But still—when Signe Luute opens the door, looking surprised and alarmed and severely put out, I have to ask. "Is Daphne here?"

"No, I thought she's with you," Mrs. Luute accuses in a worried voice. "At the castle. Why don't you know where she is?"

"She's gone." Probably not the best way to tell her stepmother this, but right now, I'm so angry at Daphne, I couldn't care less.

"What do you mean, she's gone?" she demands. "How can she be gone? She was supposed to be with you!"

"She left the premises of the castle," I tell her with a touch more patience in case Mrs. Luute is really upset. "I thought she might have come here."

"Gunnar?"

Both Stella and Sophie appear behind their mother. I'm surprised I even notice Sophie, because all I can see is Stella.

Stella, in a thick robe and wet hair, looking *happy* to see me. And also confused.

My heart gives a little thump.

"What's going on?" Sophie asks.

"Where is your sister?" Mrs. Luute demands.

"Daphne? She should be with Gunnar..." Stella fixes her gaze on me and some of the happiness dims. "What happened?"

"There's an article coming out about Camille—about her father, and how she and Odin got together," I tell her, hoping she understands not to say too much in front of her mother. "Camille won't be happy about what it says, and Odin will be furious. Kate said it'll be everywhere tomorrow."

Stella's face falls. "And you think I told them."

"I didn't say that."

"But you're here. You're here, first thing, to find out what I said. What I did." She's breathing in little pants, so visibly upset that I have to do something to settle her.

"Stella," her mother orders. "Calm yourself and tell me what you did."

"I didn't do anything," she wails.

I reach out and grasp her hand. "I know."

"You... know? But why—"

"Of course you would never betray Camille's confidence about something she thought she was telling to a friend," I interrupt before her worry can go any further. "I never thought you said anything. And even if I did, I wouldn't, because I know Daphne did."

Stella winces. "Daphne?"

"What are you accusing my daughter of?" Mrs. Luute cries.

"The same thing you just accused your daughter of," I point out. "Daphne—with Daulton's help, I'm assuming—contacted a reporter to tell a story."

Stella's hands fly to her mouth. "She didn't."

"Sure looks like she did," I say ruefully.

"You think who did what?" Sophie looks from her sister to me with dismay.

"Daphne told a reporter..." Stella stumbles. "Things that aren't true."

Mrs. Luute straightens. "She did not. She would not. Daphne would never lie."

"But she would talk to a reporter about things that are none of her business?" I demand. Mrs. Luute drops her gaze and I shake my head with disgust. "Well, we'll never know because we can't ask her because she's gone," I snap. "She left the castle early this morning. Or late last night. Along with Daulton Drake."

Both Stella and Sophie groan. "What did she say?" Stella whispers.

"It's coming out in the local paper tomorrow and there's so many reporters here for the wedding..." My heart breaks for Camille and I feel another surge of anger toward Daphne and Daulton. "They happened to go to the one reporter that isn't really fond of the family, and I'm guessing we have Daulton to thank for that. Luckily, no one else has run with it, because no one is confirming. It's only Daphne's word and—"

Stella raises her chin, clearly understanding what I'm asking. "I'm not saying anything."

The fire in Stella's eyes soothes some of my own anger. "I didn't think you would, but this is your sister."

"Stepsister. And she's lying." With a long glance at her mother, Stella straightens her shoulders. "While we were in Saint Pierre, I heard nothing to give any indication that Camille was anything but the beloved daughter of the prefect."

I can't hide my grin "I think beloved might be taking it a little too far."

"But I should say that?"

"It would be great if you were to say exactly that." I smile gratefully and realize I'm still holding Stella's hand. "For Camille."

Stella is doing nothing to pull her hand out of mine either. "Of course."

"I also have a favour," I hedge. "For Camille."

"Anything."

"Come to the wedding with me. Camille needs a bridesmaid."

43

Stella

WHEN GUNNAR OPENS THE door to the SUV, Minka gives a cheery good morning as if she drives me around all the time.

She's driving us to the castle so I can take part in the royal wedding.

What the—?

Kelly Clarkson's rich voice fills the SUV, singing about how her life would suck without someone.

Is it like a sign?

"I can't walk in heels," was my first protest.

"I don't have a dress," was my second.

"You can wear Daphne's," Gunnar soothed. "We'll take care of everything. You just need to come with me."

"I'll help Ajax at the shelter today," Sophie promised. "And they can come to the wedding with me and Silas."

"But I don't think—"

My sister *pushed* me out of the door. "Go!"

When Minka pulls away from my house, Mom is gaping and Sophie cheers.

Sophie actually cheered when Gunnar asked me. I am never sharing another pretzel with her again if she thinks I want to do this.

But I did say yes. And let myself be bustled into the SUV, still in my robe with wet hair.

"The dress is hanging up and ready to go. Thank God Daphne didn't take it with her," Gunnar adds.

"She wouldn't," I argue before I catch myself. Because after this, I have no idea what Daphne would or wouldn't do.

It's like I have no idea who she is anymore. I wonder if it's Daulton's influence or if Daphne has had a nasty streak behind the golden glow all along.

"What if it doesn't fit me?" I ask instead.

"Someone will fix it for you," Gunnar says with the utmost patience, which is exactly what I need since I'm about to *freak out* about all of this. "This is a royal wedding, you know. We have many someones ready and willing to help with whatever we need. There's a lady on call all day just in case Camille messes up her dress."

"Camille will not mess up her dress."

"I'm sure she won't."

"*I'm* going to mess up the dress," I moan. "And everything else. I really can't walk in high heels." I really can't. And while I only hesitated a moment before agreeing to be Gunnar's date, and therefore the final bridesmaid, I didn't really think it through.

Gunnar is asking me to appear in public, in a dress I've never tried on, in shoes that will have tall, skinny heels. I never wear tall, skinny heels, and now I've agreed to walk down an aisle in front of quite a few people wearing said shoes.

Some of the people will be very famous.

No one will know who I am, and I'll have to tell them something about myself.

What am I supposed to tell them? And what am I supposed to say when I trip in the church and make a fool of myself?

I've never had a panic attack before. I wonder if this is what it feels like.

And why does Gunnar still have a hold of my hand?

"I tell you what," he says as my thoughts churn. "If you can make it down the aisle, you can take off the shoes."

"And wear what?"

"Again—royal wedding. We can find something for you to put your feet in."

I turn to the window. "This is such a bad idea. I'll never forgive Daphne."

"It'll be fine," Gunnar soothes.

"How can you say that? You hate the idea of me being in the wedding party. Forget about me being your *date*, which may be the worst idea ever."

"I don't agree," he says mildly. "And I never said anything about hating anything."

"Still," I stumble, without really listening to his words. "You won't have any fun with me. Plus, after everything I did to break up you and Kate—"

"Stella. Stop. You're spiralling."

I look at him, really look at him. Gunnar's hair is mussed like he's just rolled out of bed, he's wearing a T-shirt that doesn't smell too fresh and may be on inside out.

I think it is inside out.

He looks a little rough, and very tired, with purple shadows under his eyes.

But those blue eyes are smiling at me, with one dimple on display, and there's something about the way he holds my gaze, holds my hand, that calms me.

I take a deep breath, and then another. "What is spiralling?" I ask.

"This. When you can't get out of your thoughts." He squeezes my hand and I nod. "Now, stop worrying because everything will be fine."

"Are you sure?"

I have never been vulnerable enough to ask someone if things will be okay. I'm the one who takes care of the problems, who reassures others. Asking that of Gunnar...

"I do. It will be great and wonderful and you're going to rock being a bridesmaid."

I nod again, even though I don't quite believe him. It is nice of him to say that, though.

"And as for the Kate stuff, that was a long time ago and I told you I forgive you. And so will Kate whenever I get around to telling her."

"I want to apologize to her."

"You still can."

I stare at Gunnar's hand holding mine. Why have I never realized his hands were so big, fingers long like a pianist's? "Did Camille ask you to come and get me?"

"She texted me about ten minutes ago, just as I pulled up to your house."

Ten minutes ago, he was standing at the door. "I don't understand."

"I came to pick you up because I want you to come to the wedding with me. She didn't have to ask me to get you."

The words hang between us and I'm afraid to glance at Minka, lest she gives me another *Go for it* look. "Because you need a date," I prompt. "And Camille needs a bridesmaid."

Gunnar studies the roof of the truck with a sigh. "Camille does need a bridesmaid," he admits. "And if she'd gotten to know you sooner, you would have been her first choice. She considers you a friend now, and we both know she doesn't have many of them."

"So she doesn't think I had something to do with the story."

"Of course not. She knew right away it was Daphne. And I really hope Daphne steers clear of the castle for a bit because Camille is *mad.* That girl is scary when you see her with a sword."

"A sword?"

"She and O like to spar. With swords. It might be foreplay—I really don't understand it."

My breath chokes at the word. *Foreplay.* As in before sex play.

I don't want to think about that, because even the word makes me super conscious of Gunnar sitting beside me.

"But I came to get you because I want you to come to the wedding with me. To my utter and complete amazement—" He turns to me with a grin, dimples at full strength. "I have fun when I'm with you. Even with the flyting."

Flyting sounds like a mix of *flirting and fighting.* "We don't—That's not possible. I'm not at all nice to you."

"Not usually, no." He narrows his eyes at me. "But lately, I think maybe you want to be."

"Want to be what?"

"Nice to me. Have a conversation without spitting insults at each other."

"I don't spit," I whisper.

"Oh, you do. But you also say lots of interesting things that make me look at my life from a different point of view. Like, did you know, I've asked my father if he would give me a more serious role in the family? One with duties and responsibilities, and one that might force me to stick around? Maybe you should change your opinion of me being a lazy playboy."

I laugh. I can't help it. The expression on Gunnar's face is hopeful with a little wariness, mixed with something that might be... interest? Attraction?

Maybe even love?

That might be getting ahead of things, but the expression on his face—tanned and so good-looking with those dimples—is exactly how I feel.

But my laughter wipes the expression off his face. "I didn't know I said something funny," he says coolly.

"You didn't," I assure him. And with a deep breath, the deepest I've ever taken, I clutch his hand still holding mine. "It's just that I was going to tell you that I've been thinking about you—your travelling. Where you go around the world and see things? I was thinking that I'd like to join you on your next trip."

44

Gunnar

M Y SMILE WIDENS, MY gaze skirting Stella's face, her wide, frightened eyes.

I've never seen her look so scared. She drops her head under my scrutiny and a strand of hair slips over her cheek. It's slowly drying and I realize the mermaid colours seem to have vanished.

"You cut your hair."

"I did."

"I noticed right away but there was so much to say—" I wind the strand around my finger. "It used to be this colour."

"It did."

"I've always thought the mermaid hair was cool, but I like this."

"You know about mermaid hair?"

"I know about a lot of things, thanks to Fenella. Who is coming to the wedding, by the way. I have to go pick her up later this afternoon."

"She's... here...?"

The confusion on Stella's face makes my heart sing and if I were a meaner person, or if I were still in a cold war with her, I wouldn't say anything. But I'm not that person, and I never really liked the cold war. "As my friend. Not my date."

"Like Daphne was your date?"

"Hopefully, it'll work out better than Daphne. I thought Fen would be a good person to distract the press from the Camille stories. She's good at that." I try but I can't keep the anger out of my voice. Finding out Daphne had screwed over Camille is—it's a good thing Daphne is long gone from the castle.

She better stay gone for a while.

But she's also Stella's stepsister. "I'm a little upset with Daphne," I admit. "And myself, since I'm the one who got her into this. I offered to help, and having Fenella at the wedding will help. I hope."

"None of this is your fault," Stella says vehemently. "Daphne made her choice, as horrible as it was. I still can't believe that she told a reporter—"

"*She* didn't. Daulton did. After Duncan fired him. I found that out this morning, but I left before I could hear the whole story. It's obvious Daphne shared the information, but no one can know who had the idea to break the story."

"Duncan..." Stella blanches. "That might be *my* fault then. Me and Sophie—we told him that Daphne was involved with Daulton."

"Ah." More of the puzzle clicks into place. "There's the reason for this. Revenge. Makes sense. Camille couldn't figure out why because she thought she'd been friendly to Daphne."

"Daphne has learned a lot from my mother," she says ruefully. "She likes to get her own way and she likes to have a connection to the castle. Is Camille...? I'm sorry," she stammers.

"It's not for you to be sorry because you didn't do anything wrong. And Camille will be fine. She's got Jackson and Kate working on things."

"But—"

I bring the hand not currently tangled with Stella's up and press my fingers against her lips. "You need to learn to stop arguing with me."

Those lips curve into a smile. "Not going to happen."

"It could, if you tried really hard."

"What fun would that be?" Stella's eyes are dancing, the silvery grey more green than anything.

"So when we fly off to explore Australia, or Antarctica, or wherever else you want to start, you're going to be arguing with me the entire time?"

She gives an impish smile. "Maybe."

"Good." I lean closer. "You're cute when you're riled up. And we can have fun making up after a fight."

"Making—"

That's all she gets out before I kiss her.

It was only going to be a peck because we are in the back of the car with Minka as an audience, but one became two, and then I tilt my head just so, and Stella's lips… her hand is on my shoulder and then in my hair and…

Yeah. Our second kiss was in the backseat on the way to the castle, and I know very well Minka is checking it out in the rearview mirror.

Still. It's so much better than the first time we kissed.

45

Stella

GUNNAR KISSES ME.

The way it begins could have been an accident, or a way of quieting me, neither of which I like the thought of. A soft brush of lips, like a question. But then...

I must have given him the right answer.

Gunnar's lips slant over mine and the question turns into a demand. His mouth... those lips...

I kiss him back with everything I have. All the apologies for being nasty and cruel, all the wondering why he does nice things for me, all the pent-up emotions because Gunnar has been *it* for me, always.

I finally realize he's the one.

Or maybe I've always known but it takes a kiss to wake me up, like Sleeping Beauty out of her enchanted slumber.

He makes me feel like Sleeping Beauty.

He pulls back for a moment and our eyes meet and it's like he's asking... I don't exactly know what, but I don't take the time to wonder before I reach for him. I press my lips against his before he can say anything that might ruin it.

Or I can say anything.

I feel Gunnar's lips curve in a smile even as I kiss him. How is it possible to smile when your mouth is so busy exploring a new territory?

But why wouldn't you want to smile when you're kissing the person you were meant to be with?

Maybe we aren't *meant* to be together. But it just feels right.

It feels very right.

The kiss we shared when we were young was a memory I would revisit when I couldn't sleep at night, like a handsome face on a dating app. I'd think of the what ifs, the possibilities, imagine what it would be like.

And then I would move on and fall back asleep.

This kiss is going to keep me awake. This kiss will—

"We're here," Minka sings and I jerk back from Gunnar like he gave me a jolt of electricity.

He gave me a jolt of something. That kiss...

Gunnar is grinning like the cat who caught the canary, and his hand stays on my waist. I'm not even sure how it got there in the first place. We're no longer kissing, but we're close, in a bubble filled with us. "I was planning on doing that later."

I fight to catch my breath because my heart is racing, and if Gunnar knows how much that kiss affected me, I'll never hear the end of it. "You were planning on kissing me tonight?"

He nods, looking so pleased with himself that I can't stop my own smile because *I'm* so pleased with the thought. Or offended. I can't tell anymore. "At midnight, so you wouldn't run out without your shoe."

"Like Cinderella?"

He nods. "I, of course, am Prince Charming."

"I thought I was the wicked stepsister."

"There's nothing wicked about you, except maybe how you kiss." As I puff with indignation, Gunnar leans in and brushes my lips with his again. "Wickedly good," he whispers, and I can tell my cheeks are redder than the lipstick Sophie tried to push on me last night.

"I'm glad you approve." I am *not* about to tell him how much I approve of his kissing technique, because that would only inflate his ego.

I can't believe I kissed Prince Gunnar.

Or more importantly, that I kissed Gunnar Erickson.

And that I want to do it again.

"Am I going to have to rescue you from the room of girls again?" Gunnar asks as Minka stops before the castle. "Because I know a secret passage or two."

"I think there's a lot I'm going to have to do to get ready," I admit, flushing again at the thought of being in that passageway with Gunnar. With him, in the dark, holding hands. And now—

Maybe more than holding hands.

"Nah," he says. "You'll look beautiful."

"Aren't you supposed to say that after you see me?"

He shakes his head. "I don't need to see you to know you'll look amazing." The back door opens, just as I'm leaning into him. Camille's personal secretary, Jackson, stands beside the car.

"Ms. Laz," he says formally.

"Just Stella," I manage. "I guess I have to go."

"You better get upstairs so Camille can finally start to breathe." Gunnar cups my cheek. "And I've got brothers waiting for me. Jackson." He nods. "Can you make sure she gets to Camille, which means *do not* let her visit with Bea Arthur and Betty White, or she'll never get dressed."

Is it just me or does the tightness of Jackson's shoulders relax a bit? "Will do."

46

Gunnar

THERE ARE HOURS TO go before the wedding and all I want to do is spend them with Stella.

Because we kissed and I can't wait to do it again.

I want to make her laugh and ask about more tattoos and find out why she turned her hair back to her natural colour.

It's like she's turned back to the girl I used to know.

Only better.

Instead, I spend the time with my brothers.

First, we hit the fitness centre and draw straws on who will spar with Odin. Bo wins—or loses, because Odin is just that much better than anyone with his sword. But Bo gives him a good run, and Odin is smiling when they finally hang up the training swords.

Then it's time to shower off the sweat and head into town.

The King's Hat will be open for the wedding, with extra staff brought in because both Edie and Kalle will be at the castle, but it's closed for now because Kalle arranged a wedding morning brunch for us.

"Dad and Duncan said they'll be a little late," Kalle says as he sets a pitcher of beer on the table, because beer is the best thing to have with pancakes and maple syrup.

"Not surprising." Odin is the first to pour himself a beer and downs half of it before I even get to mine.

"Nervous, O?" I tease.

He actually thinks about it. "No," he admits. "I should be, but I'm not. Camille— this feels like it was meant to be."

"Like you and my sister?" Spencer nudges me.

"Daphne?" I ask with horror. Neither Spencer nor I have said anything to Odin about the changes in the wedding party or the article coming out, and if the others know about it, they're keeping quiet as well.

"I meant Stella. How long have you been in love with my sister?"

"How long have you been in love with mine?" I counter before I think of what I'm saying.

Spencer clamps a hand over his mouth to block the spew of beer. "What the—?"

"Forget I asked," I say quickly. I've long suspected Spencer's fondness for Lyra goes beyond friendship, but honestly, I'd rather not know how deep it goes.

Besides, this is Odin's day. But thanks to Spencer, all eyes are now on me, including the groom-to-be. "We all saw you show up with her," Bo points out. "Gunnar to the rescue... again."

"You were in the car for a while." Kalle grins.

"And she looked a little flustered when Jackson brought her up to Camille's room," Odin adds.

For once I'm not going to be a gentleman and I *am* going to kiss and tell. Because it's Stella and I can't stop thinking about her. "I kissed her."

"About time," Odin grunts.

"Did you argue about it afterward?" Spencer wants to know.

"I think maybe she wanted to, but that's okay." I grin. "It was all okay."

"Just okay?" Kalle raises an eyebrow. "Because if that's all it is, bro, you might want to up your game."

"It was better... it was a first kiss," I protest.

"Nope. I remember the first time you kissed her." Bo pats himself on the back. "Thanks to me."

"Dude. We were twelve. This was nothing like that."

"I really hope not," Spencer says. "Because that was cringey. Hope you got some better moves since then."

"Spence, you realize this is your sister we're talking about?" Odin asks him.

"Oh, yeah." He makes a face. "Just make her happy. Because if you don't, you'll seriously live to regret it."

"I think she's happy." I wish I never brought it up because now I start to doubt myself. Not the kiss—because that was *good*—but Stella. Because she's been slowly growing on me for days now—

She's always been there, the fascination and slight fear of her have never gone away.

But how does she feel? It was a good kiss, but it was only a kiss. I need to know if there's going to be a second kiss. If this will lead to more.

She wants to travel with me. That's a start. But still...

Bo slaps my shoulder. "Get out of your head, bro. It won't do you any good."

"I know, but... She's the one who told Kate about me and Mabel," I confess. "She took the picture that night. She told me."

"And you still kissed her?" Spencer demands with confusion.

"Not only that, but you went and picked her up for the wed-ding," Kalle adds.

I've done a lot of thinking since Stella confessed to being the whistle-blower and I've been through all the emotions—anger, regret, sadness, more anger—and I've gone through them in a very short period of time.

Maybe I would feel different if it hadn't been Stella and I hadn't been falling for her.

I'm falling for her.

And that realization brings a smile to my face even as the same paralyzing terror washes over me, same as it does just before a race.

And just like then, it's gone. And I'm still smiling.

"I'm fine with it," I tell them. "At least, I think I am. Kate and I—it was great and amazing and *she* was amazing, but we were young. I would have eventually screwed it up."

"You don't know that." Bo's face is his usual inscrutable—we all have a variation of the expression, but he does it best—but I know there's a lot going on under the surface. And the last thing I want to do is make it worse for him.

"I do," I say honestly. "And I wasn't ready for anything more with Kate. And I hate that I hurt her, but you have to admit, it's for the best. If things hadn't ended, she never would have left and then come back to clean up Odin's mess."

"I do not have a mess!"

"You got kicked off a reality show after the first date because you confessed to having feelings for another woman," Kalle re-minds him.

"And then you wanted to marry that other woman," Spencer adds.

"Only she wasn't sure she wanted to marry you." I laugh.

"Camille wanted to marry me," Odin protests.

"Now she does," I point out, taking pity on my big brother. "And that's a good thing."

"And that's why we're here." Kalle lifts his glass, and we all follow. "To Odin. The first of us to get his act together and find the right woman."

"To Odin!" we chorus.

I can't help feeling that, maybe, I might be getting my act together too.

47

Stella

I AM PART OF the royal wedding.

Camille doesn't even bat a perfectly curled eyelash when I show up and Jackson tells her I'm taking over Daphne's spot.

She whispers something to Jackson, but I'm so busy being bustled off to try on the dress that I don't hear.

The rest of the day is a blur of dresses and makeup. Edie, who works at The King's Hat with Kalle, is there, her easy-going smile helping to relax me. Kate eventually shows up, after doing what could be done about Daphne's mess.

No one mentions anything about Daphne, or why I'm in the dress, and not her.

Everything happens in Camille's old room in the castle since King Magnus brought in Isla and Hugo to help with our makeup and hair. She trims my newly cut hair without a question about who cut it for me and then curls it in a set of ringlets cascading over my shoulders before pinning the sides back.

"To see your lovely face," Isla tells me.

I do have a lovely face.

Today I feel lovely. Beautiful. And it's not because of the dress—which fits like it was made for me since luckily Daphne is the same size as I am—or the hair. Or the makeup; my entire face is transformed and Isla uses colours that I never knew existed. Golden pink shadow is brushed over my eyelids, and she uses a pinky plum to line the corners of my eyes.

"I almost don't recognize you," Lyra admits, lounging in the chair beside me as Hugo massages her feet.

"I almost don't recognize myself."

"Hope you were in the mood for a makeover."

I study my reflection in the mirror. Mademoiselle Zoya took away my old black housecoat and wrapped me in a silk robe as she made tiny alterations to the straps of the dress. It's been a long time since I wore white, or any colour other than black or gray. The makeup has brought colour to my face, a lightness in my eyes that I'm not used to. "I don't think wedding attire will be my everyday look."

"I didn't mean the makeup."

Lyra studies me with as much seriousness as I stare at myself. I should feel uncomfortable, but there's no hostility in her expression.

Yet.

"What's going on with you and my brother?" she asks. Asks, not demands, like she's really interested in my answer.

"I'm not sure," I admit.

"Because he was a little too excited to go pick you up for this. He didn't seem all that upset about whatever mess Daphne made."

"I apologize for that."

"Why? You didn't do anything."

"She's my sister."

"Stepsister," Edie cuts in, taking the seat beside Lyra and lifting her feet with a laugh for Hugo to work his magic. "If I had to apologize for all the messes my sisters pulled, that's all I would ever do," she adds.

"Same," Lyra adds. "Except it's my brothers."

Why is she being nice to me? The question must show on my face because Lyra gives a rueful laugh. "I know, Kate informed me I gave you a hard time the other day. My bad. But we're a little protective of Duncan, and in my mind, you're the bad guy."

"It's funny how that happens when you don't know the full story." I pause and smile at Lyra's almost apology. "And I didn't."

"And now?"

"Getting there."

She smiles smugly. "Well, I will take credit for showing you the way."

"I don't think she meant that," Kate says, dropping onto the couch beside me, wearing a silky robe as well. "But I'm glad. Families are problematic enough without parents making it worse."

Kate. Kate is sitting beside me. For the first time I really look at her, imagining what she must have felt when she got my text with the picture of Gunnar and Mabel. And for the first time, I stop thinking Gunnar deserved to be caught, and look at it from Kate's point of view.

She must have been devastated. Heartbroken.

I did that.

"Have you spoken to Gunnar since we got back from Saint Pierre?" I ask her before I can lose my nerve.

"No, I—" She falters, thrown off guard. "I have, but— Should I?"

I don't even pause to take the deep breath of courage. "I told him that I was the one who sent you the picture of him and Mabel that broke you up," I confess. "And that I'm sorry. So very sorry."

Kate gapes at me. "I—that was you?"

Lyra gives a muffled curse. "Just when I was starting to like you."

"Let her finish," Edie chides her. "There may be more to it."

Is there? Or was it just a fit of petty jealousy?

"Why?"

It's Kate I turn to, steeling myself for the truth. "I was walking home from a bad date and feeling pretty sorry for myself. I saw Gunnar leaving Mabel's and... and I got mad. I was angry with Gunnar because—"

"Because you hate the castle," Lyra cuts in with a twist of disgust on her face.

"I had strong feelings for those living at the castle," I correct. "I also didn't like that he was there, thinking he could get away with hurting you."

Kate looks perplexed. "I guess I can't really be angry about that."

"You can," Lyra tells her. "It was a chicken move."

"I know," I admit. "And it was the wrong move. Because—I hope this doesn't mess things up in any way for you and Jackson—" This time I take a deep breath, praying this is the right move and this thing with Gunnar isn't going to end before it begins. "Because Gunnar told me nothing at all happened with Mabel. Not like that. He never cheated on you, with her or anyone else. And I believe him."

"Well, bully for you," Lyra sneers. Then her face relaxes. "I couldn't believe it of him either," she says to Kate. "But you're my girl, so I was Team Kate all the way."

"It made me sad to come between you." Kate smiles at her. "But thank you."

"Me, too," Edie says. "But I had a lot of trouble believing that too. Gunnar was so into you."

That provokes a stab of jealousy. But still— "I'm sorry. For everything," I apologize. "I shouldn't have assumed."

"Anyone would have," Kate says ruefully. "It's Gunnar, the playboy prince."

"Technically, he didn't get called that until after you broke up," I point out.

"Paid a lot of attention to him, did you?" Edie studies me.

"I did. More than I realize," I admit. "Because... because I think I've always wanted him for myself. And when he was with you... and then I thought he was with Mabel, it hurt. A lot." Since this seems like a safe space, I keep going. "I think I've always liked him."

"Well, duh," Lyra says and throws a makeup brush at me.

48

Gunnar

"**Y**OU ARE IN AN exceedingly good mood," Minka says after she picks me up from the pub to drive me to the airport to pick up Fenella. "Is that because of the multiple pints you drank with the other princes, or the make-out session in the car earlier?"

I'm not even embarrassed. Not in the slightest. "You caught that, did you?"

"It would have been impossible not to."

"Yeah, well, it all happened a little sooner than expected. I had planned on midnight—"

"Spare me the details," she groans. "Because I heard your conversation as well as the kissing sounds."

"Sorry about that."

"Exceedingly good mood," she mutters. "But I approve."

"And that is so important to me," I tease.

"I think little miss Goth girl is rubbing off on you."

"She didn't look Goth this morning," I point out. She was in a robe—black, but there was a softness about her. Maybe because it was a robe.

I can't stop thinking about her.

"And she won't be walking down the aisle in that."

"You sound like you're looking forward to seeing her walk down that aisle."

I am. I can't wait to see Stella start down the aisle, clutching some bouquet of flowers, wearing whatever colour bridesmaid's dress Camille assigned her. She'll be nervous, but trying not to show it, feeling horribly out of place so that she'll pretend it's all beneath her.

And she'll be walking straight toward me.

Not that I want to be the guy at the end of the aisle who has to make the statement and the promises before he gets the kiss. That would be jumping the gun, so to speak.

I just want the kiss.

"You're smiling again," Minka points out.

"I think you'll be seeing a lot of that."

We're at the airport soon after, and Fenella greets me with a hug. Minka helps me stow Fenella's bags in the back of the SUV while she settles herself in the backseat.

"How long are you planning on staying?" I call, hefting the third and hopefully final bag into the back.

"As long as it takes," Fenella says, snapping a picture of my flustered face.

"It's only a wedding, so that'll be a couple of hours," I tell her as I climb into the backseat beside her, trying not the think about how I was in the exact spot earlier with Stella. Not that anything like that will happen with Fenella. "How many costume changes did you bring?"

"I only need one perfect little red dress for the wedding. And you're lucky I had just the thing in my closet. With a little more of a heads'-up I could have gone shopping."

"I'd give you time if I had more. Things moved fast this morning." I tap the back of Minka's seat. "Good to go."

"Will we have time to stop at Soulful Silas's for his yummy coffee?" Fenella asks in a pleading voice.

"I am already on route," Minka tells her.

"You're a good woman." Then she turns to me. "I brought everything I might need because I don't know how long I'm staying. That depends on you."

"On when I kick you out?"

"Camille said you needed a wingwoman."

I stare at Fenella with surprise. "She said what? And when did she say this?"

"A wingwoman, or as she puts it, someone who can help you screw your head on straight about a woman. Her words, not mine. I might have said it a little more indelicately. And she called with a formal invitation not long after I talked to you."

I stare at the back of Minka's head with a grin. "Did Camille happen to mention who this woman might be?"

"Stella Laz, of course."

I glance out the window with a chuckle. "I'll have to thank Camille for that, but I think I'm doing all right on my own."

And then I tell Fenella everything that's happened.

49

Stella

THE WEDDING LOOKS LIKE a box of crayons.

Lyra dances down the aisle in periwinkle blue and Edie follows in turquoise, walking with a confidence among this group that I wish I shared.

Guests adhered to Camille's request for colour and dressed in all the shades of the rainbow. I would have stood out in my black dress, but not as much as I stand out in my yellow one, walking slowly down the aisle leading to an arch of flowers where Odin stands with his brothers.

All five of them are wearing colour as well—red pants with a highlighter yellow jacket and a bright blue sash. It's a lot to take in, but of course, the princes of Laandia are able to pull it off.

Gunnar looks amazing, his uniform perfectly fitted to his broad shoulders and long legs.

His dark blond hair is brushed back with a wayward curl falling onto his forehead. His blues eyes are searching the back of the church and both dimples flash as I take my turn.

He stands at the end of the row, fitting because he's the both youngest and the shortest, but it makes it easier for me to look at him.

It's all I can do just to breathe as heads turn and people I don't know smile at me. Midway down the carpeted aisle, I have to avoid glancing at Gunnar because I won't be able to stop the smile and I don't want to look like a grinning maniac as I walk down toward him.

Instead, I find my father in the crowd and give him a tentative smile. In doing that, I totally walked by my mother without a glance. Considering our last conversation, I'm fine with that.

You did great, Gunnar mouths as I make it to my assigned spot at the end.

And then, *I like the shoes.*

The heels weren't as long or skinny as I feared, but still, Edie nudges me as my shoulders shake with laughter.

And finally, as Kate appears at the door of the church, *You look so beautiful.*

I have to turn away from him then, afraid the rush of emotion I'm feeling will show on my face.

Kate, in pink, starts her turn and I'm not the only one who notices she smiles at Jackson the entire way down the aisle.

And then Camille appears and takes everyone's breath away.

Including her groom-to-be. Odin can't stop smiling. I think there might be tears in his blue eyes.

But it's another set of blue eyes that I'm more concerned with. I can't help glancing over at him while poems are read and vows are said.

He keeps smiling, his gaze fixed on me, and maybe it's being part of a wedding that makes it more emotional, but my heart is about ready to explode and all I want to do is cross the few feet that separate us and throw my arms around Gunnar and never let go.

The rest of the ceremony passes in a blur, as does the photo session outside in the sunshine and inside, in the warmth of the sitting room where Gunnar once rescued me from a tea party with my mother and the queen. Finally, with aching cheeks from smiling, the wedding party, with me holding tight to Gunnar's arm, follows Prince Odin and Princess Camille into the ballroom.

"Remember what I promised?" Gunnar asks in a low voice to be heard above the cheers of the many, many guests.

"I don't remember you promising anything, but then again, I'm so overwhelmed with all this, I don't really even know my own name," I confess with a shaky laugh.

"I told you, you did great. The understudy who did better than the star. Not that Daphne is a star *at all.*"

It's good that Daphne disappeared from Battle Harbour because there are a lot of angry people here that would love to give her a piece of their mind. The protective part of me has died down a bit, after Spencer discovered Daulton absconded with the royal plane and official pilot and flew with Daphne to New York City.

I wonder what his wife says about all this.

To say I'm disappointed in my stepsister is an understatement. At least I have Sophie here, smiling proudly as she stands with Ajax and Silas at the bar.

"So remind me what you promised?" I ask, allowing Gunnar to pull me back from thoughts of Daphne.

"I said..." Gunnar draws out slowly as he leads me to my place at the head table.

Yes, I will have to sit at the head table, which sits on a raised dais like we're royalty, which of course, they are, and let everyone see me eat.

I really hope soup isn't on the menu. Or spaghetti.

"—that if you made it down the aisle, I'd find you another pair of shoes to wear for the rest of the night." He pulls out a chair with an expectant grin.

A pair of high-top Converse sneakers with a platform sole sit on my chair. They are yellow, bedazzled with rhinestones.

They are the happiest pair of shoes I've ever seen—and totally not me.

At least they *weren't* me. I kind of like this yellow dress.

"You made it," Gunnar says from behind me. "I told you that you could take them off if you did."

"Where did they come from?" I snatch up the shoes and hug them to my chest with a silly smile on my face.

"I thought I was getting the yellow dress." Lyra squeezes behind the chairs to the seat beside me. "I had them made then, but then Camille goes and switches the order and gives me the purple." She swishes the skirt of her dress so I can see her shoes—same as the ones I'm holding but in a shade that matches her dress. "Try them on. Gunny says that amazingly, we have the same size feet."

I turn to him and frown at his smirk. "How do you know the size of my feet?"

"I know a lot about you that you don't know I know." Gunnar pulls out the chair. "Sit down."

And then to my amazement, Prince Gunnar kneels by the chair and slips off my high heels.

It's too awkward for him to actually put the sneakers on my feet, but after I get them on, he ties them up.

It makes me feel like a princess.

"Thank you," I tell him, unable to stop the smile. My entire face is one big grin— my eyes, my aching cheeks, even my nose is getting into things.

Gunnar looks the same way.

"They're not as clumpy as what you're used to, but I figured they'll be better than heels. I didn't think you'd be able to manage in them all night."

"Oh, I could manage," I say quickly. "Never doubt a woman's ability to stay on her feet in the most uncomfortable shoes."

"I will never doubt you for anything, Stella."

Gunnar gets to his feet, towering over me. I stand up, already in love with the shoes. "Don't say never."

"I can try really hard. How's that?"

"Better." I smile at him— hopefully it's an encouraging smile since I'd really like to kiss him again, but I can't seem to drum up the courage to do it myself here with all the people and if—

"I like your tattoos," a deep voice says from behind me and I turn to see King Magnus. "Nice shoes, too."

"Thank you." As I begin to drop into a curtsy, the king grabs me by the arm. "None of that, Stella. I remember you running amok through here with the rest of them, so none of that."

"Yes, sir," I murmur.

"Thanks for stepping in," he says.

"I'm happy to. I'm happy to be here," I tell him honestly.

"Well, I think there's more than a few here tonight that are very glad you came." The king jerks his head in a move that would have toppled the crown on his head if he were still wearing one, and motions to Duncan standing with the Prime Minister of Canada but watching me with a proud smile. "I'm sure he'll be wanting to talk to you tonight."

That's when I get the best, worst idea that I've ever had.

"Actually, Your Majesty, if I could have a word with you about my father?"

If I was nervous about walking down the aisle in front of all those guests, it's nothing like getting up on the platform later, with a spotlight on me.

But I'm with my father, so it lessens some of the fear.

Only some—until I start to sing, my dad joining me with his old guitar as we serenade Camille and Odin for their first dance.

50

Gunnar

I GRAB STELLA AS she steps off the stage. I can't help it. She's beautiful—she's had a glow about her ever since she appeared at the back of the church, but I've never seen her look so happy.

She's radiant.

"You were amazing." I pull her into my arms, lifting her off her feet, bedazzled sneakers swinging as I spin her around. "I can't believe you did that."

"I didn't think I *could* do it," she admits with a laugh. "I was so scared. All I could think about was it was the worst idea ever, and what if I messed up their first dance?"

Stella and Duncan sang a cover of Anne Murray's "Could I Have This Dance?" for Camille and Odin's first song, the same song she'd sung for us in Saint Pierre.

She sounded even better with Duncan.

"You can do anything you want," I tell her. Stella is still in my arms and we sway together amid the guests packing the dance floor. "You've already proven that."

"So can you." Her smile fades and there's a serious gleam in her eyes. "You can do anything. You don't have to keep running away."

"I wasn't running away," I can't help but protest.

"Now who's arguing?" Stella teases with a grin, her eyes more green than grey.

"Well, when you say things like that, I will. And even if I was running away—which I wasn't—I know that. Now. Thanks to you."

"Because I said mean things?" she asks sadly.

"Kind of," I admit, even as my arm tightens around her and I take her hand in mine.

We get a few looks as I lead her into a waltz around the floor once, twice... and then I lead her out of the ballroom onto the balcony overlooking the back gardens.

Stella looks straight into my eyes as I pause our dance and stand with her against the railing. The only light is from the ballroom and the full moon rising high in the sky.

It's a magical night for a wedding.

"I'm sorry about that," Stella whispers. "Truly—all the things I said to you. I shouldn't have."

"I'm not sorry, since it clued me in to a lot of things I needed to change," I tell her. "I don't like people thinking that about me."

"I don't think that about you," she says quickly. "I think you're so much more. I think..." Stella drops her gaze. "I think you're kind of great."

"Only kind of?"

She swipes at my arm, but there's no heat in it.

Not the bad kind of heat anyway. "I think you're kind of great, too."

"Only kind of?" Stella frowns. "Does that mean we're in... agreement?"

That makes me laugh. "There's a first time for everything." My smile fades but I keep my gaze on her. "There's a lot of firsts happening today."

"First wedding at the castle, first of the princes married," she rattles off.

"First kiss… as adults." I wiggle my eyebrows at her.

"Do you honestly count that kiss when we were twelve as a first kiss?" she scoffs.

"I honestly do," I tell her.

She drops her gaze again. "So do I."

"Again we agree."

"Don't get used to it."

"Oh, I hope to get used to doing a lot of things," I say, taking her chin in my fingers and tipping it up.

"If you think—"

I kiss her then.

I lower my head and press my lips against hers and give Stella Laz the kiss I've wanted to for years.

The kind that keeps her from talking.

We stand on the balcony as the party goes on inside and we don't talk at all.

Epilogue
Kalle

I DANCE WITH FENELLA Carrington for the third time.

She's young, she's Gunnar's friend, but she looks really good in that dress and she smells incredible.

The first sniff had me hooked and keeps me finding my way back to her between dances with wives of the VIPs.

Odin is so much better at the princely socializing than I am, but he never leaves Camille's side, which leaves me to mingle. Being the first son has taught me well, but I'll never get used to it.

"Did you take dance lessons like Gunnar?" Fenella asks, tilting up her head to study me. Those violet eyes are too distracting for their own good.

"No, this is just my natural talent." I smile, a little too grimly to be considered flirting, because I definitely don't want to give the wrong idea to the wedding guests.

Although Fenella was invited to be a distraction, so I'm sure she won't mind. The way her fingers curl around the back of my neck suggests she might not mind being on the receiving end of my considerable charms.

At least that's what women tell me—that I can be charming.

I don't see it.

"Impressive," Fenella muses. "But I'm sure you're talented in many areas."

Is she flirting with me? Sure seems like it, but she's Gunnar's *friend*, and therefore...

Therefore nothing. Gunnar is her friend and has no other claim. And the way he is carrying on with Stella Laz—

Fenella catches me glancing over at the couple in question dancing. Or if that's what they call swaying together, arms wrapped around each other with the occasional longing glances. "I knew they'd end up together."

"Interesting, since they couldn't stand to be in the same room together before today."

"You don't really know your brother all that well, do you?"

"He is my brother." I'd never admit that sometimes I have no clue what's going on in Gunnar's head. Same as Bo, same as Odin. Lyra... I can't even begin to understand.

The music stops; a good thing because dancing for a fourth time with Fenella wouldn't be a good idea.

Odin and Camille stand together on the dais. She looks every inch of the princess she now is and something swells inside me that I recognize as brotherly pride.

I haven't gotten to know Camille as well as Gunnar has, but I have time for that, in between her visits to Saint Pierre.

There's no other word for Odin towering above the guests but kingly, or as much of a king he can look like in the uniform.

I slip a finger under my jacket collar. The cut of that jacket hugs my shoulders a little too tightly, not like Odin's, which fits him like he was made to wear it. Maybe I should have taken the offer of a new jacket like Bo did, but my brother's shoulders seem to be growing wider every time I see him.

I can't help but think back to the night when they announced their engagement. It had been so awkward, uncomfortable for all, and to this day, I have no idea how none of the press caught wind that Odin and Camille weren't the love match they claimed to be.

That was then—this is now. This is my brother happily in love with his wife.

I'm not the only one who smiles at the sight of them.

Fenella leans closer. "Can I ask you a question?" she asks in a low voice. I look down with a jut of my chin for her to continue. "The colours of the uniform." The corners of her lips curve slightly. "Why?"

"Red, yellow and blue, you mean?"

"It's very... vivid," she says diplomatically.

My lips quirk. "My grandfather let his queen design it. No one realized she was colour-blind until it was too late."

Fenella laughs. "Are you serious?"

"'Fraid so."

"Maybe you should look into another designer when you become king."

My smile instantly fades. This isn't the first someone has said this tonight, and I know it won't be the last.

"Ah. Gunnar was right. You really don't want to be king."

"I'd rather not discuss it." Which is the biggest understatement of the night but it's the way I want it. Always.

"And so we won't," Fenella says lightly, tucking her arm into mine.

Until Odin starts his speech.

The first part is fine; he thanks everyone he needs to and more than a few he doesn't. And it's cute, the way Camille stands and stares at O like he's the most important person in the world.

He'd better be to her. It goes both ways—Camille needs to be a priority for Odin, more than any of us.

Maybe as the big brother, I should have talked to him about that.

It's not until Odin starts talking about Saint Pierre that I really tune in.

"...while Lady Camille has fallen in love with Battle Harbour and Laandia, she still feels a responsibility to her duties in Saint Pierre. Especially when Lord Arnaud retires from prefectship at the end of the year. Lady Camille will become prefect of Saint Pierre at that time."

Applause spreads through the ballroom. "What exactly is a prefect?" Fenella whispers to me.

"I have no idea," I confess. "She runs Saint Pierre, but it belongs to France, so they get final say."

"Isn't that something you should know?"

I wink at her. "Probably. I'll get right on that."

"Not before I get another dance."

"With me? Because I don't know if you've noticed the line-up—"

"But I want to dance with you." Her pout is childlike, but the expression in her violet eyes is anything but. I adjust my hand on her lower back and wonder how far I can take this flirtation.

But then—

"As her husband, I will be living on Saint Pierre with Camille and helping her with her duties," Odin continues. "Because of this,

I don't think it's plausible to hold responsibilities for both Saint Pierre and the crown here in Laandia. So after careful thought and much discussion with Camille and my father, I have made the difficult decision to abdicate my position of second to the crown."

Murmurs flood the ballroom like a wave. "What did he just say?" I jerk away from Fenella and take a step closer to the dais. Guests move away from me and Odin meets my confused gaze. "I won't ever be king," he says with true regret in his voice. "Even if Prince Kalle doesn't succeed our father, I am giving up my place in the succession."

"What the—?" I thunder.

Kalle has always been next in line for the throne but hated even thinking about it. But with Odin's abdication, will the royal rogue take his rightful place?
Find out in Royal Rising—book three in the Love in Laandia series!

Subscribe to my newsletter for a BONUS EPILOGUE—The Bridesmaids!

Thank you!

THANKS SO MUCH FOR reading Royal Retelling, the second book in my Love in Laandia series

I knew Gunnar's story was going to be next in line even before I finished Royal Rumble, but I wasn't convinced who would be a good match for him. I think I found her in Stella—even though some might think she's a little too hard on him. It all works out though. Of course!

Fun facts:

Fenella Carrington—remember that name.

I'm planning a trip to the archipelago of Saint Pierre, and Newfoundland and Labrador—which I kind of annexed to make room for Laandia. Big apologies to all the Canadians I've offended with geography magic!

I think Duncan needs a love story...

A huge thank you goes out to you, my readers, for if it wasn't for you, I wouldn't be doing this. Thanks to the IG booksgrammer community and all my new followers; to Regina, and Blu, and Dylan for my people!

And always, thanks to Mom and Dad, E, and my kids for their support!

Thanks so much for spending your time with me and my books!

Suitor Science

Hating the Chemistry Teacher
Falling for The Suitor
Fraternizing with the Ex
Marrying the Billionaire Best Friend
Loving the Wrong Guy
Finding the One

Love & Alliteration

Perfectly Played
Beautifully Baked
Pleasantly Popped

Don't

Don't Tell Me You Love Me
Don't Want to Be Friends
Don't Stop Me Now
Don't They Know It's Christmas

Sisters in a Small Town

Coming Home
Hanging On
Stepping Up

Charlotte Dodd

The Secret Life of Charlotte Dodd
The Missing Files of Charlotte Dodd
The Best Worst First Date Ever
The Hidden Past of Pippa McGovern
The Last Stand of Charlotte Dodd

Love in Laandia

Royal Rumble
Royal Retelling
Royal Rogue

Unexpecting
Unexpectingly Happily Ever After

Absinthe Doesn't Make the Heart Grow Fonder

Oceanic Dreams – I Saw Him Standing There

Kid Lit

The Dragon Under the Mountain
The Dragon Under the Dome